POTTER'S FIELDS

Frank Roderus

POTTER'S FIELDS

WHEELER
PUBLISHING, INC.
ROCKLAND, MA

★ AN AMERICAN COMPANY ★

Published in Large Print by arrangement with Bantam Books, a division of Bantam Doubleday Dell Publishing Group, Inc., in the United States and Canada.

Wheeler Large Print Book Series.

Set in 16 pt Plantin.

Library of Congress Cataloging-in-Publication Data

Roderus, Frank.
    Potter's Fields / Frank Roderus.
       p. (large print) cm.(Wheeler large print book series)
    ISBN 1-56895-492-1(softcover)
    1. Western Stories. 2. Large type books. I. Title. II. Series
[PS3560O346P6 1997]
813'.54—dc21   97-034341
                                                         CIP

For Betty Richardson Roderus,
who looked into the abyss
and had the compassion to wonder
where the evil sprang from

POTTER'S FIELDS

SILENCE, *eerie and utter silence. Not a mere muffling of sound but the absence of it. Total silence. Frightening silence. He could feel the thump-thud, thump-thud, thump-thud of his heartbeat beneath the scratchy wool of the heavy overcoat. He could feel the searing cold of each indrawn breath. He could hear... nothing.*

He took a blind step forward. The fog was as thick and heavy as the silence. It lay close around him like great sheets of cotton, but insubstantial. Gossamer ice that ebbed and shifted, white and ghostly in the quiet.

White fog. White snow. White on white, impossible to see. He blinked, conscious of the frigid air that burned his eyes and turned the hairs inside his nose to sharp, brittle needles.

He took another step forward. Felt the hard, crusted surface of the snowfield resist his weight, then give way. His boot broke through into the soft snow beneath and plunged to a depth well over his ankle.

There should have been sound to accompany what he could feel. There should have been the crunch-flutter-crunch of old snow being broken, but there was not. Around him in all directions there was nothing but silence. And shifting, wispy whiteness.

He looked down. His trouser legs and knees and boots, what he could see of them above the snow, were black. Except they were not black. He knew that. His trousers were a very dark and elegant blue. They looked black now, as if the white of fog and white of snow together leached away all color, as if the only choices remaining were purest

1

white or starkest black and nothing was left over to permit the introduction of any gay hue. Black and white, severe and frigid. Nothing more. He began to shiver and tremble.

Forward. A step. Another. He looked about wildly, but there was nothing to see. Nothing but swirling white fog and slogging black bootsteps. And still there was no sound, not even that of his own labored breathing.

He could feel the burn of the cold in his lungs. He should have been able to hear... something.

He was weary. His lungs were afire, and his arms ached. He looked down. The rifle, too, was black against white. Even the scratched and battered wood of the buttstock was black in this strange light, with no hint of brown wood tones, although he could see the patterns of the grain beneath the rubbed oil surface. It all, everything, appeared black against white.

He stepped forward. Felt the crunch of the snow surface giving way. Felt the drag of snow heavy and clinging around his lower legs. Felt the pounding of his heart.

He was frightened. He did not know why. Confused. That was much easier for him to understand. It was the silence. The silence surely was causing both his fear and his confusion. It had to be the silence.

The cold stung his eyes and burned his cheeks. His lips were dry and cracked and stinging. Air reaching his lungs was painful, and yet he gasped for more. He hacked and panted and moved stolidly, persistently ahead into the impenetrable white of the fog.

White there and then... dark. A shape. Something lying dark in his path. Only a few paces distant but impossible to make out through the shifting, ethereal fog.

Closer. A step and then another, deliberate and cautious.

The shape shimmered and flowed as if of liquid, and he blinked to clear the cold tears from his eyes. He shook his head and blinked rapidly, and after a moment his vision cleared.

A blanket lay in the snow. Crumpled, snow-crusted, black against the white. The blanket was plaid. Bright colors. Red and green and cream. He could see only black and white, but he knew the colors of the plaid. How odd. The oddity of it almost made him smile. Almost.

He stepped forward again. Peered down upon the crumpled blanket to the pale center. There was an object there like the pale center of a dark blossom.

Except this center was a face. Serene and very round. A child's face. White. As if dusted with powder. Except this powder was frost-rime, frozen, thickly coating puffy cheeks, tiny delicate eyelashes, pale and motionless lips, dully staring eyes that looked out through their coating of frost and far, far beyond him.

A child's face. Immobile. Frozen. Arrested in time and dusted with rime.

Beneath the white coating there was dark skin, dark eyes, dark dark hair lying still and stiff where once sweaty curls were frozen in place.

Movement. He sensed or perhaps saw the motion with peripheral vision. Certainly he could hear nothing.

He glanced up. Gasped.

A shape bounded toward him from the mists.

Black shape. Batlike. A dark blanket flapped.

3

Furry leggings scattered clods of snow crust. Black hair streamed and black eyes accused.

There was hate in those eyes. Evil.

The woman's hands curled into claws, fingers extended like talons to rip and injure.

Her mouth gaped and twisted, hurling obscenities that the fog muffled and mercifully contained. He could hear nothing. He needed to hear none of the sound to know what she said. The language was not his and he knew that, too, and that mattered no more than the sound did.

He shuddered, conscious of the thump-thud, thump-thud, thump-thud of his racing heartbeat.

Evil. The woman was evil. A harridan. A harpy. He cried out, but no sound escaped his lips. His throat ached and became raw, but still there was no noise.

And the bounding, horrid woman came closer. Ever closer. Ever more intent on rending him asunder.

His eyes stung and burned from the cold. There was a surge of sharp pain deep in his chest.

If he merely stood… if he failed to act…

He braced himself. Lifted the rifle. Peered down the long, steel-banded barrel, pointing—not aiming, pointing. The bayonet extended slim and deadly, glittering and ugly.

The woman's mouth opened and closed.

The child's body in its swaddling of blankets lay between them.

The woman rose into the air in a leap that appeared to him as if she were floating. As if they somehow were in water and her movements were slow and weightless.

If she touched him, he would die.

He knew beyond certainty he would die. He knew it.

Crying out with soundless terror he braced himself, the muzzle of the rifle tracking to meet the woman's leap.

She floated toward him in a graceful arc. Ominously silent. Hateful. Deadly.

Met the bright, sharp point of the bayonet. Met it and welcomed it into her breast. Impaled herself onto it with horrid eagerness as he stood braced above the body of her child. Took into her body the cold, implacable steel.

He staggered under the jolting weight of her. Stumbled. Fell onto his knees in the crusty snow.

Blood flowed from her breast. Sprayed onto the child. Onto the snow. Ran dark and dripping down the barrel of the rifle. He did not want the blood to touch him. He did not know what might happen if the blood were to reach him, but he knew he did not dare allow it.

He tried to pull back, to pull away. The steel was held tight by the pull of her flesh. He began to sob.

Frantic, gasping and afraid, he grabbed for the huge curved hammer of the rifle. Dragged it back to cock the weapon. Jerked furiously at the trigger.

Flame, bright and beautiful, blossomed at the muzzle of the gun. The cloth of the woman's blanket burst into smoldering, smoky fire, and the force of the gunshot dislodged the bayonet from her clinging flesh.

Oddly, there yet was no sound.

Only the eerie, muffling, terrifying silence.

He came to his feet, choking from the force of his own sobs, and the woman's body toppled face forward to cover that of the frozen child.

He turned, abandoning the stark scene.

He turned and he ran. Into the white, cotton-mist fog.

Into the silence.

Leaving horror behind.

Chapter 1

1

Belle Creek, Montana
Friday, January 19, 1906

The sound of a rasping cough and stamping boots quickly followed by the click of the door latch being opened interrupted the constable—or patrolman, police officer, deputy town marshal; there was some dispute as to the title depending on which city councilman was asked—in the act of pouring his morning coffee. He turned away from the softly purring stove and gestured with the pot in his right hand. "Morning, Mister Mayor. Care for an eye-opener?"

Mayor Willis Bowers ignored the question. With a scowl he hurried to unfasten the toggles of his buffalo coat and spread the heavy garment open to admit the heat from the coal fire. He stamped his feet again, littering the floor with chunks of snow that quickly began to melt.

"No?" Joe Potter said. "To look at you I'd've said you needed this more'n me, but everybody to his own taste. As the goat said to the gander." The constable replaced the pot onto the potbelly stove and carried a brimming cup full of coffee around the desk. He glanced down into an open desk drawer but did not bring out the flat, brown pint bottle that lay

7

there. Instead he bumped the drawer shut with his hip in passing, shutting away the sight of the bottle. He settled into the spring-loaded swivel armchair behind the police chief's desk and held the unadulterated cup close under his chin. Steam from the coffee lifted warm and aromatic from the dark brown surface. Joe Potter enjoyed the smell of fresh coffee on any morning but most especially on a cold morning. This morning was past cold. It was squeak-walking cold, the snow so hard frozen and dry that a man's boots squeaked when he walked in it. On a morning like this one, coffee was meant to be appreciated, he figured.

The mayor of Belle Creek stripped off his coat and muffler and wolfskin hat and unceremoniously dumped them all onto a side table, then helped himself to a seat in front of the chief's desk.

"Sure you wouldn't like a taste of this coffee, Willis? It's mighty good even if I did make it myself."

"Let me see your hands, Potter," the mayor demanded abruptly.

The constable lifted an eyebrow. He also shrugged, patiently set the coffee cup down—onto the blotter sheet, not on the wood surface itself—and showed Bowers first his palms and then the backs of his hands. "Not that I care, Willis, but what's this about?"

"You know what it's about, Potter. Damn you."

"Damn me? Willis, I declare I'm beginning to think you're having a bad morning." The constable's smile was more smug than

8

serene, although it was serenity that he was trying for.

"Damn you," the mayor repeated.

"Maybe you ought to roll yourself a pill, Mayor. Something to make you feel better."

"Don't get smart with me, mister."

"No, sir. Sorry," Potter said politely, leaning forward amid a screech of protesting chair springs and taking up his cup again. He smelled of the coffee, then tasted it. In comparison with the delight of the aroma the flavor was anticlimactic. Good but without zest. Oh, well. "Was there something I could do for you, Mayor?"

"Where were you this morning, Potter?"

"Come again, sir?"

"You must have heard the bells."

The constable raised one mobile eyebrow again and shook his head. "Sorry, Willis. I'm sure I don't know what you're talking about."

The mayor's face darkened and became mottled with barely suppressed anger. "You, sir, are a liar."

"Am I, Mayor? I'm sorry you feel that way. But I have no idea what you are talking about." He sipped of the coffee again and belatedly, insolently, added, "Sir."

"I don't suppose you heard the ambulance bells this morning, then?"

"Bells? No, I didn't hear no bells that I recall. As for what I did see an' hear... give me a second to recollect what all I done. I woke fairly early. Went out to the backhouse. Huh. That trip didn't take long, believe me. Cold? I reckon. Then back in here. Got bundled up good and heavy for going out again. Went

9

over to the café for breakfast. On my way back walked the alleys to check door latches and windows and like that. Then walked the storefronts, too. Hap Harper was open. I stopped in and visited with him a minute. Then I came back here. Put that pot of coffee onto the stove and used the first half of the water to shave with." He fingered his chin as if to demonstrate. "Which about brings us up to where you come in just now. But it was bells you was asking about, wasn't it? No, I don't recall hearing no bells while all of that was going on."

"I say you are a liar," the mayor said with perhaps less heat than the last time.

"I'm sorry you feel that way, Willis, but there's nothing I can do expect to tell you the truth here. Now what was all this about bells? The ambulance, you said?"

"Exactly."

"Somebody slip and fall or something, Mayor?"

"Damn you, Potter, you know..."

Joe Potter's lips thinned. The expression fell short of being a smile, but it did convey a message of sorts.

"If I could prove it, Potter, I'd have you on murder charges."

"Murder, Mayor, that's a real serious thing to say about a man."

"But it wouldn't be the first time someone has said it of you, Potter. Would it?" Bowers glared across the desk at the town constable.

"I don't know what you mean, Mayor."

"Don't you, Potter? You don't remember a man in Cohagen? Or those three Indians who

10

were beaten when you were the marshal of Glendive? You don't recall anything about them, eh?"

"You were talking about murder, Mayor. No one ever said anything about murder in those—"

"Oh, shut up, Potter. Just shut up."

"Yes, sir. Whatever you say." The thin, mocking smile was back. "Sir."

Bowers fixed his constable with a glare, but it took little time for him to realize that Potter was oblivious to anything so insubstantial as an implied accusation. Considerably more than that would be required if he wanted to rattle Joseph Bascomb Potter.

And the longer he sat there the more Willis Bowers found himself wanting to break through the cold, brittle, uncaring shell that Constable Potter showed to the world. Lord, but Bowers had come to detest this man.

"He was only seventeen years old, Potter."

"Who's that, sir?"

"Arnold Littlefeather. Did you know his name, by the way?"

"I don't know what you're talking about, Mayor. And I don't recall anybody named Littlefeather. Some Injun, I take it?"

"Arnold was in my wife's Sunday school class. I'll bet you knew that much anyway. You resented the boy, didn't you, Potter? You didn't want some stinking Indian getting uppity and sitting in the same room with white girls. Was that it, Potter? It was something very much like that, I'll wager."

"I still don't know what you—"

"It was murder plain and simple," Bowers

11

declared hotly. "Murder, damn you. You beat him senseless and you left him lying there on the manure pile behind Gartner's barn. Busted him up so bad be couldn't crawl away to find help and then left him. Left him there to freeze to death."

"I'm sure I don't—"

"Where are your gloves, Potter? You showed me your hands aren't marked. Fine. Now where are your gloves?"

The constable inclined his head in the direction of the doorway where his coat, a shaggy and crudely made but blessedly warm army surplus buffalo coat much like the mayor's, hung on a stout peg. "In the pockets."

Bowers jumped for the door as if he and Potter were engaging in a race for the evidence. But Constable Potter remained seated behind the police chief's desk and enjoyed another sip of the excellent—if as yet unfortified—morning coffee.

The mayor found the heavy, gauntleted, and fur-lined gloves in the flap pockets of the big coat. He practically ripped the gloves free, his expression a mask of triumph. Triumph turned immediately to tragedy and he scowled. "These are..."

"Brand new, that's right. I told you Hap's store was open this morning. I bought the gloves off him just this very morning."

"Where are your old... ?"

"I dunno, Mayor. Lost one, you see. That would've been yesterday sometime. Threw the other away since one glove won't do much to keep a body warm."

"Where... ?"

12

Potter inclined his head again. This time in the direction of the gently chuckling stove, where a deep bed of red, pulsing coals breathed and cackled.

Potter's grin was mocking and nasty.

"You son of a bitch," the mayor said.

The mockery fled from Potter's expression. He tensed and bolted onto his feet, slamming the coffee mug down onto the desk so hard the steaming liquid splashed out onto the blotter and beyond it to the polished wooden surface that Chief Bennett was so fussily careful about.

"Don't you never," Potter hissed.

The mayor recoiled, drawing involuntarily back away from this man, whose rage he had never before seen.

Potter's eyes were colder than the temperatures outside and harder than frozen glass.

"Don't you never call me that," Potter warned. His voice was low and soft and all the more menacing for that. "Never."

Bowers wasn't even tempted to bluster or threaten back.

He was, he was sure, seeing very much the same sight that Arnold Littlefeather last viewed in this vale of tears.

And Willis Bowers was afraid that if anything happened now to trigger the violence that so patently coiled spring-wound and lethal within Joe Potter, he would not live to see the constable's comeuppance.

The mayor was not so anxious to see justice served that he would sacrifice himself on its altar.

13

"That isn't... we're getting sidetracked here," he sputtered and spat, his heart thumping at a dizzying rate.

"You heard me. Don't you *never*," Potter said, "not ever again."

"Like I said, we're getting sidetracked. I was talking about Arnold Littlefeather. He, uh, he's dead."

"You said that."

"You beat him to death."

"You said that, too, but you haven't showed your proof. You got proof, Mayor? Or just that mouth of yours?"

"I know what I know. That's all."

"Knowledge and a nickel, Mayor. Which one of those will buy you a cup of coffee?"

"I'm putting you on warning, Potter. As soon as Chief Bennett gets back from Miles City, I'm calling a special meeting of the town council to ask for your resignation."

"Don't bother. I'm tired of all you bastards anyhow. You want Harry to fire me? Well I quit. The hell with you and the hell with him and the hell with your Sunday school Injuns, too. The hell with all of you."

Potter fumbled at his shirtfront to rip the badge from his breast and realized only too late that he hadn't yet pinned it on. Cursing then and muttering he found the shiny piece of tin on the file cabinet behind the desk, snatched it up, and flung it in the direction of the swiftly retreating mayor.

"There. You happy now, damn you?"

Bowers grabbed his coat and muffler and escaped, leaving his wolfskin hat behind and leaving the police station door open to the frigid elements.

Potter charged across the room and kicked the door, sending it crashing shut.

He grabbed Bowers's hat off the table where it lay crumpled like a dead rat, and he shook it like a terrier snapping a rat's neck. That accomplished nothing, so he whirled and threw the hat into the stove.

Burning hair sizzled and stank, filling the small room with a stench that was almost as bad as the smell had been when Joe burned his stiff and blood-sticky gloves earlier.

Damn them anyway, he fumed. Damn them all, the bleeding-heart politicians and the vile, stinking Indians and all their kin and sympathizers, too. Damn them each and every one.

After a bit the roaring in his ears subsided, at least a little, and he felt himself growing calm again.

He almost wished now that he hadn't been quite so quick to acquiesce to the mayor's plan to get rid of him.

Belle Creek wasn't such a bad town. With some exceptions, that is. More to the point, it was not apt to be easy for him to find another job as a peace officer.

Damn politicians were a bunch of gossipy old sons of bitches. That was plain enough, or Bowers wouldn't have heard those lies about him out of Cohagen and Glendive. And who knew where else besides.

Damn it anyway.

If he was done for in Belle Creek, then he likely was done for in Montana. He'd just about used the place up.

15

Maybe Wyoming next, he thought. Perhaps he could find something there. Preferably something in the line of peace officering. He did so love the feel of a revolver heavy on his hip and the stand-proud sense of knowing there was a badge on his chest. A gun and badge made a man taller and stronger. It swelled his neck and let him breathe deeper than any ordinary man, and Joe Potter loved it.

Wyoming then, he decided. And the hell with these miserable bastards in Montana. The hell with all of them.

2

Manwaring, Wyoming
Tuesday, April 21, 1908

Police Chief Joseph Potter leaned against the back wall of Stimson's Hardware, one foot propped lazily onto the husk of a broken bucket that lay amid the alley litter. The hour was late and the alley dark and there was a chill in the air. The police chief slouched warm and comfortable inside the protection of his coat, his hands shoved deep into the flannel-lined coat pockets and chin tucked tight into the upturned collar. Judging from posture alone he might have been thought to be drowsing there. Except for his eyes. His eyes were bright with alert interest beneath the short, greasy bill of his fur-lined cap. Appearances aside, Chief Potter was very much awake and aware.

A series of dull, partially muffled sounds reached him—footsteps coming from within

16

the building he leaned against—and Potter straightened into an upright position, abandoning the support of the milled lumber wall and distributing his weight lightly and evenly with his feet placed shoulder width apart. He removed his hands from his pockets—he wore no gloves—and slowly, carefully unfastened one coat button at waist level.

A hint of eager smile thinned his lips—or that might have been a trick of pale moonlight as a cloud scudded across the face of a cold, distant moon—and he sidled closer to the hardware store wall where the shadows were deepest.

A dozen feet away there was a brittle screech of metal upon metal as an ill-hung door moved on unoiled hinges. A dark void in the wall became darker still, and then there was movement within the framework. A figure, slight and hunched low, came into sight from within. The small figure was hatless and round, swaddled heavy in an oversized greatcoat and scraps of old blanket pressed into service as muffler and head covering alike. The figure could be only dimly seen, black outline against charcoal background. The person appeared to carry a bundle clutched tight to his—or to her—belly. The person paused at the door and with some difficulty managed to balance the bundle with one hand while with the other he reached out to find the knob and pull the door shut with another thin creak from the hinges.

Potter withdrew his hand from beneath his coat. He definitely was smiling now.

" 'Ey! Pablo. Kay passo, little buddy? Eh?"

17

The lumpy figure by the door jumped, startled, but continued to cling to the bundle that was held so tight against his midsection.

"Doing a little robbery, eh, Pablo? Little bit of breaking an' entering?"

"N-no, I—"

"Don't you be lying t' me, boy. I got you dead t' rights, Pablo. I seen you hanging around this evenin', you know. Seen you watching, waiting for old Stimson to lock up an' go home. You're dumb, Pablo. A damn blind man could see what you was up to. You might as well hang a sign round your scrawny neck an' ring bells to call attention to yourself. I seen you pick that lock and I seen you go inside a while back and now I seen you come out carrying that there loot that belongs to Mr. Stimson. I got you, Pablo. I got you dead to rights."

"Señor, please, I... I don't take much. Here. You see. You look, please." The man called Pablo—his name was Emilio Cantiflores Estevan Suarez-Morales, but here he was known only as Pablo—took his carefully wrapped bundle of stolen goods, none of the individual articles of any great moment or value, and held them out to the chief of police, held them out with both hands as if offering them to the dour and brooding *yanqui*, held them out on upturned palms as a supplicant beseeching a boon. Held them out as proof of his own veracity or, if the other wished, if the other would accept, as *mordita*, as what they called here the bribe. "You will see. I don' take much. Here. Take. Please. You take."

Potter sighed and shook his head. Sadly. For a moment Pablo had hope. This man, he

18

would see, he would take, the moment would be past, no harm would be done. Pablo would be no better off than before. But no worse off either. It would be all right. And tomorrow... but now the *yanqui* with the cruel lips and the empty eyes snickered. It was a small sound. Cold laughter as empty as the eyes of the *yanqui*. It chilled Emilio Suarez-Morales and cut through him the way the cool of the night air never could. It brought a leap of fear into his heart and sent his pulse to racing.

"Señor. Please."

There was a flare. Sun-bright in the darkness. And something hard and heavy crashed into Pablo's throat. Had the tall *jefe* struck him? No? He was too far away for that. What then? Pablo felt numb. He could not get his breath, and there was a wet, gurgling noise. He was weak, weak. His knees would no longer hold him. No matter, for he no longer stood. He was lying down now—ah, but that was good, for now he could rest—and the cold was receding. Of a sudden Pablo-Emilio was surrounded by warmth. He felt good. Light. So light he seemed to float. He closed his eyes. Ah, this thing was not so very bad. He no longer hurt. No longer ached. No longer felt hunger or pain or...

"I sure as hell thought he had a gun. You know? I mean, here he's coming out of the hardware store and it's black out as an Injun's heathen soul and I can't see a damn thing. But he's coming outta the hardware store an' you and me both know the most valuable things Fred Stimson has in stock there are them guns he sells. So I naturally figure that thiev-

19

ing sonuvabitch Pablo... which I didn't know at the time was him, you understand, I only found that out later, too... anyway, I figure whoever he is he's stole some guns an' is coming out armed. And the first thing when I try and take him he drops what all he's carrying and jerks his hand. Now I can't tell you what he had in mind when he done that. He can't neither. But I can tell you what I *thought* he was doing and that's going for a gun so's he could shoot me. When I fired, Your Honor, it was purely in self-defense. Nobody felt any worse than me t' learn Pablo didn't have no gun on him after all. But at the time, Your Honor, I didn't know that. All I knew at the time was that he was jerking around like as if he was going for a gun an' I was right in front of him too close to miss. If he'd had a gun an' I hadn't shot first, well, he'd've had me sure. The way I saw it at the time, Your Honor, it was him or me. I'm sorry as hell it worked out the way it did, but what I done last night was pure self-defense."

"That is your sworn testimony, Chief Potter?"

"Yes, sir, it is. I've wrote it down right here, pretty much like I just told it to you, an' signed it. Whit Bayliss and James Burdett witnessed my signature to the statement."

"Neither of them witnessed the incident, I take it?"

"No, sir there wasn't nobody in that alley last night but me an' old Pablo. I wisht there had been. Maybe if there'd been more folks there he wouldn't've done what he done and I wouldn't've had to shoot him."

The justice of the peace sighed and tapped a polished oak anvil with his gavel, the sound loud and sharp in the town hall office the JP shared with the assessor, the town clerk, and the president of the town council. "I will enter a ruling of self-defense, Chief Potter."

"Thank you, Your Honor."

"But... Potter."

"Yes, sir?"

The judge frowned, hesitated, finally shook his head. "Nothing, Potter. I was going to say something else. But I don't think there would be any purpose to it."

"Whatever you say, Your Honor. Can I go now?"

"Yes, certainly."

"Thank you, Your Honor. Thank you very much."

The JP said nothing as Joe Potter turned and sauntered, whistling, out of the town hall building.

3

Saturday, June 6, 1908

"Twenty-five, gentlemen. The price of cards is going up a quarter."

"I'll see your quarter, Potter, and"—Whit Bayliss fingered the loose mound of change in front of him, then pushed three coins into the center of the table—"raise you another four bits."

"I'm out."

"Too much for me." The other two men at

21

the table shook their heads and dropped their cards facedown.

"Call," Joe said. He tossed fifty cents into the middle and plucked one card from his hand, placing it to the side. "Take one."

"Opener takes one," said one of the men who'd dropped out. He picked up what remained of the deck and slid one card off the top to deliver it to Potter. "Whit?"

"Two, please," Bayliss said, his smile deliberately smug and his eyes squarely meeting Potter's.

"You're bluffing," Potter said.

"Could be," Bayliss agreed pleasantly. "The question now is, are you willing to back that claim with cash?"

"I opened. I bet ten cents."

"Your ten and up fifty." The table limit was a half-dollar per raise, no more than four raises per round.

Joe Potter peered at his hand for a moment as if assessing his chances. Well, he was doing that all right. But his quandary had nothing to do with the cards he'd drawn. He'd started with two pair, jacks and treys, and he hadn't improved on that. Hadn't expected to either. He hated to get two pairs in the first deal. You could as good as never improve on them. He suspected Bayliss started with one pair and was trying to run a bluff on him by asking for only two cards. Whit did that sort of thing sometimes. Dammit. The question was, was he doing it now? And if he was, had he drawn a third card anyway? Three of a kind beat the crap out of two pair.

But did Bayliss have three of a kind? Or only the pair Joe believed he'd started with.

It would cost another fifty cents for him to find out. There wasn't much on the table in front of Joe by now. He could ill afford to lose another half-dollar. But if he won this pot...

"Shit," he grumbled, although with no particular heat or emphasis in his voice.

Bayliss winked at him.

"I still say you're bluffing."

"So call me. Four bits buys you a look."

Potter frowned. And folded his cards, dropping them facedown onto the pile of money.

Bayliss smiled and raked in the pot.

"Did you have them, Whit?"

"That's something you'll never ever know, Joe."

Joe Potter had a gut-deep hankering to reach out and pick up the cards Whit Bayliss laid down. He wanted to know, dammit. To *know*. But he stifled the impulse and, he hoped, kept the desire from showing where any of the others might read it. There are some things a man simply doesn't do.

"Ante up, boys. Who's light?"

Joe tossed his nickel into the middle of the table and watched Gene Comer pull all the cards of the much used deck to him, mixing them together and forever eliminating any chance for Joe to know if Whit bluffed him or not. After all, at this point even if Whit confessed to it Joe wouldn't know if he was lying or not.

Dammit, now he regretted not calling Whit. He was sure it'd been a bluff. He should have

23

spent the fifty cents. His two pair might have won. Probably would have. He would never know. Not for sure.

"Pass," Gene said.

"Pass."

"I'll bet a dime," Joe said. He had four clubs and the ace of diamonds in his hand, but the table rule was that a man could open on nerve alone if he wanted.

"I'm out," Bayliss said. Joe didn't care much for that. He wanted to get some of his money back from Whit.

"Beats me."

"I'm out, too."

Joe left a nickel in the middle and dragged back the rest of it. Fifteen cents. Big deal. It wasn't enough to wipe out the sour taste of having been bluffed by Whit Bayliss. Not by a long shot, it wasn't. Still...

Joe accepted the deck from Comer, shuffled, and began to deal. Properly speaking the dealer had the choice of games, but there was no need to announce what was being dealt. Not with this bunch. With Whit and Gene and Carl Morton the game never changed. Straight draw poker, unadulterated and never anything wild. Joe dealt, glanced down at the junk he'd given himself, and passed.

He sighed. Another Saturday night and it looked like he was going to make his usual contribution to the well-being of the others at the table. Dammit. He should have called Whit. He really should have.

"Chief Potter. Are you all right, sir?"

Joe stopped, caught at the doorjamb to

24

steady himself, and gave the kid—what the hell was his name anyhow? He couldn't recall it for some reason—a cold, hard glare. Yes, he was all right. Shit, yes. What did this guy think anyway?

"You forgot your hat, Chief." The young man—he worked for the saloon owner, Al Benjamin; Jimmy? Johnny? Jerry? something that began with a *J*, Joe thought; but not Joe; wouldn't that have been funny, ha ha ha—held the hat out to him. Ugly damn thing, that hat. Old and sweat-stained and beat all to hell, full of camp dust and dried dung, so sun-bleached and water-leached that you couldn't hardly tell now what color it used to be. Used to be a proud damn hat, it did. Campaign hat. Kossuth. Hell, they didn't even issue them like that anymore. Hadn't in years. But Joe had this one. Earned it too, by damn. Came by it honest and square. Damn kid—*Jeremy,* that was the kid's name—damn Jeremy wouldn't know about stuff like that.

Joe pinched his lips tight shut against an impulse to belch and reached out to take his hat from the kid. Jeremy, he repeated silently to himself. Jeremy. Gotta remember that. It seemed important at the time. Gotta remember. So much to remember. Too much. All the time something else. Sometimes a man just got plain tired of remembering all the time.

He reached forward, and his shoulder slid away from the doorjamb and he lurched, nearly taking a tumble. Jeremy grabbed at him to restore his balance and at the same time, ignoring Joe's outstretched hand, draped the old hat atop Police Chief Potter's thinning hair.

25

"Quit that, dammit." Joe slapped at the boy's arm. He hated it when somebody did something like that. Didn't this kid know that nobody could set a man's hat onto his head except the person himself? Stupid little sonuvabitch, Jeremy. Insulting. Oughta take the little bastard in and lock him up.

"Yes, sir. Sorry, Chief."

That was better. Little respect, that's what was called for here. Just a little respect. Joe took hold of the doorjamb with one hand and with the other carefully, very carefully, resettled his hat. Now it was comfortable. Yeah, much better. Some things a fellow just has to do for himself. Like put on his hat. Or hold it when he takes a leak. Couldn't ask anybody else to do that, could he?

The thought of asking somebody else to unbutton a fly and hold the old blind snake for you struck Joe as being uproariously funny. Funniest damn thing he'd ever heard, you bet. He commenced to laugh. Stood there in the doorway of Al Benjamin's saloon and laughed until he hurt from the laughing. Laughed until he hurt so bad it wasn't funny anymore, then stopped just long enough for some of the hurting to subside and, thinking in spite of himself again about getting this Jeremy—or maybe some fine-looking little hoor, now wouldn't *that* be fun—to hold it for him went to laughing all over again. He laughed so hard his knees buckled, and he found himself sitting on the floor in the open doorway of Al Benjamin's stinking damn saloon. Didn't remember getting there, but next thing he knew he was sitting on the floor all right.

"Can't I help you, Chief? See you home, maybe?"

"Get away from me, y' little bastard." Joe slapped the offered hand away and, a little shaky but otherwise fine, really, just fine, managed to climb back onto his feet again.

"Yes, sir. Anything you say, Chief."

"Tha's better. Ri'. Damn ri'." Joe squared his shoulders and shot his jaw. Shit, he was all right now. Just a mite tired, that was all. Tired. Needed a little sleep. Be just fine again come morning. "G'ni', kid."

"Good night, Chief."

Shoulders rigid and eyes locked straight forward, solemnly and with his dignity intact, Chief of Police Joe Potter marched slowly to his quarters at the back of Mrs. Sherrod's boarding house.

4

The only good thing to be said for Sunday mornings was that all the hypocrites—which is to say all the town big shots and most everybody else, too—were off the streets. Instead they were all in church singing hymns and playing at being pious. Well, Joe Potter wasn't no hypocrite. He was a lot of things—including, at the moment, damned well hungover—but he wasn't no hypocrite.

Hypocrite. Good word, that one. A two-bit'er if ever he heard one. He snorted. There were those, he could name the sons of bitches if he had to, who looked down on Joe Potter and said he wasn't as good as they were. Well,

27

they were the ones that were the hypocrites, not him. And he knew a thing or two. He could handle some fancy language when he wanted. Fancy language, fancy women, all of that.

Damn them all anyhow.

He squinted, the glare of the sun bright on the empty main street of Manwaring, and tugged the brim of his hat a little lower. Lordy, but his head did hurt this morning. More so than usual, he thought. Which was what had driven him out of his blankets at this unusual-for-a-Sunday forenoon hour. Generally speaking, Chief Potter's weekends held to a pleasant enough routine. A few hands of poker with the boys on Saturday night and a few drinks afterward. Then on Sunday he'd sleep in until midafternoon or thereabouts. At five on Sunday afternoons he'd have his regular, once-a-week visit with whichever one of Fat Edna's girls he wanted. No charge for the chief of police, of course. And no harm done to anyone, not even the girls, because on Sundays there wasn't any trade to speak of anyway, all the married men being at home sleeping off their Sunday dinners, and always after five because Fat Edna claimed it wasn't moral to open for business any earlier than that on the Sabbath. Joe figured Fat Edna was a hypocrite, too, but not so offensive a one as the men hypocrites in town. At least Edna was willing to give a little something if she also expected to get. Edna, she was all right compared with most of them.

Still, it was way too early in the day for him to be thinking about Edna and her girls.

28

There was no point in showing up there for another five, six hours.

Right now what Joe wanted—no, what Joe *needed*—was a hair of the dog. His head hurt so bad and his tongue felt so dry and awful that he needed a drink, maybe two, to kind of smooth over the lumps and lay a little padding atop the worst of the pounding.

Al wouldn't be open at this hour—he'd be down the street at the Methodist church helping them prove they were louder and therefore more pious than the stiff-necked Lutherans—but Joe knew where Al hid the spare key to the back door. One drink, maybe two. He could pay for them later.

The key was... no, that wasn't it, now where was the damn thing anyhow. It wasn't tucked inside the knothole in the framing like he'd thought. Joe commenced to sweat just a little. He really wanted that drink. Did he remember Al saying something about the key two, three weeks back? Like moving it to... ah, sure. Now he remembered. Caught inside the downspout, that was where it'd been moved to. Sure.

Joe took the few steps to the back of the alley beside Al's place and, his head thumping and thudding like a bass drum, knelt to reach inside the rusty tin opening of the downspout pipe. Normally he would've bent over to reach the thing but he was afraid if he bent so that his head was lower than his heart he might bust something inside his skull. His head was hurting him that bad.

"There you—"

Something clattered behind him and Joe like

to came out of his pelt. He said something aloud—he didn't recollect what—and jumped like he'd been jabbed with a cattle prod. He grabbed for the butt of his Army Colt. Then scowled and shook his head. Carefully so as not to make the pounding any worse.

Damn cat. He'd have shot the thing if it wouldn't have been for the noise.

Ignoring the tabby—and the fright it had given him—he resumed his search for the key.

There! That was better. He drew it slowly out of the pipe and quickly unlocked the back door to the saloon.

It's a funny thing about a saloon when it's closed and no one else is around. There is a lonely, empty sort of feel about it and a smell like nothing and no place else on the face of this earth. A closed saloon smells sour and stale, and there is a sort of shabbiness about it no matter how nice or how new it might otherwise be.

Even the light seems different in a shut-down saloon, filtering in through drawn blinds so the whole place takes on a fuzzy gold coloration and the dust motes drift in the nearly still air without energy or purpose.

At night when the boys are hoisting a few there is a world of energy in even the worst of such places. But on a Sunday morning... Joe shivered, cold ghost fingers tickling his spine like the hand of some ghastly dead piano player.

He jumped again, different this time from when the alley cat had startled him, and quick grabbed for one of the cheap bottles behind the gouged, stained old bar.

He'd only intended a drink or two, but he sure as hell didn't feel like hanging around in here for the purpose. He figured he'd just take the bottle with him. He could pay for it later. If Al wanted him to, that is.

Chief Potter carried his bottle with a grip so tight his knuckles went white. Without stopping to look around anymore he got the hell out of there and only remembered at the last minute to go back and replace the key in the downspout.

Then he took his jug and carried it out of town and on down the creek toward the patch of shade he went to down there sometimes, past the bend where the town kids drowned crickets in the hope of finding some sunfish or, the great trophy, an actual trout.

He sat at the bole of a sickly cottonwood, his legs spread wide and his hat snug against the brilliance of the sun, and he uncorked the bottle. Two drinks. Absolutely no more than four. Then he'd stash the rest to come back to some other time and go back for a quick walk-through checking doors to the town business. It was the weekend, but he wasn't completely off duty. But then a police officer never is.

5

Chief of Police Potter took hold of the doorknob, twisted, pushed. Nothing. The door was locked. Just like it was supposed to be. A man never knows, though. Lots of times people would close up for the night and forget

31

to check their back doors. Maybe they hadn't known the thing was unlocked sometime during the day. Maybe they just forgot. It was a cop's job to check, to make sure, to go and get the business owner whenever a door was found open. A good part of the time when that happened the guy would discover that someone had slipped in and helped himself to something. Cash mostly. The owners generally knew it when cash was taken. Little things, though, they generally missed seeing. Or rather didn't miss. Little things could disappear and nobody would ever know or notice. Joe Potter knew that because quite often he was the one who picked up some little something for himself before he went to fetch the businessman. Never anything important, of course, and never anything that could be traced. A penknife, sure. A twist of tobacco, of course. But never anything big like a new suit of clothes or a Gramophone. Never anything like that and never anything with a serial number like paper currency. There were some businessmen in town who deliberately wrote down the serial numbers of some bills and then left them in the cash drawer hoping to locate a thief by that method. Joe knew good and well they did that because they told him so. They let him know so as chief of police he would be prepared to hunt down and apprehend any backdoor thief who made the mistake of taking that bait. Joe thought it pretty rich that the stupid sheep in town told him all about their silly traps. Hell, he knew all about stuff like that anyway. Every copper does. And every copper regards backdoor scrounging as simply one of the little perks that comes with the job. Just like every copper knows that it's only safe in a situation like that to take the coins and leave the bills alone. Silver you don't generally mess with, not above maybe a couple three silver dollars. The gold coins, though, the eagles and double eagles and half eagles and $2.50 quarter eagles, those were meat on the table if any businessman was dumb enough to leave them laying around unlocked and untended. Hell, taking those was practically a public service. It taught the people something. Joe knew that for a fact because it'd been, what, more than a month anyway since he'd found any gold coins lying around loose.

Anyway he checked the back door of the barber shop, moved down the alley and tried the door behind Mrs. Damar's ladies' wear, and stopped outside Doc Trenton's pharmacy. He didn't bother to check that door, just leaned close to it and listened. After a moment he began to grin.

Yeah, it was Sunday afternoon, all right. And Charlie Trenton, Doc to most of the town, was inside as usual. Not that the pharmacy was open. Not hardly. And if anybody needed Doc in a hurry at this hour of a Sunday afternoon they were gonna be disappointed. Nobody could ever find him at this time on a Sunday.

Nobody but Joe Potter. Him and Ernie Hipplewite's daughter Peggy. Peggy Hipplewite was fifteen years old, a giggler and a simperer with bad teeth and big bazooms. Joe had seen her kind often enough before. Inside a year young Peggy would either be knocked up and sent off to a home for wayward girls or she'd be found out and thrown out. And by either of those paths Joe figured inside two years old Peggy—for she sure as hell wouldn't still be young then no matter what her age would indicate—inside two years old Peggy would be selling the same stuff she was giving away free for nothing to Doc Trenton these days.

Joe leaned against the pharmacy door and grinned while he listened in. That Peggy, she was a squealer and a thumper, she was. Made a guy kinda horny just listening to her. Joe figured he was going to have to hurry his route through the alleys and get over to Edna's place soon to kinda scrape off the edge Peggy Hipplewite was putting onto him. And if Peggy wound up working at Edna's someday, why, Joe would just have to try her on himself. This was something he'd resolved for himself every Sunday afternoon since Doc started in on Peggy two, three months back. Reluctantly he stood upright, withdrawing from the tantalizing sounds inside the pharmacy.

It pleased Joe to know things like that, though. Things that nobody knew that he knew. Things nobody was supposed to know. But then that was another of the perks that came with the job of being a copper. You got to know all the good stuff. Or almost all of it. Joe hadn't found out yet what it was that Trenton gave to Peggy to make her do for him like she did. It was something out of all those jars and bottles and chemicals and shit that Doc kept in the place there. Whatever it was it seemed to work like magic, and Joe wished he had some of it.

And so he might, one of these days. That was yet another thing a copper had going for him. Once you got to knowing the good stuff on a guy there was generally some leverage that could be applied, but quiet like, to loosen a fellow up and convince him to come across with a little assistance. Like whatever it was that Peggy liked so much she'd turn herself inside out if that was what Doc wanted from her on a Sunday afternoon. Jeez, it'd be wonderful to have that kind of power over a woman. Joe could think of four, five… hell, a dozen… women in town he'd like to slip some of that stuff.

Thinking about that prospect made Joe shiver. And grin.

He left the alley and crossed into the next block to start along the backs of the stores there.

6

Joe wasn't feeling any too good. His stomach was sour and the sun was still so bright it hurt his eyes. He needed… hell, he didn't know what he needed. Not for sure. He needed to go over to Edna's for one thing. Go over there and have a few drinks, let one of the girls pull his boots off and rub his feet for him. And whatever else, of course. But first he needed… he didn't know. Something. Dammit. He scowled and rattled the knob of George Morgan's back door, then moved along to the hardware.

He stopped short and blinked. Jesus! The door was all right. But the window in the back wall was cracked a good two or three inch-

35

es. The last time Joe was through here that window was closed and locked. And that had been last night, long after Fred closed for the weekend. Somebody'd come along and opened that window since then.

Joe moved closer and peered carefully along the window frame as best he could without exposing himself to the sight of anybody that might still be inside.

There weren't any pry marks. Not that he could see.

Joe's mouth felt kinda dry, and his eyes burned. He was staring so hard he didn't want to blink lest he miss seeing something, and he was listening so hard he scarcely wanted to breathe lest the sound of his own breathing cover over some sound inside the hardware store.

The thing was, there wasn't no way to know if whoever opened this window was still inside or not. The guy could've come along sometime last night after Joe already made his rounds, sometime past midnight, say. It'd been, what, eight-thirty or nine o'clock when Joe checked the alleys last night. He always did that early on Saturdays, knowing he wouldn't be in any shape for it later on in the evening.

This thief here could've gone in and robbed Fred Stimson at ten last night and by now be all the way to Cheyenne. Hell, by now he could've reached Cheyenne all right and taken a train. By now he could be well on his way to Omaha or Ogden or some such place. Or just as easy the sonuvabitch could still be inside there, and if Joe peeked in to try and find out he could get his brains blown out of his hat.

Helluva thing to let happen to a man's hat, that would be.

Joe smiled a bit at that thought, pleased with himself for being able to come up with it. Being able to make light of a situation like this, Joe figured that showed some nerve.

He took hold of the butt end of his Colt's patent revolving pistol—that was what the old hoglegs were officially termed, although practically nobody ever knew that; but Joe did— and leaned against the side of the building to listen and think and wait to see what happened next.

Jesus, but he was sweating. And it wasn't all that hot a day.

He held the barrel of the revolver carefully in his left hand while just as carefully he wiped the palm of his right along the seam of his trousers. Then he resumed his grip on the gun and, leaning his head against the peeling, splintered wood of the siding at the back of Fred's store, closed his eyes for a moment while he focused all his attention on listening.

Jesus! Oh, Jesus, Lordy, have mercy. The sonuvabitch was still in there. Joe could hear the clink of something—glass against glass— and then a thump. Two more thumps. A muffled sound that might've been cussing. Something else that sounded like Fred's old gray mouser running across the floor. And another thump.

Yeah, the SOB was in there all right. Joe took some deep breaths and got hold of himself. It was all right. He knew what he was facing now. Knowing that there was a live thief roaming around loose inside Fred's hardware, bad as it was, somehow seemed to make things better. Like it was the uncertainty and not the thief that was a bother to him.

And, hell, he supposed that was true. He'd faced thieves before—thieves and worse than thieves. If this one didn't give it up nice and easy, Joe would just put a hot round in his belly. That would take the fight out of anybody even if the guy was eight foot tall. Joe was a born-again believer in that old saw about God creating all men equal but Sam Colt making them all the same size. Joe didn't fear no man, not so long as he had his .45 in his hand. And knew what he was facing. Joe would go head-to-head with any son of a bitch and not back down.

He would... he'd quit thinking about anything except what was happening inside that hardware store, that's what he'd by-damn do, for now he could hear some of those noises heading back toward the open window where Police Chief Joseph Bascomb Potter was waiting, gun in hand, ready to make himself a hero to the town yet again.

In fact this couldn't hardly be better, what with Fred getting himself elected to the town council. It never hurt to give one of the bosses reason for a mite of gratitude. And this would be twice now that Joe Potter foiled a breaking and entering at the hardware.

Joe quickly wiped his hand on this trouser leg again and licked at lips that'd gone dry on him. That was all kind of backward, wasn't it? Palms wet and mouth dry. It was supposed to be the other way to. Ha. Oh, Joe was proud of himself. He was doing fine here. Everything good and under control. Everything…

The window shot up, and a leg and butt appeared on the sill.

Little sonuvabitch, Joe saw. Not that that mattered. Little men shoot bullets just as big as anybody else's.

The thief ducked low to clear the bottom of the window. When he was half outside the store, hanging there with one leg still indoors and Joe standing ready not a yard behind him, Joe took one short step forward and, gauging his blow with some care as to placement, bashed the crap outta the little bastard.

The barrel of Joe's Colt came down just a little way behind and slightly above the guy's ear. It landed with a solid thud like somebody thumping a melon to see was it ripe enough to split open. And ripe enough or not this guy's scalp split right open just as pretty as you please.

There was the thud of the gun barrel hitting its target and then a low, strangled sort of grunt, and next thing there was blood flowing and the guy was dropping like a felled shoat, dropping clean out of the window into a rag-doll lump on the ground smack in front of Joe's feet.

Joe followed that first swipe just natural as could be and kicked the silly sucker in the kidneys. The guy squealed and turned, curling into a ball, and Joe kicked him this time in the ribs. He could feel something let go, so he kicked him again.

"No, no, no myGoddon'tyoudothat-nomore…."

Something small and screaming came fly-

39

ing out the open window to smack him hard and wrap itself around his head, sending Joe stumbling off balance and half-blind, his boots crackling through the littered junk on the ground inside the alley. He tried to swat the thing off him like you'd swat at a bat that tangled its claws in your hair, but the damn thing kept screeching at him and hanging on to him and after a half second's panic—it was a damn good thing he never thought to bring his gun around to bear on this thing that'd gone and jumped him through the hardware store window—he got wits enough about him to figure out that it was a kid he was carrying like a monkey on his back and that the kid was screaming something at him and had both arms wrapped clean around Joe's head and neck and, the most important part of this, around his throat, too, so that he couldn't hardly breathe much less think properly.

"Chief Potter, please don't, sir, don't shoot Jimmy, Chief, please don't hurt him no more, please."

It occurred to Joe that maybe things here weren't exactly like he thought. He shoved his gun back into its pouch and took hold of the boy who was riding his shoulders. It took both hands to pry the kid loose, but after a few moments Joe got the job done and set the kid down onto the ground to where he could get a look at him.

"Shit, you're Fred Stimson's boy Asa, aren't you?"

"Yes, sir, and that's Jimmy Taggert laying on the ground there, Chief."

Jesus God! Joe felt the blood rush out of his

head and his face go numb. And not from booze neither. Jimmy Taggert was Mayor Merle Taggert's boy. And Joe Potter had gone and half killed him thinking he was some sneak thief.

"What the hell were you kids doing in your papa's store there, dammit?"

"We was sneaking some fishhooks and line, that's all. I swear that's all. Papa said we couldn't have no more, but we only..."

Joe groaned. He looked down at the kid who was writhing on the ground nearby, blood still flowing and ribs likely broke and who knew what else wrong with him.

This wasn't gonna go over real well with the town council. That was the one thing Joe could be real sure about right now. This kid, dammit, was white. And his papa was respectable. There's things a man knows not to do, and this right here was one of them in the not-to-do category. One that Joe had gone and done before he ever realized it.

Jeez!

"Look, uh, kid, I think maybe you'd better run get Doc Trenton to come take a look at your little friend. But don't go to his house. He ain't there." Joe sighed. This wasn't going to do him no good neither. But what choice did he have? If Taggert's shitty little thief of a kid went and got complications or something, if the little bastard died or something... "I know where you can find him, kid, so run quick an' fetch him, will you?"

"Yes, sir, you bet."

Reluctantly and with great foreboding, Joe told the Stimson kid where to find the closest thing Manwaring had to a doctor. Then he stood leaning against the back of the damn hardware store waiting for people to start showing up. It wasn't going to be long, he knew that.

FLOWERS IN THE SNOW. *Blossoms. So pretty. Ah, and color. This time color. Pale and delicate yellow. Bright and bold scarlet. Dark and earthy brown. The blossoms came in such wonderful colors.*

They burst forth as if by magic. Quick eruptions rising out of the pure, clean white of the snow.

A spray of palest yellow fire here. A scattering of clay and old grasses there.

And every now and then the bright, bright red of the blood.

Oh, God, the blood. Spreading wide across the snow, its brilliant red contrasts stark upon the purity of the snow. Speckled, streaked, lying in runnels and rivers and tiny ponds with still, reflective surfaces. So much blood. Hot against the snow, with wispy tendrils of steam rising from it. Living blood so quickly become death. And yet… beautiful. The color was strikingly beautiful. Did it follow that the death was, too? Surely it must, for the blood was death. The fire, the eruptions, those brought the death and the death brought the blood and the blood was beautiful against the snow.

Blossoms. Flowers rising briefly in the snow and quickly falling back to earth again to be swallowed by the snow and forever lost.

Flowers without sound. There should have been sound. Without any sensation of turning, or being turned, his gaze swept slowly round. White of snow, still with blossoms. And now, too, with the dark and formless lumps that lay, each surrounded by a halo of boldest red, upon the field of white.

And there, off close to the horizon, the dark and

simple silhouettes. Sticks and wheels and tiny, human-shaped figures. Cannons and cannoneers. Tiny yellow blooms—not yet blossoms but merely buds as precursors to the blossoms—winking and chuckling at the mouths of the cannons.

Ah, it was beautiful. It was.

He would have smiled. If he could have.

Instead he brought the blossoms into his heart and enclosed them there.

Chapter 2

1

ZK Ranch, Northwestern Nebraska
Thursday, August 12, 1909

"Gawddammit!" Potter barked his sudden anger and flung the claw hammer down into the slippery wet clay at the base of the tower. Pete Bower jumped out of the way, damn near went down into the slimy stuff when his boots slid on the greasy clay, and glared up at Joe.

"What the hell's the matter with you now?" Bower demanded.

"A splinter. I got me a damn splinter here."

"If you go an' hit me with something, Potter, I'm gonna give you more'n a splinter to worry about. Now hurry up, will you? I don't wanna be late getting back."

Joe glared right back at him. But didn't carry it any further. Pete was a little sonuvabitch, but mean. He was one of those lean, sawed-off little runts that didn't know or just plain didn't care that he was half the size of a regular human person. Pete would fight anything, man or beast, that had hair, and likely win, too. He was known to be the best bronc peeler on the outfit—or for that matter probably the best in this part of the country—and he was proddy today anyhow on account of being told to drive a wagon and help

45

Joe tend to the windmills. Pete Bower came from the old school of cowboying, from back when a man felt insulted whenever he was asked to do a job that couldn't be handled off the back of a tall horse.

Joe, now, he wasn't from anybody's school of cowboying. To him the business of nurse-maiding cows was just another way to draw pay. In his time he'd done some of this and a lot of that, lifted shovels and cut sod, laid up walls and swamped floors, cut hay and... upheld the law. That had been the best. This... who gave a fat crap if some stupid cow had to walk to the next tank over or not?

Well, there was an answer to that one, wasn't there? Old man Schumacher cared, that's who. And it was Schumacher that laid out the payroll, so Schumacher was the man whose opinion counted out here.

Joe clung to the wooden ladder with one elbow hooked through a rung while he sucked and nibbled at the heel of his hand. Damn splinter. It was bad enough it'd stabbed him. What was worse was the sweat running into the wound now, and the salt of that was stinging like hell. Joe got the sharp bit of creosote wood out of the meat of his hand and spit on the still smarting wound to try and clean some of the salt away. He should've worn his gloves, but it was too late for that now. He sure as hell wasn't going all the way back down the ladder to get them. As it was his knees were shaky and his breath coming kind of quick. Joe didn't like heights, and if there is one thing that can be said about a windmill tower it's that the son of a bitch is tall. Joe was real careful to not look out across the grass when he was atop one of the miserable things. All he looked at up there was whatever was smack in front of his nose. Nothing more.

"Are you gonna do this or not?"

"You wanna do it instead?" Joe called back. "Just say the word an' I'm on my way down." That would shut Pete up. With his stupid pride, Pete never did any actual tower climbing. Joe had to do all that. What Pete did was drive the damn wagon and fill the grease bucket whenever it needed it. Lazy little SOB. One of these days him and Pete were going to get into it. He was sure they would.

Joe spat again, not very particular about which way the wind might carry it, and scrambled the rest of the way up the ladder. He felt a little better, not much but anyhow a little, once he was safely on the platform that surrounded the mill head.

The mill was already shut off. Joe locked the mechanism in place—just this summer there'd been a boy, a dumb kid thirteen or so, who hadn't bothered to tether the mill he was working on; the wind shifted and the tail vane snapped around and bumped the kid clean off the tower; busted his back, they said, and he wouldn't never walk again; Joe Potter wasn't about to let something like that happen, not to him—then began checking each and every nut to see was it tight on its bolt. The stupid things worked loose and had to be checked all the time. Whenever he found one he could turn with his fingers he used the patent wrench to tighten it.

Once that was all done and he'd looked

47

the thing over to make sure everything seemed to be where it belonged and that nothing looked busted or missing, he pulled a lump of twine from his back pocket and, tying the wrench on to give the free end some weight, lowered one end.

"Okay," Pete hollered a moment later. Joe lifted the twine, considerably heavier now, and brought up the grease bucket and flat wooden paddle they kept in it.

The grease was plain old axle grease, thick and gooey and stinking, but for all that fairly effective. Axle grease could take the abuse of a lot of sun and wind and rain. Joe slathered it onto the gears good and thick—he wasn't paying for it, after all—then stuck the paddle back in and lowered the bucket to the ground, letting the twine fall once he felt the ground take the weight.

"Coming down," he called unnecessarily. Pete Bower wouldn't care if he came down or not. But what the hell.

"Hurry up, dammit. We got two more to look at before we can head back in, and I don't wanna be late for supper again tonight."

Joe thought about telling Pete what he could do with his supper tonight but decided not to. He was busy taking care to not get any more splinters and could only concentrate on one thing at a time, after all.

2

Joe wrinkled his nose and looked at the window to make sure the thing was propped

48

open as wide as it could get. Bad enough that it was hot. What was worse was that the stinking bunkhouse... well, the damn thing stank. Eight men living inside one small cabin with all their dirty clothes piled in heaps at the foot of their bunks—nobody in his right mind put his laundry pile under the head of a bunk— and the days so hot this time of year that a guy came in from work all sweaty and covered with dust, there wasn't no way a bunkhouse could be anything except ripe. The worst part of it, of course, was all the blankets. Wool blankets have an awful stink by the time you get around to the heat of August. And by September? Come October, of course, when the hands were paid off for the winter the old blankets would be burned—and none too soon for it—and new ones bought. But by August every year the blankets that'd been so new and fresh and nice last October or November were rank and nasty and smelled like moldy buffalo hides. If a man was old enough to remember what buffalo hides smelled like, that is. Joe only remembered it because the army had still been issuing buffalo coats when he was young and wore blue britches. The truth was that he'd never once in his life seen a live buffalo nor smelled a recently dead one. But that was neither here nor there, was it? He peered up at the nearest window with a scowl ready in case some stupid SOB had let the thing fall shut and sat on the edge of his hard, creaking bunk. The windows, what few of them there were, were all open, half a dozen tiny little things tucked

49

up high under the eaves where they would be protected from hail or whatever.

He pulled off one boot and then another, wrinkling his nose again and thinking he was for sure going to have to get some new socks, too, when the ZK, mostly known as the Zeke, paid the hands off for the winter.

"Jesus, Potter, whyn't you wash your feet?" a complaint came from the far end of the bunkhouse.

"I will, Hostin. Meantime whyn't you wash your ass? It's got some tobacco juice in the corner. Like right here." Joe fingered the corner of his mouth to show Hostin the spot he meant.

Emil Hostin did not take offense. But then he never did, no matter what. Hostin, a youngster of twenty or so with a soft belly and softer head, grinned and pulled one of his own boots off, then loudly sniffed and rolled his eyes.

Joe Potter went back to tending his own knitting, satisfied with the exchange. He hadn't taken any crap off Hostin. The rest of the guys, including Pete Bower, would see that. Joe didn't like Bower but was expected to take hind tit off him just because Bower had been on the Zeke for eight, ten years or something like that. That was dumb right there. Anybody could see that Joe Potter was the better man, older and more experienced and better all the way round. The problem was that Andy Plasser didn't see it. And Plasser was the general manager of the Zeke and acted as his own foreman, too. Plasser and Bower went back together too far for Plasser's judgment to be sound when it came to Bower, and that was the pure and simple truth so far as Joe saw it. He'd be willing to swear to that in any court of law.

Which brought a twitch to his thin lips. There was one hellacious fine collection of things that he'd be willing to swear to in a court of law, wasn't there?

With a sigh he stripped off the limp, soggy shirt he'd worn that day, held it up for a critical inspection, and decided it could go a spell longer before it hit the pile underneath the foot of his bunk. He tossed the shirt atop the trunk that was tucked between the head of the bunk and the roughhewn log wall. That trunk, about the size a swell would use to carry his dress shirts in, held a lifetime collection of valuables. Nobody but Joe ever touched his trunk. Not if they knew what was good for them, they didn't.

He unbuckled his belt and slithered out of his britches, tossing them onto the trunk along with the shirt. The britches, copper rivet jeans they were, were so crusted with old sweat and sun-dried manure that they'd begun to take on shapes and colors the maker would've marveled to see. But, hell, jeans are more durable than blankets, even, and there wasn't call to wash them. A man was expected to have his working britches and a separate pair of go-to-town britches, and that was that. Joe's go-to-town jeans had a worn, shiny spot on the one leg where his holster rubbed, but the work jeans had never been touched by gun leather. A man who weighed himself down with a belly gun while he was trying to work cows from horseback would get himself laughed off an outfit quicker than some sour-faced, hidebound jehu who couldn't take horseplay. It had taken Joe a spell to learn that, and he sure hadn't liked it, not after the years he'd spent wearing a gun to go along with his badge, but he wasn't stupid and he did learn it. Now he only actually wore his gun when he went to town to raise a little hell. But the rest of the bunch knew it was there in his trunk where it wouldn't take him hardly any time to grab hold of it.

He stretched out flat on his bunk and raised his arms to cross them behind his head like a sort of bony pillow. A hint of warm breeze— well, it was air movement if not an actual breeze—was refreshing as it drifted over him, cooling him and soothing too. He closed his eyes and let his muscles relax so that he had a sensation almost like he was melting down into the grass-stuffed ticking that covered his bunk.

From a little way off he could hear a low, fluttering noise. A moment later there was a heartfelt groan and a disgusted voice complained, "For God's sake, Taylor, go out to the dumper if you're gonna do that."

"Hey, it wasn't me, Mike."

"That's right, Mike. Old Taylor, he didn't fart. He shit his drawers. I can see it starting t' leak out on this side."

Potter didn't bother to open his eyes. There wasn't need to. At least for the moment everything seemed pretty much all right with the world.

3

Monday, September 20, 1909

Joe hauled the muleheaded, leather-mouthed brown sonuvabitch to a stop and warily shifted to one side in the saddle. The brown was a contrary SOB, apt to play possum until its rider decided this was going to be one of its rare good days, then pick the exact worst possible moment at which to blow up and put a fellow into the dust. And generally where every other hand in a ten-mile radius would be there watching and laughing at the person's shame. Well, not Joe Potter, thank you. He was on to this idjit animal and knew better than to trust it. This was the second year in a row that he'd drawn the brown as part of his string for the fall working. It wouldn't happen a third time. Not if Andy wanted Joe Potter to keep on working for the Zeke, it wouldn't.

Joe shifted his butt another fraction of an inch and twisted just a mite, careful of the treacherous brown and keeping a close eye on the horse's ears. If those ears dropped flat against the brown's skull, it likely meant there was fixing to be some fireworks. So far so good, though. Joe kept his hold on the thick, inch-wide reins—a man didn't use delicate gear on a horse he might have to drag down to its damn knees; all that pretty, prissy stuff was fine for some dainty little mare that a lady would ride through the park of a Sunday afternoon

53

but not for a working mount—and shrugged out of his coat, first one arm and then the other.

It had been a bone-chiller before dawn, with frost lying on the low ground in fuzzy white patches and coating the grass stems like each individual leaf had been dipped in sugar icing. Now, two hours or so past sunup, the heat was too much for comfort and it was time to shed the coats and mufflers and sheep-skin vests that came out of the men's war bags every year about this time.

Joe got out of his coat without the brown so much as turning its head to glare at him. In addition to all its other faults the brown was a nipper. The sonuvabitch would act at being oh-so-innocent, yawn and flop its tail around, and turn like as if it was going to nose a deerfly off its shoulder. Next thing a fellow knew it'd have its yellow old teeth clamped down on his boot, and if his toe happened to be in that same spot, well, he'd be limping for the next couple days. Once or twice like that and a man learned he needed to either put tapaderos over the fronts of his stirrups or else learn to kick the cranky brown bastard in the mouth every time it turned its head back toward him. Joe didn't own any taps and wasn't fixing to go buy any neither, not for the sake of a horse as miserable as this one. By now the brown pretty much knew what to expect if it turned its ugly head too far around.

And today it really did seem like the brown was going to do all right. That was some-thing could be said in the brown's favor. When it had a decent day it really wasn't such a bad old horse. The stupid thing was as tough as oxhide. A man could take off on a big circle in bad country and ride the brown uphill and down from dawn to don't-see and hardly get the horse to break a sweat. Two, three hours at a hard run—uphill—and Joe figured you *might* be able to put a lather on the brown. Maybe. If it wasn't at the top of its form, that is.

The son of a bitch was tough, and that was a natural fact. And on a good day, well, it'd get the job done. A man couldn't ask much more of a horse than that.

Joe shifted around a bit more so he could fold his coat and lay it behind his cantle. He folded everything nice and careful so the dust would only lay on the outside of the coat and not get into the liner where it would chafe and itch him. Then he reached down for the saddle strings to tie everything in place nice and snug and secure.

That was when the sneaky bastard of a brown blew up.

He should've known. Right from that first split second when he felt the brown's shoulder drop he knew he should've known. That was all the warning he got, though. And that wasn't in time to save him.

The shoulder dropped—hell, the ears didn't even wiggle—and the next thing Joe knew the brown's butt was headed for the clouds and taking Joe Potter along for the ride. If he'd ever wondered what it would feel like to ride a mortar round as it was shot toward the sky, well, this was his chance to figure it out.

That speckled brown butt shot high into the air, and Joe's legs clamped hard around the horse's barrel. The problem, of course—and the damn horse knew it, Joe would swear to his dying day—was that Joe wasn't sitting square on the animal so he might be able to get a nice, firm scissor clamp with his thighs and calves and, hell, with his spurs, too, for that matter. No, he was half-turned, trying to tie his damn coat on behind the saddle, so all he could do was try and turn back around in time to get a good grip with his legs.

Well, there wasn't half enough time for him to do that. It's like asking that same mortar round to decide against going into the sky and grab hold of the gun breach. By the time the thought could be formed it was just naturally way too late.

Joe yelped, his voice pitched high and thin from the unexpectedness of it all, and had the momentary satisfaction of feeling his one spur rake hell out of the damned brown's hide as he was propelled into the air like a beanbag coming off a kid's slingshot. And because he'd been fiddling with the saddle strings he didn't have a good grip anymore on his reins so he lost hold of them, too.

One second he was mounted. The next he was sprawled flat out in midair. And no angel wings to flutter and glide on.

He spun end over end just as pretty as you please and came down hard on his back.

Dust flew and the wind got driven out of him, and for about half a minute there Joe couldn't see, hear, or smell.

He just lay there, stunned, wondering if he was ever gonna be able to breathe again or if this time he was gonna lay there and drown in the dry dust that swirled all around him, getting into his nose and finding its way inside his clothes and making his mouth and eyes both feel gritty and nasty and miserable.

Then pretty soon he could hear again, and what he could hear was laughter.

All the rest of the bunch was laughing their damn fool heads off. All eight hands from the Zeke and half a dozen more from the Pinetree and five or six from the T-Bar and ten or so from the Lewis Ranch and all those one- and two-man scrub outfits, too, all the damn riders and cattlemen who'd gathered for the fall working. All of them laughing their fool heads off at Joe Potter laying there on the damn ground like a green kid fresh from the farm.

Jesus! Joe hurt. Damn but he hurt. His head was pounding and his back felt like it was afire and there was that awful taste in his mouth and the grit stinging his eyes.

He bounced to his feet and grabbed his hat off the ground—he had no idea when he'd gone and lost that—and swept it low in a grandly theatrical bow, standing there and grinning like he was as big a fool as all of them were. He managed a laugh and then another one, joining in on the fun so to speak—fun! yeah, sure—and making like it was all a big joke on him.

Fun, shit.

A toothy little redheaded bastard from the T-Bar whose name Joe didn't remember came loping up dragging the brown by the reins. "You lose something, Potter?"

"Who, me?" Joe pretended to look around underneath and behind him and his eyes got wide like as if he was just then noticing that he wasn't no longer riding a-horseback. "Why, I reckon mayhap I did." He grinned at the red-head and took the ends of his reins and thanked the kid.

With a wink he stepped back onto the brown and settled deep into the saddle. He paused for only a moment, then turned and retrieved his coat, which was hanging off one side of the saddle by the one string he'd managed to get tied already. Deliberately he dropped his reins behind the horn and turned far around so he could use both hands to secure his coat snug to the cantle.

All the rest would be watching him, he knew, even if they made like they weren't. They sure as hell would be, and Joe knew it. He tied the coat down and even went so far as to unfasten the one set of strings he'd tied earlier and redo them so the coat would lay proper.

The brown horse stood as calm as a pigeon-shit statue in a town square and never so much as rippled its skin until Joe was done with his chore and turned back around to pick up the rein ends once more.

Then the horse moved out like a regular little gentleman and the rest of that whole long day never gave him another moment's trouble.

4

"Potter." The word was spoken once and soft-ly, but that was all that was needed. Joe was instantly awake and fully alert. He grabbed up

58

his hat and came to his knees blinking and looking around for his boots. "What is it? What's wrong?"

"It's all right, Potter." Andy Plasser's voice in the night was calm and reassuring.

"We don't gotta roll out? There's no stampede, nothing like that?"

"Nothing like that," Andy told him.

Shivering, Joe pulled his boots on anyway and stood, shoulders hunched against the predawn chill. His hat was dragged tight to his ears and his mouth tasted foul. His eyes stung from the bit of breeze that crept along the bottoms of the gently rolling land, and his stomach gurgled. "Did I miss a night trick, Andy? I swear I don't remember...."

"No, Potter, it isn't anything like that."

Joe looked around in confusion, then shrugged and bent to retrieve his coat and put it on. The inside of the garment was chillingly cold, but only for the first few seconds. Quickly his own body heat began to overcome the cold of the night air, and the coat began to hold the heat he gave to it. Once he started to warm up he was able to relax the tightly hunched set of his shoulders and pay more attention to the world around him.

The Zeke foreman Andy Plasser gave Joe little time to waken and get his wits about him. "You remember that brown horse you rode yesterday, Potter?"

"Hell yes, I remember that son of a bitch, Andy. You was there. You know I do."

"How was the horse when you turned him into the remuda last night, Joe?"

"I dunno what you mean, Andy. I mean, he

wasn't sweating bad or nothing. I rubbed him down some and checked his feet like I always do. There wasn't nothing special about him."

"I don't suppose you've seen the horse since you unsaddled, have you?"

"No, an' don't expect to for another five days till I got to use him again, the sorry sonuvabitch. I don't like that horse, Andy. I'm telling you right here an' now if I draw him t' my string again—"

"You wouldn't know anything about that brown stepping in a prairie-dog hole last night then, would you?"

"Dog hole, Andy? I ain't seen many ground holes around here."

Plasser reached into his pocket for his pipe, already loaded with the particularly nasty cut-plug tobacco he favored. He snapped a kitchen match aflame and took his time about lighting the pipe. Joe said nothing while the boss went about this small task. "That's kind of what I thought, too, Potter."

"You thought what, Andy?"

"That I haven't seen much in the way of holes in the ground around here. That it's a pretty unlikely coincidence that..." He stopped there and stood for a moment, eyes half-closed against the smoke that was trickling out of his mouth and collecting under the brim of his hat like a Christmas wreath. "You know?"

"Do I know what, Andy?"

"About a coincidence like that?"

"You mean the brown horse got hurt and you think I might've had something t' do with it?"

"I didn't say that."

"No an' I hope you damn sure won't, neither." There was a hard edge in Joe Potter's voice.

"Mind that I didn't say it, Joe."

"All right, I'm keeping that in mind, Andy."

"Fact of the matter is that the horse stepped in a dog hole last night. Or something. Whatever happened, it's got a broke leg this morning."

"I ain't sorry to hear that, Andy. Not in a way. That brown, it's a bad horse. Always has been. But I know it costs the outfit fifteen, twenty dollars to replace a horse. I'm sorry about that. But not about the horse."

"I hear what you're telling me, Joe. What I come by to ask you is, since the horse is in your string and everything, do you want to be the one to put it down?"

"Naw, I wouldn't get no satisfaction from something like that, Andy. Besides, my gun is back at the Zeke, locked away tight in my trunk. If you got a gun on you, go ahead an' use it. I don't want no part of putting the horse down. It'd be like I was wanting revenge or something. And you know that's stupid. Hell, it's just a horse. A dumb damn animal. A man I'd expect to go after for doing me a trick like that, boss. But not a dumb horse."

"All right, Potter. I, uh, just wanted to know."

"Sure, Andy. I understand." Joe stretched and yawned. He could see by the stars overhead that it wouldn't be long before they'd all be rolling out anyway. "I don't suppose Coosie has the coffee ready yet."

"Should be. Come on. I'll walk over with you."

Joe paused long enough to flip his blanket roll closed so the dust wouldn't get into it during the day—for the time being they were staying put in one camp and wouldn't even have to move their bedding for another three or four days—and joined the foreman making his way toward the cook's wagon where a large, cheery fire presented itself as a beacon in the night. By the time they were halfway there Joe could smell the rich, enticing aroma of coffee boiling and burbling in the big kettle.

"Say, Potter," Plasser said as they neared the flames and the foreman began to strip off his gloves.

"Yes, boss?"

"You didn't ride nighthawk last night, did you?"

"Nope. Wasn't my turn yet."

"Stay in bed the whole night through, did you?"

"That's right, Andy. Unless you count the one time I had t' get up and go take a crap. And before you figure you have t' ask, as far as I know nobody seen me get up an' nobody followed me out t' watch me. Which means nobody would've seen me even if I had taken a walk round to wherever the remuda was grazing last night. Which of course I didn't." Joe grinned at the foreman and reached for one of the tin mugs that dangled from a rod fitted to the side of the cook wagon. He handed that mug to Plasser and took another for himself. "Hold that still, Andy, an' I'll pour for the both of us."

"Potter, if I thought you were lying..."

"If you did, Andy, you'd be right t' do

whatever you have in mind to say. But o' course you don't." Joe's smile got bigger and bolder. "Do you?"

The foreman paused, but only for an instant. Then he shook his head. "No, of course not, Joe. Not at all."

"Careful, Andy. I wouldn't want t' slip and pour none of this coffee on you. It's mighty hot. Hold still now. There, that's better."

5

It wasn't the heat of the days nor the cold of the night that was so stinking miserable bad. It was the dust. Damn the dust anyway. Hundreds of cattle and dozens of horses, and every time any one of them took a step there was more dust lifting into the air and not half enough of a breeze to carry it away. It just hung there, waiting for more to rise up and join in, and there was no getting away from it. Your horse rode through clouds of dust. You breathed dust. You ate, drank, and bathed in dust.

Joe Potter loathed, despised, and damn well didn't like dust. Not after this and never would again in all his lifetime, he knew.

Oh, you tried to fight it, tried to keep it out of your nose and mouth as best you could. You tried wearing a kerchief tied over your face. You tried buttoning your shirt tight at the neck and wrists and using a bandanna like a scarf to keep the itchy, filthy dust out of the sticky sweat on your chest. But there wasn't anything that did any good. You knew all your attempts

63

were doomed to fail. Joe Potter knew that. And Jesus, he hated dust.

It crept in underneath your kerchief and into your nose, clogging your nostrils and making it hard to breathe so that every once in a while you had to lift the mask away and blow out great stringy wads of snot that was the same red-brown color as the dust. Breathing the dust you had to smell it, dry and sunbaked and reeking of dirt. It got into your mouth, and so you had to taste it and feel the grit of it in your teeth and lumping up between your tongue and your gums, so every once in a while you had to lift your kerchief and try to spit the dust from a mouth that was dry... from all the filthy dust robbing you of your spit.

It came in underneath the scarf at your throat and collected in the sweat there, driving you half-mad from the itching under your shirt collar and making dark, muddy runnels down your chest and under your arms.

At night there was nowhere to bathe or otherwise escape the dust, and so it got into the fibers of your blankets and you slept in dust, your body still caked and coated and covered in it. You went to bed in dust and woke to dust and worked in dust, and there was nothing on the face of this earth that seemed worse than the dust that made up the face of this earth.

It was filthy and pervasive and awful stuff and Joe Potter hated it.

Harold Adams and the cat-quick gray horse he favored hazed a leggy short-yearling calf out of the bunch, and Joe flipped a loop over

64

the calf's head and dragged it bawling and complaining to the three-man crew waiting by the fire. Joe was glad he wasn't having to work the branding fire today. That was the hottest, sweatiest, dustiest job of them all. But everybody had to take his turn at the fire. Everybody except the foremen and owners, and a few show-off sons of bitches among them took turns along with the hired hands.

Joe took a wrap around his saddle horn to get a good purchase on the end of his catch-rope and by means of the rope and the brute strength of his horse dragged the calf along close to the fire. The calf braced its legs in protest, but all that did was make it bounce and skip over the hard, stony, dust-lousy ground. The calf's bawling and twisting and sullen resistance weren't near enough to save it.

Once Joe had the skinny red calf close by the fire, Mike Shay, who was another one of the boys from the Zeke, and Harold Mulfern from the Lewis outfit grabbed hold of it and dumped it onto its side. Mike stripped Joe's lariat off the calf's neck, and then the two of them held it by the legs and dragged it a few feet closer to the fire, turning it and holding it down hard on the ground so it couldn't get away nor hardly move.

Meanwhile Joe was calling out "Pinetree," for that was the brand the calf's mama wore.

Dave Pittman took the Pinetree brand off the coals, the brand being formed with one long vertical bar and three shorter horizontal ones. There was a long horizontal bar about midway up the vertical one, then a middling long

65

bar atop that and a very short one close to the top. All in all it made for a fairly good representation of a pine tree. Sort of. Close enough for brand purposes anyhow.

While Shay and Mulfern held the calf still, Dave pressed the glowing hot metal into the calf's hip. There was a sizzle and a bawl of pain, and the sharp stink of burning hair and singeing meat joined all the other smells of a cow-working.

In its pain and frustration the calf's bowel emptied in a squirt of yellow-brown, and there was that smell to contend with, too. The calf wasn't particularly tidy about what it was doing, so much of the delivery spilled across Mulfern's right thigh, making him cuss and holler even though it was his own damn fault for not paying attention to where he was kneeling. Joe thought that was kinda funny.

As soon as Dave was satisfied that the brand was burned deep enough to take but not so deep as to cause damage, he pulled the iron away. Shay knelt on the calf's neck while Mulfern held its leg out of the way—likely with a good deal of satisfaction, since the damn creature had messed on him like that—and Shay used two quick swipes of his pocketknife to cut the calf's scrotum. Mulfern squeezed the plump and slick-shiny gray nuts out and ripped them free of the thin strings and webbing of membrane that had held them. Mr. James Lewis's kid, a button of seven or eight, came running over with the bucket for Mulfern to toss the testicles into. Later on there'd be a helluva fine feed made up of all these mountain oysters sliced and floured and fried in hot lard. There wasn't any better eating than that.

But that would be for later. Right now Mulfern let the leg down on the former bull calf, now a steer calf, and sort of sat on its hindquarters to hold it down—a cow gets up ass end first and a horse the other way around, so to keep a calf from standing you sit on its butt while to keep a horse down you push its neck hard to the ground—while Shay used his knife again, this time cropping the tip off the calf's left ear and slicing an underbite off the right ear, that being the ear markings that signified a Pinetree animal as clear as did the brand.

Once they were done with the calf they turned it loose to run around kicking and slobbering until it found its mama again and the comfort she represented.

Long before that could happen, of course, Pittman had the Pinetree iron back on the coals to return it to the particular heat he liked for branding—not yet a cherry glow to the iron but hotter than an ash white—and Joe was, or should have been, turning back to drop his rope onto the next calf's neck.

This time, though, he angled away from the herd where the cattle were being sorted, calves out for branding, marketable steers into a separate herding area for shipment and sale once this working was over and done with, cows together to wait for the return of their offspring if they had any. Joe moved away from the men on foot beside the fire and from the rest of the crowd and, well away from the others, lifted his horse into a lope over to the cook wagon.

"No handouts, damn you, I've told all you asshole cowpunchers that—"

"Don't dribble in your drawers, old man. All I want is a drink outta that barrel."

"Well, all right then," the cook said with a grunt and a grimace.

Joe nudged his horse close to the wagon and, still mounted, leaned down to flip the lid of the water barrel open and take up the dipper. He held the first half-swallow in his mouth for a moment and swished it around to try and wash some of the dust out of his teeth, then instead of spitting the water uselessly onto the ground opened his mouth and let it spill down onto his chest where it was cool and at least for the moment refreshing. The second swallow he savored, enjoying the cool, sweet flow of it down a dry throat.

"Damn," he said. "That ain't bad."

He drank again, then lifted his hat and poured a full dipper over his scalp and down the back of his neck. "Jeez, yeah," he said.

"If this country was any drier I'd have your balls in the nut bucket for wasting water like that," the cook grumbled.

"If this country was drier you'd never see me do it," Joe returned.

"You want coffee before you go back?" the aging, arthritic cook offered.

"No, thanks. I been gone too long as it is."

"Tell 'em to hurry it up. I don't want supper all burnt up before you bastards call it quits for the day."

"Up yours, Coosie," Joe said without rancor. He leaned down to close the lid on the water barrel, then gave the cook a friendly wave—it's one thing to engage in a little harmless banter but quite another to actually make a trail cook angry—and carefully walked his horse clear of the cooking area before he bumped it into a lope again and headed back to the herd.

6

Potter stood in his stirrups, searching the brush in the coulee ahead for glimpses of color that would disclose the presence of hidden cattle. With a grunt of satisfaction he saw what he'd been expecting, a flash of that peculiar red hair that distinguished the white-faced Hereford cow that had become so extremely popular in recent years. The old-time cowhands complained about the Herefords, comparing them unfavorably with the skinny, long-legged, many-colored longhorns that first were brought in to populate the vast northern grasslands. Joe Potter never participated in those discussions. The damn things were all just cows to him. And all cows are stupid and most cows are predictable, and that was what Joe was counting on right now.

The job today was to gather in more cows for sorting and branding and whatever else needed doing to the things, and right now he'd found a bunch of them brushed up in the shade down inside the coulee.

Joe scratched his backside, then resumed the hard leather seat of his saddle and wiggled around a bit to make sure he was settled down as tight and secure as he could get.

The idea of working cows was to do it as slow and lazy as possible—not for the sake of the cowhand's comfort, for damn sure not that, but because the less agitated and more content the cow the less spooky and hard to work the stupid creatures were... and the less tallow was run off them, too—and a slow walk was the best of all possible gaits to employ. Of course the fool cows didn't always let a man work them slow, and if one of them took a notion to booger they would all run and then it was all flying feet, boiling dust, and a race to see who could reach hell the quickest. In rough country that could make for interesting times.

Joe tugged the brim of his hat to make sure it was tight to his head, then gave his horse a nudge to ease it forward nice and slow.

Two, three hundred yards in front of him there was movement down inside the brush-choked coulee as the cows—he couldn't see yet how many there were in the bunch—became aware of his approach, either winding him or catching sight of the motion. One thing sure, even though the Hereford breed hadn't been in the country all that long it hadn't taken them any time at all to return to being half-wild creatures just like the longhorns they were replacing. Longhorn or Hereford either one, range cows were vigilant, spooky sons of bitches. Which at times, like right now, could be used to work against them.

Without making any noise or deliberate show of what he was up to, Potter placed himself and his horse where they could be seen

70

and just sort of ambled forward slow and easy.

The cows did the rest of the work for him.

The leader of the bunch, probably a dry female with no calf this year, stamped and shuffled around until all the others were alert to the danger. Then with a toss of her head and a flick of her tail she commenced to sneak down the coulee, staying tight in the thickest part of the brush and likely thinking she couldn't be seen. The others followed close behind.

Joe couldn't see all of this, just enough of a bit of color here and a hint of motion there that he could guess at what all was happening down below.

Still at a slow, leisurely walk that did not give away to the cattle that they'd been seen, Potter followed along the north rim of the coulee, staying skylighted and far behind the now moving cattle.

The bovines reached the mouth of the coulee and, obviously nervous about being exposed once they had to leave the protection of the brush, broke into a trot as soon as they were on the open grass. They swung to the south. The gathering point for the day was off to the northeast.

Joe grimaced and curbed his inclination to jump after the damn critters. As patiently as he could manage, he waited until the cows— there were eight in this bunch, he'd seen now—were out of sight behind the south ridge that marked the southeast end of the coulee.

Then he wheeled his horse and put the spurs to it, jumping the animal down the

71

slope to the gravel bottom and crashing hard through the thick brush to race up the opposite slope. He rode hunched over the neck of the horse, elbow crooked in front of his face to protect his eyes from the whip and slash of the branches he crashed through and feet socketed deep in his stirrups. This would be no damn time to come out of the saddle, after all.

Before he hit the top, though, he hauled back on his reins again. By the time he was in the open where the cattle could see him—at least he damn sure hoped they would be able to see him there—he was moving at a slow and lazy walk again.

The cows were right damn where they were supposed to be, off to the east of where Joe now was and slightly behind him. Perfect.

They saw him. He could see the old cow's head toss when she spotted him and the horse above and slightly ahead of her. Not taking any chances with this human, the cow blew some snot and threw her head in minor annoyance, then angled away from horse and rider.

Joe let the bovines settle on their new direction, then reined the horse a bit to his left and squeezed with his legs just enough to increase the horse's speed a mite but, carefully, without breaking into a trot. A smooth walk was still what was wanted here. A trot would give the game away and let the cows know that they were being chased. The ticket was to avoid them knowing that so they would think it was all their own idea to move well ahead of the man.

Horse and rider angled eastward, and three hundred yards away the cows responded, changing their direction ever so slightly again to make sure the man would not be allowed closer.

Joe angled a bit further left. Again the cows responded. And once more. By now the small group of cattle were walking head high but not excited toward the northeast while the horse plodded, its rider deliberately slowing it, along behind.

Satisfied, Potter slouched deep in his saddle and allowed himself to relax. There wasn't going to be any hard, brush-snapping run this time or any dash across open ground that might be littered with the treachery of loose stones and prairie-dog holes. There wasn't going to be any danger. He reached into a coat pocket and brought out his pipe. Now all he had to do, just as slow and gentle as possible, was let these stupid bovines lead him to the gathering place where they could be counted on to join the herd that would be assembling there as one by one the circle riders brought their gathers of range cows into an ever-growing herd.

Three, four more days like this and this whole part of the country would be covered. They would do the groundwork, taking care of this year's calves and sorting the market steers out from the cows, then move along to another part of the range and start the process over again. By the end of October the whole basin would have been worked and the hands could be paid off and sent packing until spring when the range work would begin all over again.

7

Jeez, he hurt. Ached was more like it than hurt, really. His muscles ached, his joints ached, the very marrow of his bones ached. This was a young man's trade, and Joe Potter wasn't young anymore. Not that he was old, dammit. But he wasn't young either.

He turned his horse loose in the rope corral the nighthawk had made, and the animal kicked and whickered and lay down to roll and wallow in the dust so as to dry the sweat off its back and bring some relief after the wet heat of a saddle blanket the whole day long.

Potter picked up his saddle and bridle and humped them to the tarp the nighthawk had laid out nearby. Not that there was much chance of rain or snow in the night, but a man never knew. The men who'd drawn night herd duty would take their gear with them, but everybody else could pile their stuff on the tarp where the nighthawk, the kid in charge of the remuda, would cover it once everyone was accounted for.

Holding himself stiff against the sharp pains that nagged at the lower part of his back, Joe hobbled to the cook fire and helped himself to a cup of coffee. Coosie bitched a lot, but he never minded a man having himself some coffee.

"Potter."

Joe looked around to see who was calling out to him. It was the Zeke foreman Andy

Plasser and therefore had to be answered. "Yeah."

"You got a minute?"

That was a dumb damn question, Joe thought. He had whatever minutes the boss said he had. And Plasser knew that as good as anybody. "You bet, Andy." He took his coffee mug with him and legged it over to where the boss was seated on one of the campstools the Lewis outfit had brought along. Campstools! Really.

"Sit down if you like, Potter."

Joe gave the canvas and hickory contraption a skeptical inspection and decided to remain standing. "You want some coffee, Andy?"

"No thanks, I just had some. Tell me, Joe, did you hear what happened to Peter Bower today?"

Potter shook his head.

"He was chasing a pair of beeves through some brush and took a tumble. His horse came down on top of him and busted his leg."

Andy paused, and Joe drank some of his coffee. After a moment he realized the boss was expecting him to say something. "Which one got the busted leg, Bower or the horse?"

"Pete. It was Pete that busted his leg. The horse rolled on him and got right up again. Pete's just lucky there was somebody close by to see what happened."

Joe grunted. He didn't know what the hell Plasser wanted him to say, for Christ's sake. It wasn't his leg that got busted. And he damn sure didn't give a shit what happened to Pete Bower.

"I thought you'd want to know, Pete being top hand on the Zeke and everything," Plasser rambled on.

"Yeah, o' course," Joe said. It was what he figured was expected of him.

"We sent the wagon in to carry him to a doctor, but his leg don't look good."

"That's, uh, a real shame, Andy."

"I suppose somebody will be coming around to take up a collection."

So that's what it was about, Joe thought. The sons of bitches were wanting him to kick in out of his pocket to give to that no-good Bower. He'd have to give something. He knew that. The question was how little he could get away with without making Plasser mad and maybe costing Joe his job.

"The reason I wanted to talk to you now, Potter, is that Pete has been our main hand for a long time. You know?"

Joe shrugged and drank some more of the coffee. It wasn't bad stuff.

"With Pete laid up… for that matter, maybe out of the saddle for good if that leg doesn't come right again… we'll be needing someone to winter over in the line camp."

"Yeah?"

"You haven't been with us as long as some, Potter, but I've always favored an older, steadier man for winter line riding. You know?"

"Yeah, sure." Joe frowned.

"Well, what I was thinking is that maybe you'd want the job this year."

Joe' frown deepened. "I was kinda looking forward t' going down to Denver, Andy. There's a fat little old gal down there... ," he laughed. "You know what they say about fat women, Andy. Always a new wrinkle t' try out, ha ha."

"Yeah, well, if you change your mind, Potter, you let me know, hear? The job's yours if you want it."

Wintering over on the Zeke, with pay the whole time, was kind of a compliment, and Joe knew it. The problem was that he really was looking forward to spending a few months in Denver. Helluva town, Denver. Cheap whiskey and easy women. Or vice versa. Whatever a man liked, Denver had it aplenty. And there was something to be said, too, about being able to lay around and enjoy life for a few months. Of course winter always got kinda old along about February or so when a man ran out of money and started to get bored.

But then there were women in Denver. And none in a snowbound line camp out amongst the brakes and brush bottoms of the Nebraska plains. And broke and bored with women around was always better than flush and bored with nothing but a couple long-haired horses for company.

"I thank you for thinkin' about me, Andy, but if it's all the same t' you I'll go on down t' Denver and look for new wrinkles in that fat lady. Y' know?"

Plasser nodded, not seeming particularly upset by the rejection, and looked out over the plains to where the sun was setting. "I sure hope Pete's gonna be all right," the foreman mused.

"Hmm?" Joe had already forgotten about Bower, and now it took a moment for him to recall what Plasser was talking about. Then he put on a long, sorrowful face and solemnly agreed.

If he could just figure out who'd be coming around taking up the collection for Bower maybe he could avoid the guy and get out of having to pay anything, he was thinking.

8

Hyde's Crossing, Wyoming
Friday, October 29, 1909

"Cold, ain't it?" Berty Conover clapped his gloved hands together and stamped his feet. While he was so occupied the others of the Zeke crew were sorting through the bedrolls and baggage in the back of the wagon, digging out what was theirs and throwing it down into untidy piles on the pale, half-frozen ground.

It was midday on a Friday, not a time when the men from the Zeke would normally be in town—or in what passed for a town this far away from the real thing—but this particular Friday was an exception from the norm. This particular Friday the men had drawn their final pay and were not expected back at the Zeke, those whose chose to return, until spring. April, May, some of them might not straggle in again until June. Any who did elect to report back to the Zeke would be welcomed. There was no written rule to that effect, but it was the practice. In the meantime they were on their own, whatever was in their pockets now being all they could count on for their winter's living expenses.

"Give me a hand with the harness, would you, Joe?"

Potter scowled a little, but that was mostly a matter of habit. He disliked being singled out for any sort of chore when there were others who could have been imposed on instead. Still, he understood that Berty asking the favor of him now was a sort of compliment. Berty was acknowledging Joe's rank—an achievement of age, not longevity—as one of the senior members of the Zeke. But then Berty knew he would not have drawn the winter's work, complete with full pay and found, had it not been for Joe's refusal of the offer.

While the rest of the men gathered up their things and lugged them all off, Joe Potter set about helping Berty strip the team of their harness and turning the horses into the corral nearby. The corral and accompanying half-walled dugout/soddy were part of a stagecoach relay station that had been abandoned years earlier. Both were kept now in a state of semirepair by whichever cowhand or transient felt like wiring a fallen rail back in place or packing a new clot of mud into a chink in the crumbling wall. There was no hotel or boarding house in the crossroads community. Nor post office or telegraph station, for that matter. There were only the beaten earth of the intersecting roadways, five cabins, a combination saloon and store-of-all-purposes, and a smithy with the best bellows and firebox to be found within a hundred fifty miles. Or possibly further. It

79

was the smithy more than anything else that accounted for the continuing existence of the Crossing. The old stage station with its remaining corral and ancient dugout were regarded as community property, free for use by anyone who chose to take shelter in them.

Hands from the Zeke and every other outfit for many miles around came to the Crossing to drink, to carouse and—as they were now—to find transportation to and from the cities where they spent their leisure between seasons. Or between jobs.

No longer a recognized way point, the Crossing was still at a crossroads, and so coaches continued to come through on a more or less regular basis and from here a man could find his way west to Casper or east to Chadron, north to Rapid City and Deadwood or south to Cheyenne. All he had to do was wait for a coach that happened to be going his way. One was sure to be along by-and-by.

Joe and Berty stripped the big cobs of harness and bridles and turned the animals loose inside the corral. While Berty carried water from a community hand pump to the ancient and battered trough, Joe tidied harness and lines and laid everything out in the back of the wagon ready for Berty tomorrow. Or whenever Conover should choose to go back to the Zeke. Joe knew for a certain-sure fact that Berty didn't have to be back until Monday morning, and a man with a winter job could afford a blowout if he wanted one.

"You playing tonight?" Joe asked over his shoulder as that thought prompted others in a quite natural order of progression.

"Yeah. Likely," Berty said as he dumped a bucket of water into the trough. By morning there would be a hard film of ice over the trough and someone would have to break it or the horses would not be able to drink.

Joe smiled. It was well known that Berty Conover was one of the poorest judges of cards west of the... Joe had been thinking Mississippi, but he doubted that did justice to the subject. He figured it would be more accurate to say that Berty was one of the poorest card players anywhere between the Atlantic Ocean and the Shining Sea. Call it roughly an area bounded by England on the one hand and China on the other. Yeah, that ought to be about right.

With his own pay in hand plus Berty's, Joe was figuring, he could have a right comfortable winter to look forward to.

"You'll save me a place at the table, won't you, Berty?"

"Sure, Joe, if you want."

"Yeah, I think I do."

"Fine by me, Joe."

Potter made sure the lines were all lying free and untangled and that there wasn't any obvious filth encrusting any of the buckles, then lifted the heavy tailgate and latched it into place. He thought about unrolling a tarp to drag over top of everything but decided not to bother. The sky was bright and clear. There might be frost tonight but there wouldn't be snow. And a little frost never hurt anything. No point in bothering with the tarpaulin.

Joe stood facing the back end of the Zeke's big freight wagon and Berty was at least forty feet away by the water trough, and without any meager hint of warning there was a stink of wild onion and a voice hissing practically in his damned ear.

"Beef, mis'er. Sugar, mis'er. You help please, mis'er."

Joe jumped, startled by the unexpectedness of it.

And when he turned to see who'd snuck up behind him like that it was a dark, wrinkled, toothless old son of a bitch of an Indian.

The sight—so close, so sudden—was enough to send Joe's heart shooting into the back of his throat to lodge there in a great, awful lump.

His vision blurred and wavered, and his heartbeat began a crazy race like it was trying to blow itself up inside his chest. Just run wild faster and faster until it burst. Until it exploded like a... never mind like a what. Until it exploded, that was all.

Joe's mouth opened and he had to stifle a mad, surging impulse to cry out. Instead his right hand formed into a fist and he swung his arm in a hard, sweeping arc, his clubbed fist lashing out without thought or reason.

Joe's wrist and lower forearm chopped hard across the old man's face, by accident really and not design, but if the intent was lacking the effect was not. The Indian's nose and upper lip split, and blood sprayed onto the old man's dirty brown blanket and Joe Potter's best boots, too.

The old man staggered backward and dropped to his knees, head down and arms uplifted to ward off any more blows that

82

might follow. He cowered there, trembling, saying nothing.

"Jeez, Joe, you didn't have to do that." Berty came running over, still carrying a forgotten bucket in one hand. "He was only wanting something to eat, for Christ's sake."

Potter, still shaken by the fright the old Indian had given him, scowled and shook his head. "The old bastard snuck up on me, damn him. He deserves whatever he gets, coming up behind a man like that. Old sonuvabitch!"

As if to emphasize the righteousness of his point, Joe took a step forward and kicked the kneeling Indian in the ribs. The old man grunted and scrambled to turn half away, presenting his hip and thigh as targets but protecting his more vulnerable midsection from the white man's blows.

"Dammit, Joe, don't do that."

"Are you gonna stop me?" Potter demanded, his fury directed at Berty Conover just as quickly as it had been launched at the old Indian.

"I'm just saying, Joe, that you don't gotta do that. Jeez, Joe. Look at him." Berty pointed. The Indian was on his knees facing away from Joe, his forehead pressed into the dirt and both arms raised to cover his neck and the back of his head. Even with the dirty, ragged woolen blanket draped over his lean form it was easy to see the shaking that racked his body. He was terrified and appeared capable of offering no resistance.

"Looks don't mean nothing with an Indian, Berty. They playact like that, but he could have a gun, a knife, some damn thing under that blanket. Don't never trust an Indian, Berty. They're treacherous sons o' bitches. I'm telling you they are. This here one just like all the rest. Count on it."

"Well, this one ain't gonna hurt nobody, Joe. Not right now, he ain't."

"He snuck up behind me, didn't he? How the hell was I t' know what he was up to?"

"Fine. You didn't know then. Now you do. So let it be, Joe. Will you just let it be now?"

"Just keep him outta my way, that's all I'm saying. Outta my way and out from behind me. You hear?"

"Hey, it wasn't me that done any of this. All right?"

Potter took a slow, deep breath and then another. After a moment he nodded. "Yeah. I hear you, Berty. It wasn't you."

"And this here Indian, he..." Conover took a look into Joe Potter's eyes and shrugged. There was no point in trying to get Joe to agree to anything on that subject. He could see that there wasn't. "Look, uh, thanks for the help, Joe. You go along now. I'll, uh, finish up and be right along. You hear?"

"Yeah, Berty. Right. Whatever." Potter sent one last, furious glare toward the blood-spattered old Indian, then stalked around to the other side of the wagon to pick up his gear—it wasn't much, a bedroll, a saddle and saddlebags, and the small trunk that was never allowed to stray far from his possession—and awkwardly managed to gather them up in one wobbly, unbalanced load.

Joe started off toward the abandoned way

station and the other men of the Zeke, ignoring Berty Conover behind him and the sneaking old son of a bitch of an Indian who'd crept up and startled him like that. Berty, the soft-hearted and gullible little SOB, was kneeling down beside the Indian. Joe snorted. So let him. He was stupid, Berty was. He'd be taken in by the old bastard now. Probably end up buying the old fool some stuff. Well, let him if that's what he wanted to do. Berty Conover could make an idiot of himself over some useless old thing like that, but Joe Potter wouldn't.

"Stupid bastard," Joe mumbled as he took his things over to the musty, crumbling dugout where all the rest of the Zeke crowd was.

9

"That'll be two bits."

Joe nodded and laid down his quarter and took his two drinks—you had to buy them two at a time or be charged thirteen cents apiece instead of the regular one-bit-per-drink, two-for-a-quarter price—back to the makeshift table where Berty Conover was dealing stud poker.

That same table, makeshift though it was, had been in Walt Hyde's store for as long as Joe Potter had been in this part of the country and likely for a whole lot longer. It consisted of a pair of sawhorses with some loose planks laid over them and a rat-chewed square of poorly tanned elk hide laid over the planks to kind of hold it all together. There was no telling where the elk hide would have come from

85

because there hadn't been a live elk seen this side of the Bighorn mountain range in a generation. Not out here away from the timber, although there were some old-timers around who swore elk used to be common in the breaks and even out on the grass in the early days. Joe wouldn't know about that, nor would very many other people he knew of either. This country simply hadn't been settled, not by white human beings anyway, long enough for there to be many folks with true memories of the early days.

Joe set his pair of whiskeys down with great care to not spill any of the amber nectar, wiped both hands along the sides of his britches, and resumed his seat on the upended keg that served as a chair.

"You're light, Potter."

"Well excuse me all t' hell, Dolman. I been busy. Y' know?" Joe used the tip of a finger to slide a nickel across the slick hair surface to the center of the table. "Happier now?"

Mike Dolman grunted and Berty Conover picked up the cards. Berty flexed the fingers of his left hand before studiously gripping the deck with all the precise concentration of a jeweler mounting a damn diamond—a mannerism of his that for no good reason annoyed Joe Potter almost beyond endurance—and licked the ball of his right thumb before methodically dealing out cards to each of the five players, one card down and one card showing for each man, nothing wild and nothing drawn. "Place your bets, gentlemen, place your bets." It was early in the evening, and already Conover was down six or eight dollars from

86

where he'd begun. This was going to be a good night. Joe could feel it in his bones that it was.

"Queen showing," Berty intoned. "Your bet, Johnny."

Johnny Lee Jaimeson was sitting immediately to Berty's left. Then there was Joe, Mike Dolman, Carl Taylor, and back to Conover.

"Queen checks," Jaimeson said, rapping the table lightly with his knuckles to so signify.

"Check," Joe said.

"Trey bets a nickel," Dolman said.

Joe concentrated, trying to decide if Dolman had the second trey down or if he was just bluffing. It was a little early to know how Dolman was playing this time. And with him a guy never knew. One day Dolman would lie, bluster, and bluff damn near every hand he drew, the next time he played he might bet only on the surest thing. You couldn't ever get a good handle on Dolman's game, dammit.

At a mere nickel raise everybody stayed, but nobody went any further with the betting yet. Berty picked up the cards again—flexing his fingers again and placing the stupid deck just so into his hand—and dealt a round of cards. Nobody had any power showing yet, but Berty gave himself a king over Johnny Lee's queen.

"King bets ten cents," Berty said firmly and tossed a dime into the pot.

Joe didn't even have to think about that one. Poor Berty was as transparent as spring water. And a lousy card player to start with. He didn't have a thing to ride on and was just running the bet up thinking he could buy this pot before the betting was done. It seemed to be working, too. Johnny Lee dropped out rather than meet Berty's dime raise.

Mostly for the hell of it Joe saw Berty's dime and raised another. Dolman, who probably did have a pair of threes, stayed with the play, but Taylor folded.

Berty dealt cards to the remaining three players.

Joe was careful to show nothing. But his fourth card was a mate to the ten he had in the hole. He figured that put him on top of Dolman's small pair and way above Berty Conover's king high.

"King bets another ten cents," Berty said.

"I'll see that and up another ten." Joe tossed a quarter into the middle and dragged back a nickel.

"Call," Dolman said.

"And call." Berty put in a dime and picked up the slender remnants of he deck. Why the hell did he *do* that? Joe groaned to himself when Berty once more went through the flex-and-fit routine.

Berty dealt himself a deuce, Joe a seven, and Mike another deuce. "King still high? King's still high, gentlemen. King bets a quarter." Berty looked Joe square in the eyes when he said it. He even grinned. Call me, he seemed to be challenging.

"I'll see your quarter and up a quarter." Joe met the challenge.

"Too much for me," Dolman said.

"Call." Berty tossed his quarter into the pot and, still grinning, flipped his hole card face-up. The sonuvabitch was a second king. He'd gone and paired after all.

Joe cussed just a little. Then put on a grin to show that he hadn't meant it. Even though of course he really had. But then, hell, the night was still young. And Berty Conover was still one of the worst damn card players Joe Potter ever in all his life did see. There was plenty of time yet to get that little bit back and a lot more on top of it.

"Whose deal?" Joe asked, sweeping the cards into a loose pile and pushing them toward Johnny Lee Jaimeson, whose turn it was as they all knew right good and well, including Joe Potter.

"This time, gents, let's play a round of plain ol' draw poker. Nothing wild, jacks or better to open, and heaven help the hindmost."

Joe tossed back one of his whiskeys, the liquor warm and friendly in his belly, and watched Johnny Lee lay the cards out.

10

This was not fun. Potter's eyes burned and stung. His head throbbed. There was a foul, acid taste in his mouth, and his belly ached. His butt hurt from sitting too long. And there was a nagging, insistent nausea building inside him, a growing urge to puke and get it over with, that the whiskey could no longer quell.

It was... he blinked and rubbed at tired eyes and tried to work it out... Sunday morning?

He thought probably it was. Sometime Sunday anyhow. Middle of the day or close to it. No longer Saturday anyway. He was sure of that. And they'd started, what, Friday night? He thought so.

He scowled and looked across the table. Taylor was gone. His place had been taken by Boyd Shirer. And Howard Moore had brought a sixth chair to the table some time early on Saturday, so there were six in the game now.

Everybody looked the worse for wear. Everybody was red-eyed and haggard. Everybody looked rumpled and unshaven, skin greasy with half-dried sweat and clothes smelling of stale smoke and spilled liquor.

What started out to be a normal pastime card game was turning out to be one of those marathon affairs that guys would talk about this whole winter long and maybe for years to come.

That wouldn't be so bad except that Joe Potter was on the losing end of things.

And to add insult to that injury the big winner so far was that asshole Berty Conover. Conover had five, six months' wages piled up in prissy little stacks in front of him, damn him. He wasn't even decent enough about it to show some modesty and hide the big coins away. Instead he rubbed it in, leaving the gold stuff right out there with the silver and the nickel so as to show off all that he'd taken in, a glittering column of bright yellow ten-dollar eagles right next to the same-sized silver dimes. If Zeke hands were rich enough to deal in twenty-dollar doubles, then that SOB Conover would probably be stacking them next to the same-size quarter-dollars. But that would've been only if this was a table of rich swells. These were working boys, though, and there wouldn't be a one of them so much as see a double eagle in half a year's time. To working men an eagle was big money.

Except, that is, to Berty Conover, damn him anyway.

This day if he left the lousy table he'd likely find himself walking in circles from being weighted down on the one side by all that money in his pocket. Not that the sonuvabitch showed any inclinations to leave the table. Good thing, too. Anybody who won that big owed it to his victims to stay while they tried to get their losings back. Or at least get back some kind of a stake.

Jesus Christ, this was gonna be one long, stinking winter if he had to go into it broke as he was right now.

Potter had no idea how much he had left from his winter savings—you don't count your money while you're yet playing, everybody knows that—but then it was getting so a glance told the story good enough to bring a fresh rush of chilled sweat to his forehead. Everything in front of him was small, nickels and dimes, and only one two-bit piece that he could see. No gold at all. He'd lost the last of that hours ago. Now if he did get a good hand he wouldn't be able to run the betting up enough to make it worthwhile.

Smart play, of course, would be to cash in and walk away with what little he had left. But if he did that, dammit, there wasn't any chance he could get even again.

The only way to win, by damn, is to play.

That's something that everybody knows, too.

You just can't hardly win unless you play.

Joe shoved a nickel forward. "Come on, damn it. Are we playing cards or what? Ante up, everybody. Ante up."

It was the four kings that did it to him. Stupid, he thought. Stupid, stupid, stupid. And cruel. The only son-of-a-bitching decent hand he'd gotten the whole son-of-a-bitching game long, and there wasn't any point to it. Not to any of it.

Johnny Lee was dealing. Five card stud. Joe pulled a king down and a king showing. He opened the betting at a dime. Got another king showing and bet another dime. He'd have gone for broke on that pair-up, three-kings-down deal except he had to have something left to stay in the play through all five cards and he was down to having just what he'd put into the pot—and of course that was gone now, too, unless he stayed for the rest of the deal—and thirty-five cents, two dimes and three nickels, on the table in front of him.

He was dealt a seven and bet a dime on the strength of his pair of kings showing. Conover and Jaimeson and Moore were out. It was just him and Shirer and Mike Dolman left.

Damned if Joe didn't pull the fourth king for his last card. Three kings up and the fourth one down. It was a helluva hand. A wonderful hand. A hand to brag and crow about. A hand to remember.

Except... everybody else dropped out.

He was left with four kings on the table and chickenshit for winnings.

The pot—he counted the son of a bitch; you aren't supposed to but he couldn't stand it and counted it anyway—amounted to a useless, lousy one dollar and eighty lousy cents.

A dollar and eighty cents. Not even two stinking dollars.

There wasn't any justice. Well hell, he'd known that. Everybody knew that. The idea of justice wasn't nothing but a joke anyway.

But... four kings. The best hand he'd seen in hours. Hell, in days. And all he won was a buck eighty.

He had that and the dime and three nickels on the table in front of him. Two dollars and five cents. To see him through the coming winter.

Jesus!

Sick and weak and trembling, he shook his head and cursed some and pushed back away from the table, scooping his pathetic handful of coins into his palm where they didn't have heft or bulk enough to make a decent lump in a vest pocket.

This was what he'd worked the whole year for.

Christ!

"You cashing in, Potter?"

"Yeah, I reckon, George."

"Mind if I have your chair then?"

Joe didn't even answer. Just turned and walked outside, blinking in the glare of the sunlight that made his eyes water—they were already doing that anyway if the truth was known about it—and swaying unsteadily on legs that hadn't been used in too, too long a time.

He leaned against the wall of Hyde's store, the unpeeled bark of the log walls prickly against the back of his neck and the smell of his own sour sweat rising up out of the collar of his shirt to churn his stomach with the stink of it.

He wished he could puke and get rid of the mess that lay heavy in his belly but knew he couldn't. He hadn't been able to throw up in... years. Not since... not since too damn many years had gone by, that was what it'd been not since.

He thought about lighting a pipe, but that would just add to the many tastes in his mouth. What he needed was to get rid of tastes, not add to them. There were already too many. And what was already there was too nasty. He didn't need any more, dammit.

What he needed was... shit, he didn't know.

He closed his eyes and felt cold sweat running down the back of his neck and trickling over his ribs after leaking out of his armpits. It was a cold day, sunny but chill, yet he was sweating and at the same time shivering. Crazy. There was no sense in that.

He felt his stomach gurgle and churn from the bile that was stored inside him. He belched and the taste of it in his mouth was horrid. It tasted... green. That didn't make sense. He knew it didn't, but it was true. The flavor of his stomach gases was green.

"Joe."

He hadn't heard anybody come out, but when

he opened his eyes Berty Conover was standing there.

"If you tell me you're sorry you won, Berty, I'm gonna punch you right square in your fucking mouth."

Berty grinned. "Sorry, Joe? Damn right I'm sorry." The grin got bigger. "What I'm sorry for is that you didn't have any more t' lose to me."

Joe grunted. That was all right. That at least was honest. Joe couldn't understand these mealymouthed sons of bitches who pretended they weren't looking out for themselves when something like this happened. At least Berty wasn't trying to pull any of that bullshit on him.

"Got any plans for the winter now?" Berty asked.

Joe grunted again but didn't say anything. What would've been the point? Denver was out, that was for damn sure. He didn't have money enough for the fare south now. Hell, after this he couldn't get there, much less live there until April.

"If you want, Joe, whyn't you take the wagon back and tell Andy you'll work the line camp for him."

"I thought you was gonna do that."

Berty's empty, graceless grin got all the wider. "You think I'm gonna walk away from here with all this in my damn pocket an' not go spend it? Work, hell, Joe. Come morning I'm for Cheyenne. They got some women there... bunch of sweet-talking little ol' French gals... you know what I mean, ha ha." Berty winked and nudged Joe in the ribs. "Hell,

Joe, Andy won't mind. All he wants is the work to get done. Besides, he offered it to you before he ever did to me. Just take the wagon back t'morrow and tell him I'll be back in the spring same as always."

Joe had been looking forward to the winter all summer long.

But then his choices had kinda gotten themselves limited over the past—what?—forty hours or so.

"I'll tell him for you, Berty."

Berty grinned again. Damn him. He grinned and grinned and grinned. "You do that, Joe."

It did not occur to Potter to thank Berty for the job. But then the show-off little son of a bitch was doing it for his own self, not for Joe Potter. It wasn't that Berty wanted Joe to have a job through the winter but that Berty wanted to go to Cheyenne and huddle up in a whorehouse for the next however many months.

Joe grunted something that Berty could take as a good-bye if he wanted to, then slouched over to the damn dugout where the beds were laid out.

He still felt like shit, of course, but it was true that his head wasn't pounding quite so bad as it had been for a while there, and his stomach maybe wasn't quite so awful sour either.

What he needed, he supposed, was one good night's sleep. Then come morning he'd be ready for anything again.

GOD, THE NOISE. *His ears. His ears hurt. His head throbbed. Resonated with the pounding, crashing, inescapable sound.*

Explosions great and explosions small. One after another after another. Boom and crunch and thunder roll.

God, if only he could escape the noise.

It was constant. Unending. One horrible sound blending into another so that it was all one vast noise. And yet each individual component remained identifiable within the mass.

Rackety-clackety-crack of volleying musketry. Pum-pum-pum of the Hotchkiss guns. Sharp, bright-flashing snaps of the shells exploding. All came together in a crashing, crushing symphony of horror.

The guns, the shell bursts, finally the screams.

Dear God, the screams.

Terror ripped out of throats.

So many throats.

So very much terror.

Screams and cries, agony and confusion. Small voices crying. Bigger voices seeking. Gentle voices begging.

Voices without words. Voices became mere noise added to all the other noises.

Noise. Dear God, the noise.

It surrounded him. Overwhelmed him. Pervaded all existence and pressed in against him. Pressed hard about his head, wreathing him in noise, crushing him with the power of sound, pushed tight around his skull so that, too much for mere ears to accept, the noise drove and pounded and throbbed direct inside the skull, filling his head to overflowing so the pressure was excruciating and there was no more room inside his head. No room for thought. No space in which to think. Able only to feel, to sense, to hear the many noises.

Crump and boom and thud of explosion. Rattle of gunfire. Horror of screams.

He tried to run. Lord, but he tried to run away. He could not. He was surrounded by noise so tangible he could not force his limbs to move within it. Noise so thick it became a solid presence, trapping him, holding him captive, crushing down upon him from all sides at once. Noise so great it could have been no louder had he been reduced in size to that of a mite and loaded between shot and powder charge in a mighty cannon. Noise so hard it fixed him firmly in place. Noise so great it sickened him.

He felt the noise invade his belly, his bones, his loins. He felt it take him, hold him, drive deep inside his marrow and make a jelly of the very core of him.

God, this noise. There was no escaping it. Nowhere to run, no way to run, no ending to the awful, ugly, sick sounds of all the noises.

Hail Mary, full of grace... now and in the hour of... noise, death, Jesus.

He floated, suspended within a pool of noise so great it had become substance. Floated in noise. Drowned in noise. Died in...

No!

His eyes flew open and he sat upright. Sweating. Terrified. In silence now and yet surrounded by the memory of noise.

Grimly, defiantly, he closed his eyes and cursed all the deities that were the soporific of lesser men than he.

Chapter 3

1

ZK Ranch line shack
Southwestern South Dakota
Thursday, November 4, 1909

Potter scowled. He considered himself to be a man who tried to put the best possible face on things and to take whatever came his way, take it and throw it right back in the devil's face if ever the need be, take what came and make the very best of it, by damn.

But the best and most charitable thing it was possible to say about the Zeke's line camp was that the place looked like shit.

It wasn't so bad in summer. Joe had seen it in summer—not ever actually stopped in here, mind, but had ridden close enough to catch sight of the place a time or two whilst chasing cows—and it wasn't so awful bad when the trees and alders and wild plum and whatnot were leafed out.

Then it was damn near pretty, what with being set down near the head of this shallow valley, like, or drainage, with the creek running through from northwest to southeast and the brush meandering alongside the stream and the grass and wildflowers spread out over the slopes beyond.

But of course that was in summer. Now in winter with the leaves long gone and the grasses browned off and frozen back and the hillsides brown and barren there wasn't much to look at down the valley except shades of gray and shades of brown depending on whether it was wood you were seeing or dirt.

Whoever had picked the spot did so with an eye to summertime pretty, true, but also with some thought to practicality, Joe grudgingly conceded, for the winter winds would come down the valley but be mostly blocked by the low bluff that lay back of the cabin.

And after picking such a generally good spot, the person had gone ahead and done right by the rest of the planning in that instead of relying on the creek for water, which was sure to ice over and become a nuisance each and every winter without fail, the person had gone ahead and put in a spring box someplace well upstream, piping the water from the sunken box deep underground so the pipe wouldn't freeze and running the source pipe into a standing pipe that came out over top of a wood tank at the creekside rails of the corral. That part was damn clever because the always-running water from the standpipe wouldn't freeze, and the line rider could either draw off his household water into a bucket or divert the flow into the stock tank or else let it dump free onto the ground where it could return to the creek it'd come from all that way upstream. Clever indeed, Joe thought.

Not so clever was what they'd built with, although likely there hadn't been any choice about that.

The line shack was built of cottonwood logs trimmed and laid up eight logs high, then roofed over with saplings and sod. The problem was the cottonwood logs, since cottonwood won't hold up worth a damn and tends to warp and split and twist over time. A good deal of a line rider's problem in a cottonwood shack was trying to keep ahead of all the holes where wind could slice through and find a fellow. That's a chore not so easy done when all the mud is frozen thick or else buried under ice and snow, or both.

Still, that was getting ahead of things. The first problem would be to set up housekeeping and try and get the SOB warm. He just hoped whoever put the fireplace in knew how to build a chimney to make it draw right. There is nothing on the face of this earth calculated to make a man more miserable in winter than a fireplace that won't draw so that the fire is all the damn time dying and having to be relit.

At least it would be a while before Joe had to worry about wood for the fire. When that crew of Mexican hay cutters came through in August, the foreman had thought to send a pair of them up here to fell timber and cut and split it into stove lengths, and as he rode up from the Zeke home place way the hell and gone to the south, Joe could see that the Mexes hadn't shirked what they were told.

There was firewood, sixteen maybe eighteen cords of it he judged, stacked tall and tidy against the north and the west walls where it would act as insulation against the wind until it was needed inside for burning. Smart. But of course the Mexes would just have been following what others had done before. They would've seen how the wood had been stacked in years past and just gone ahead and done the same without paying any mind to what a good idea it was to make the stacks like that.

Joe rode into the small corral and carefully tied his horse before tiptoeing across the frozen dirt clods to reach the gate poles and haul them across the opening. It sure as hell wouldn't do for a man to let himself be caught afoot out here. Not at this time of year, it wouldn't.

Then he went back to the animals and one at a time unloaded and then untied the packhorses. They'd been brought along on a string, one's head tied to the next one's tail and so forth, three packhorses and Joe's saddle horse. Of course any of the heavy-bodied horses could be put under saddle. There's no room for lazeabouts on a winter string. Every animal has to be able to handle any job or it isn't worth feeding and watering through the hard months.

Working quickly, if only because he was anxious to get himself settled, Joe stripped the horses, piling their gear outside the rails close by the lean-to, which was really more a windbreak than a shelter, and stacking his own supplies over to the other side where they would be easier to transfer indoors later on.

He found a piece of tarp that he used to cover the packs, halters, lead ropes and such crap, then dropped his saddle and bridle on top of the household supplies. Those would go indoors. Not that Joe gave all that much of a damn about the horses, but he couldn't see any sense in putting his butt in a frozen saddle each morning when it could hit a warm one instead. As for the bridle, a horse with a frost-bit tongue isn't going to be of as much use as one that's whole, so why take the chance?

He turned the wooden gadget—someone had carved it out of a block of pine, and a cunning thing it was, too, like a miniature sluice that mounted underneath the standpipe and swiveled to send water most anywhere you wanted it but mostly onto a low bench where a bucket would nicely sit or else into the trough or out onto the ground downslope from the corral so there wouldn't be ice for the horses to slip on—so as to run some water into the trough.

He slipped through the rails and walked over to take a look at the tarpaulin-draped haystack that had been made between the shack and the corral.

Again it was some clever thinking SOB who'd done the planning. Not particularly protecting the summer's hay against deer and cows. That was only sensible. It was the placement of the stack itself that pleased Joe. Again the guy had been thinking. There were posts surrounding the haystack, of course, for the tarps to be laced to, and Joe could see there were eyebolts on the one that was in a direct line between the southeast corner of the cabin and the corral fence beside the water pipe. He looked back, and sure enough, there were more eyebolts fixed into one of the fence posts close to the water trough.

Damn good idea, Joe thought. Before the big snows came a man could run a lifeline from the cabin to the haystack and on to the corral. With a line to hold on to there was no chance he could get lost between the shack and the corral. And most every year there would be at least one storm, sometimes more, with the blowing snow so dense that it'd be dangerous to be afoot, even in broad daylight, without a lifeline for safety. Men had been known to die within shouting distance of their own firesides if they once got themselves discombobulated. The way this deal was worked out, even if a man found himself down, say he was broke-legged or half-froze or something, he could still find his way to the haystack and burrow into it.

Whoever had thought this place out had known what he was doing, Joe admitted.

If things were as well thought out indoors as out, why then... then this would still be a stinking damn line camp, empty and lonely and a miserable sonuvabitch place to be.

With a frown, Joe gathered up his saddle and a few other things to make the first of the many loads it would take for him to get everything inside where it belonged.

2

Joe was impressed. Instead of doing the cheap and easy thing, which was to build up a fireplace and chimney with rocks and mud available right outside the door in the creek bed, somebody had gone to the expense and the trouble to haul in a real stove. A round-bodied cast-iron patent stove with a damper built into the sheet-steel pipe and a wide flaring surface big enough to cook on. The main thing, though, was the way that stove would throw heat in the winter. There's nothing, but nothing, that can compare with a cast-iron stove for giving off good heat. And the fire-box in the worst patent stove is better for holding coals than the finest fireplace ever made. Seeing that stove gave Joe hope that this winter wasn't going to be so cold as he'd expected.

The cabin walls weren't such-a-much, he quickly saw as he dumped his first load of gear onto the floor and paused before turning back for another.

In more than one spot, standing just inside the door and not really taking the time yet to examine things, he could see daylight show-ing through the chinks. He'd have to fix those spots—and the smaller, sneakier, hidden ones, too—before things got too cold.

The stove was a definite plus, though, and the weathered-out daubing was only to be expected.

All in all, he conceded, the line camp was-n't so bad. For damn sure he'd seen worse quar-ters in his time.

The shack, naturally, consisted of one room. There was nothing fancy about any line shack Joe'd ever heard of, and the Zeke's was no exception. One room about—he eye-balled it as close as he could out of a mild sort of curiosity—call it ten foot deep from front to back and a bit wider across than it was deep. Twelve foot across, maybe.

The stove was centered against the back wall and set out from the combustible wall logs a good two and a half, three feet. Someone had taken the added precaution of flattening a bunch of food tins and tacking them to the logs behind the stove, forming a metal reflector there that would do a fine job of keeping the heat from getting too intense on the wall no matter how hot the stove got.

The pipe, ordinary sheet-steel sections, went straight up through a chimney box in the roof. From where he was standing Joe couldn't see what had been used for roofing material around the pipe, but the woodbox that surrounded it was plenty big enough for safety, and the chimney pipe was guyed with steel wire to make sure there was no way in hell it could come in contact with the wooden roof supports.

And the floor of the whole place was packed earth, so there was no need for a firebrick base underneath the stove. Ash and live coal could dribble out of the joints and clinker-shaker all day and all night and never do a lick of damage nor set anything afire unless a man was damnfool enough to be deliberately stupid and store combustibles right underneath the stove box.

Whoever had built this place made damn sure he wouldn't burn up in his sleep some night.

Joe liked that.

As for the furniture, there was a spindly table or stand sort of rig with a bucket on it—to serve as a sink and counter—tucked into the back left corner as seen from the front door. Which itself was centered in the east wall.

There were shelves, still holding an assortment of tins and pails and pasteboard boxes so dust-covered it wasn't possible to see what each of them was, or had been, built into the back right corner. That would be the pantry.

In each of the front corners there was a bed frame pegged into the wall on two sides and supported by hefty wood chunks at the outside foot corners. The frames were laced with thick rope—probably worn-out catch-ropes—to serve as springs, and at the head of each of the two beds there was a clean-looking mattress cover carefully folded and laid ready to be stuffed with fresh grass or pine needles or whatever else the owner's pleasure might be. Joe favored blue fir for filling a mattress with because it smelled so damn good when it was fresh. On the other hand any of the evergreen needles turned brittle and hard and tended to spike their way through even the heaviest ticking to poke and prickle once they got dry. Anyway he'd have to take a look around and see what might be available before he made up his mind about that. Likely he'd end up doing the easy thing and sticking some hay into his bag. Or not. He could worry about that later.

There was a cabinet sort of thing set in the middle of the left wall. It didn't have a proper door across the front, but a square of long-ago red calico cloth had been tacked in place as a drape sort of thing.

He went over and took a look behind the drape and discovered that this was his dish cabinet, so to speak. The two shelves behind the drape held three plates, two bowls, four cups, some spoons and forks, a big skillet and a small one, and a couple pots, one with a lid. There was no coffeepot, but that was no problem.

It was Joe's experience that water would boil regardless of what kind of pot you put it in. In a pinch even a skillet would make do for the boiling of coffee.

In the middle of the place, and pretty much dominating everything else, there was the sit-down table. There were two actual chairs on either side of the table, one of them with arms, and an upended keg nearby could be used either as a third chair or to prop one's feet on whilst sitting in the more comfortable of the real chairs.

Some thoughtful soul had left a pillow on the seat of the armchair, but whoever left it there hadn't taken into account the pleasure mice would take in the thing once the shack was left empty. There wasn't a whole lot of the pillow left. There was still enough cover remaining so that Joe could see that it had used to be blue. Most of the stuffing, though, was long gone, likely having served to warm and comfort several generations of young mice by now.

A pewter lamp with a filthy, smoke-grimed glass globe was suspended from a wire more or less over top of the table, and an equally dirty lantern sat at the foot of the bed on the right-hand side of the door. Which meant whoever spent last winter here—Pete Bower, that would've been—likely chose to use that bed for his own.

Pegs driven into the logs here and there around the walls served as wardrobe and casual storage. Hanging from them now were a small assortment of things like a Swedish bow saw, an ax, a shovel, and an ice auger.

There was only one window in the place. That was in the front wall just to the left of the door. It consisted simply of a piece of log being cut out and a piece of glass puttied firmly into the gap. The window couldn't be opened, but there was the door for that on a fine day. All the window was expected to do was to admit a little light. When there was light to let in. There would be days, maybe weeks at a time, when there mightn't be daylight enough to be worth the bother.

Joe looked around carefully for a few seconds, then shrugged and with a grunt turned to go fetch in his next load of stuff.

The Zeke's line shack wasn't bad. Not bad at all, actually.

3

This was a fat and easy time of year. The weather was fine and there wasn't much to be done except ride out a few times and get to know the country he'd be holding come the hard snows. This early in the season, though, all the beeves had been left well north on their home ranges and there was no need for them to be moving south. Yet.

That would happen later, animals from the Deuce, the KMT, the Barlow—their brand was a rough set of lines that were supposed to represent a pocketknife, sort of—the 23 Bar and whatever others were up there in Dakota, they would start drifting south once the cold north winds commenced pushing them. That was when Potter would start earning his keep by shoving the interlopers back off Zeke grass and keeping the sons of bitches more or less where they belonged.

Somewhere down to the south there would be some other line rider from some other outfit working to keep the Zeke stock from eating the winter forage on that range. But that was his problem, not Joe's. Joe would have all he wanted right here.

For now, though, it was nice and easy. Just get acquainted with the country and take things slow.

Eat, sleep, and on weekends take a few days off—nobody would care—and go up to Cam Peaker's hog ranch—from here it was closer by half a day than Hyde's Crossing—and have a drink or two.

Except for being so broke that he couldn't buy a woman when he wanted one, this wasn't turning out to be so bad after all, Joe had to concede.

4

Joe hauled the horse to a halt and stepped down onto the slick, damp gravel that bordered the creek. He gave the animal enough slack rein that it could reach the water if it wanted, then squatted and lifted a palmful of water for himself. He stayed there for a moment squinting up the far slope toward the rider coming down off the ridge to meet him. Joe had no idea who this man was. He was sure he hadn't seen him before.

The rider came on, his horse descending the

steep slope with that waddling, butt-swing gait that is so hard to sit with any kind of comfort. When he reached the creek opposite Joe he nodded and touched the brim of his hat. "Howdy."

"Howdy our own self," Joe said. "Step down if you want." The offer was his to make, or to withhold, since he was the one who'd been here first.

"Thanks." The rider first splashed across the shallow run of icy water, then dismounted and let his horse water. "You'd be Potter, I believe," he said.

"That's right. How d'you know me, mister? I don't recollect we've met." The man was only of average height, but he had shoulders that looked like he could juggle anvils. If he knew how to juggle. And he had the sort of clean, molded features that artists draw when they're wanting to advertise something, a fancy shirt or new suit of clothes or expensive cigar or the like. Women probably thought this man was swell. Joe didn't much like him.

"Once. It was up in Montana."

"I see."

"No reason you'd remember. I was just a face in the crowd."

"And now?"

The fellow pulled out the makings for a cigarette, offered the pouch to Joe, and when refused began to roll one for himself. "I'm McCarthy. Foreman for the 23 Bar."

"I've heard of the outfit," Joe conceded.

"We're located up on Sugar Creek."

Joe shrugged. He'd heard the name but had no idea where it was. This right here was as far north as he'd been on the Zeke range.

"Riding line for the Zeke this season, are you?" McCarthy guessed.

"That's right."

"In that case you'll likely be seeing some of our beeves directly."

"I expect I will."

"'I was kinda hoping to run into the Zeke rider," McCarthy said. "I heard about Pete getting himself hurt and was wanting to make sure his replacement had the lay of things."

"Is that right?" Joe said without enthusiasm. Obviously this man, who wasn't no way shape or form his boss, was one of them that could be counted on to have something to say whether it was his business or not.

"That's right. Now let me tell you...." He launched into a description of the drainage basin, buttes, and other terrain features that marked the boundaries—more or less—of the unfenced land that was used by the Zeke and the other larger outfits. It was pretty much the exact same stuff Andy Plasser had told Joe before he rode out from the Zeke. He'd had to pay attention when Andy said it. He didn't particularly have to listen again now.

"When you turn our 23 Bar stock back, I'd appreciate it if you'd drive 'em on into the next drainage over instead of just dropping them here. It'd save you and me both a lot of work if you'd do that," McCarthy concluded. "Keep 'em from coming back on you all the time if you do that, and there isn't so deep a drift likely over there so it could save me some winterkill if you'd be kind enough to help out like that."

"If I have time," Joe agreed, not meaning it. He was here to protect Zeke grass, not to play nurse to any 23 Bar stock. The hell with this McCarthy and his 23 Bar.

McCarthy lit his cigarette and cocked his head to one side. That was something a man did to let the smoke slip out from underneath his hat brim, but Joe had the notion McCarthy had something else in mind. The man sure seemed to be giving him a hard looking over.

"Something on your mind?" Joe challenged. Piss on him. Whatever McCarthy was thinking, piss on him.

"Just thinking how funny it is to find you here. Or have you changed the way you used to think about Indians?"

"I don't know what you mean, mister."

"You. I mean, you always used to have a real hard-on for Indians."

"Anything wrong with that?"

"No, I reckon not. A man's entitled to his opinions. It's just... you know."

"Damned if I do. I don't know what in hell you're talking about, McCarthy."

The 23 Bar foreman grinned and shook his head. "Really?"

"I said so, didn't I?"

"Don't get yourself ruffled. I was just finding it funny, that's all. I mean... you working here on reservation land and everything."

"The hell you say."

"You really didn't know?"

"Hell no, I didn't."

"Oh, yeah. Everything from Six Mile Creek north for, oh, seventy, eighty mile or more, it's all reservation land. Leased by white cow outfits of course but reservation all the same. Belongs to the Sioux."

"Shit!"

"You see any Sioux around here, Potter, you're supposed to act polite an' say sir."

"That'll be the damn day. Look, you're pulling my leg, aren't you? Just trying to get my goat? Did I ever run you in when we was up in Montana or something that you're trying to get even with me now?"

"No, I'm telling you true. This here really is reservation land."

"Shit," Joe repeated. Of course McCarthy was crazy as hell if he thought Joe Potter was ever going to say sir to any Indian. But the 23 Bar man was twitting him about that part of it anyway. No white man would ever do that. Not any white man who had any pride or dignity. Not to a damn savage Injun.

But jeez...

"You know," McCarthy said, "it's close enough to noon that some coffee would taste pretty good. How's about you join me for some, Chief."

Joe gave the man a hard look. He couldn't tell if this McCarthy was pulling his chain about Indians again or if the guy was referring back to when Joe had been chief of police in whatever Montana town it was where McCarthy and him had met. And he wasn't sure he wanted to stay around and find out which way the man meant it neither.

"Thanks, but I'll be getting on."

"You got the lay of things worked out all right, do you? If you have any questions I'd be glad to help."

"I got it down, all right," Joe said. Which was a healthy exaggeration if not an actual lie.

114

But dammit, he wanted to get shut of this McCarthy with his fine job and fancy looks. Damn him anyway.

"Thanks for the offer of the coffee. Next time, all right?"

"Sure."

Joe nodded and stepped into his saddle, wheeling his horse west, off toward Wyoming, off toward the low hump with the rock outcropping at the south end where the Zeke range more or less ended. Or at least where Joe's responsibilities ended.

He rode off without remembering to say a good-bye to the 23 Bar foreman.

GOD IT FELT GOOD *to be young and strong and full of pep. All piss and vinegar, energy and grinning goodwill. Get up in the morning after four hours' sleep and feel nothing but go. Not a pain or ache or so much as an upset stomach.*

Payday. Was there ever anything better in this whole world than payday when you were eighteen and eager and proud?

There was always an inspection first. Buttons polished. Shoes shined. Rifle bore so clean it gleamed. Hair fresh cut by your bunkie; I'll do yours if you do mine and laugh like hell when somebody makes remarks about all the ways a comment like that could be taken; it's all part of the good feeling, part of the joy of being young and strong and proud. Hair fresh cut and fresh shaved, too, even though there's no real need for the shave part of it. It's just that it wouldn't be a proper payday if you didn't shave as part of the getting ready for inspection.

As you stood stiff and straight in the long blue line waiting for the lieutenant to come around, the sun would be hot on the back of your dress blouse and the smell of laundry soap would sneak up out of your collar as sweat, fresh, and not unclean really, began to soften the starch in your best shirt.

Then the man would stop in front of you, make a snappy quarter turn, maybe ask a question, and you'd play the game the whole way through, eyes fixed sternly forward and level and bark the answers back to him crisp and loud. He'd start to move and you'd snap through the much-practiced motions. Slap of leather on flesh as the perfectly tight sling pounded into your palm. Slap of flesh on wood as he'd snatch the rifle right away from you. Ring of metal on metal as he'd click the breach open and glance inside. Tiny grunt as he reversed the piece and peered down the bore. Grunt of approval? God, you hoped so. Grunt of approval or grunt of disgust. One gave you the afternoon free. The other gave you hell. But it was all of your own making whichever way he found it. The rules were as clean as the rifle was supposed to be. All you had to do to get that lazy afternoon was do everything else just exactly right. Perfection, that was all they asked. And hell, the young always figure they can give perfection, so there wasn't anything wrong with that.

The lieutenant shoves the rifle back at your gut and you take it without even having to look where you're grabbing, take it just right, at that perfect point of balance, and once more there is a slap of leather on flesh and the man executes a smart quarter turn to the left and takes one more measured step and it's all behind you now.

You look at the sergeant who's trailing the lieutenant and he nods about a quarter inch and you know you did fine—perfection, no problem— and you're free until next reveille, don't even have to make retreat tonight if you don't want, and what could feel better than that?

What could? Well having the free time and a weight of coins in your pocket, too, that's what. And that comes next. Shuffle forward in the long line. Come to attention before the table and throw a stiff salute and bark out name, rank, and unit. The dog-robber corporal mumbles too low and fast to be understood. A bunch of gobbledygook to say what they've credited you with and what they're taking back in fines or charges and what

117

for. It doesn't matter what the corporal says anyway because right or wrong they're always right. The main thing is that the corporal raises his voice enough to be heard when he comes to the final amount owed, and that is what the paymaster counts out of the steel-banded lockbox and pays over to you. You sign the pay sheet, pick up your money, salute smartly, and wheel away to make room for the next guy in line.

But oh, that money does feel fine in a blue woolen pocket. The coins are thick and cool and heavy and they make a soft, almost fluttering sound as they slide over one another when you walk.

First thing you do is head for the post trader's store. The inside isn't segregated by age, but it might as well be. The old men all turn to the right toward the counter where the beer and spirits are dispensed. Some of the young guys go there, too, the tough ones and the ones who want to make everybody think they're tough. The rest of the fresh fish turn left to pick over the geegaws and the goodies. Maybe buy a piece of ribbon to mail to a girl back home. Those that have homes. Or paper and ink for mail to send off. For those who have someone to write to. For the rest, well, there's always something needed. A silk kerchief to tie round your neck—you can't get away with it on the parade ground, but on detail or out in the field it's all right—so the wool shirt collars won't chafe.

Or candy. Horehound is the best. Impossible to describe, really. You know because someone—who the hell was that, anyhow?—asked once and you couldn't do it. Not really. The closest you could come was to say it was like root beer but with a hint of licorice as an aftertaste and a smidgen of sassafras as an overtone. Which makes no sense at all if you haven't ever tasted the stuff. And which isn't necessary if you have. Point is, of course, that horehound is the best. Every payday you buy enough horehound candy to last the whole month through until next payday.

And every time all the candy is eaten and gone five, six days later.

Still and all, the next month you'll do the same thing again.

And once you ever do taste horehound you never forget it. Anytime you want thereafter you can call the taste back to mind just as if you finished some five minutes ago even if it's been twenty-five, thirty years since you've had any. Even if it's been...

Eyes. The thought of horehound candy makes you see eyes. Huge eyes. Black. Shining. Eager. Supplicants yammering in a tongue only their heathen forebears could understand. Ugly little nits, damn them. Somebody should keep the little bastards away on paydays. It isn't right they be allowed in to beg on paydays, damn them.

Loud, pushy little sons of bitches with their hands out and lies on their lips, crowding and tugging and whining. No pride. Not one single stinking one of them has the least scrap of pride.

Except... one of them that isn't loud or pushy. Just quiet. Awful quiet. And with the biggest, saddest eyes of them all.

Little son of a bitch. Like a whipped dog with no fight or heart left in it.

Looking. Eyes following every damn move. Every time you reach into the poke and lift another tar-drop nugget of horehound to your mouth there're those damn eyes. Not saying anything. Not coming forward. Just standing there, looking.

Eyes shiny and full of water, but not crying. Not a bit of that. And not begging. Just... watching.

You know at the damn time it's a mistake. It's a stupid thing to do. But then all young men are stupid. Pity, but it's the truth. Nobody ever learns except too late to avoid the mistakes that are our ladder from young to smart, from stupid to maturity.

So once, just one damn time, you reach into the bag and put the candy not in your mouth but in the blanket-ass kid's grimy hand.

Stupid. It is a stupid thing to do.

Thank God the young can learn. What a shame they have to learn the hard way.

He sat up, frowning. There was a faint, lingering memory that he'd been having a dream. He couldn't recall what the dream was about, but he had the vague, uneasy sense that he hadn't liked it, not worth a damn.

He wasn't going to worry about it now. It wasn't important.

He shivered beneath the thick wool blankets piled atop the bunk. He had no way to tell what time it might be. Late enough that there was no heat coming from the stove.

Still shivering he went barefoot to the stove, opened the firebox, and pushed some fresh chunks of split dry wood onto the bed of red, softly pulsing coals. Yellow flame lifted around the edges of the stove lengths and began to dance and flicker. He shut the door with a clang and, still barefoot, went to the door. It was too cold to walk all the way back to the outhouse. For that he would have to dress, at least pull his coat on, and struggle into this boots. Instead he stood in the doorway to quickly relieve himself and then, thoroughly chilled, scurried back to the comfort of the bunk and blankets, pulling them high under his chin and burrowing deep into the warmth that remained there.

What in hell had he been dreaming about anyway?

Not that it mattered. He closed his eyes and put the dream out of mind, wanting to get back to sleep quickly so he could take advantage of whatever was left of the night.

Damn but it felt good to lie there warm under the blankets.

Was there any feeling better than dozing warm and comfortable on a cold morning? Probably not. If there was he sure as hell couldn't remember what it might be. Couldn't think of a single thing that would be better.

Well, maybe one thing. But there weren't any women nearer than, what? Twenty miles? Thirty? Might as well be a hundred.

But no, except for that he couldn't think of very much at all that would feel better than this right here.

Chapter 4

1

ZK Ranch line shack
Southwestern South Dakota
Monday, November 29, 1909

Christ, it was cold. A bitter, dry, nasty cold. Had been for weeks. What, two? Three? At least two weeks without seeing a thaw even in the middle of the afternoon. But dry. This time of year you would think there'd be snow on the ground, but no. The most there had been were some flurries so light he could have imagined them. And even then the flakes were so dry they were brittle. Tiny and with no substance whatsoever. They hit the frozen ground, too few of them to hardly color it, and stayed there until they shriveled up and evaporated clean away.

Still, if it stayed like this he would have an easy winter. It is wind and blowing snow that the cattle drift in front of, not cold. Weather like this wouldn't move them any.

Not that there wasn't work to be done in the cold. Damn cows. They always meant work of one sort or another. That was something a man could count on. Cows are a pain in the ass, pure and simple.

Joe Potter saddled the second-best horse in his short string and jammed the bit between its teeth. He led it outside the corral and carefully tied it to a post, then just as carefully slid the poles across the opening to close the gap. A man alone for months on end learns to take care.

And it was probably a good thing that he was alone, too. He'd make a helluva sight if there was anybody else around to see.

He had on oversized boots that were stuffed with newspaper. That helped keep his feet from freezing. Barely—they sure felt like they were froze by each day's end—but enough.

He'd put his wide-brimmed hat up on a shelf more than a week ago in favor of a homemade rig that he'd sliced out of a scrap of old wool blanket. It was part hood and part helmet, the itchy-scratchy wool cut and folded and stitched up with waxed harness thread to shape and then tied in place with strips cut off the same blanket so that the strips kind of acted like a muffler in addition to holding the hood on.

The contraption likely made him look like he was wearing a flowerpot upside down on his head, but better that than freeze his ears off.

And that wasn't just a figure of speech either. Joe had met more than one old boy who had stubs where his ears ought to be after they got taken with the frostbite.

Hadn't hurt hardly at all, they'd told him. You go to ride a big circle in the wintertime and not pay no attention. First your ears went numb. Hell, that happened practically all the time anyhow, so who'd ever think twice about it? But when it was really good and cold there'd sometimes be a whole lot more to it than that. The ears would get numb and

123

then sometime during the course of the day they'd start going white. And then that night or the next day or whenever the guy managed to get himself warm again they'd thaw out. Next thing you'd know they'd turn black and the spoiled flesh would rot away and slough off until of a sudden the fellow wouldn't never again look like a normal human person.

No sirree bob, Joe Potter didn't want such as that happening to him. Better to walk around looking like an animated ragbag than lose his ears. Or other parts.

He was always careful about such things. He owned a pretty decent coat with a lambskin collar and the best long johns money could buy, pretty near, and a pair of sheepskin chaps. And of course his fur-lined gauntlets. Without a good pair of gloves a man wouldn't be able to work at all in this country. Not during winter, he wouldn't. Joe had even less desire to lose his fingers than he did his ears. He was always careful of his hands.

Without ears he'd have trouble getting a two-bit hoor to lie with him. But without hands he wouldn't be able to make a living and might just as well ask someone to do him the favor of shooting him. If he had a good enough friend to do it, that is.

He tied the horse, a stout creature of a muddy shade of grulla, to the post, checked the latigo to make sure it hadn't loosened any, and let the stirrup drop. Then he picked up his ax and slid it into the scabbard that had been made to hold a carbine but served every bit as well to carry the ax.

He thought about going back inside for

one more cup of coffee, then rejected the notion. It wasn't that he was in any particular hurry to get a start on the day's work, just that if he had any more coffee he was going to have to stop that much more often to take a leak. And in weather like this that wasn't very damn comfortable. Better to let the coffee wait until he got back, he decided.

Resigned to the necessity, Joe untied the grulla and climbed slowly, joints protesting and tired muscles aching, into the saddle.

Another day closer to payday. Hurrah.

2

There were twenty-five, thirty head or so gathered close around the deep spot in the creek. All the damn things thirsty and complaining about it.

Joe hadn't been to this water hole in, oh, three days now? Something like that. Likely the opening in the ice froze over again the first night after he last chopped it loose. So the cattle hadn't been able to water here for a couple days or thereabouts.

Stupid damn things. A horse or a deer, now, will bust its own hole through ice unless the ice is awful damn thick. A cow will find a thin skin of ice covering a water hole and stand right there complaining until it thirsts to death. Stand hock deep in snow and thirst to death instead of pawing and stamping through to the water or eating snow for the water in it. That's what everyone said, anyway. Joe didn't know enough, or for that matter care enough, about cows to claim it for himself. When it came to cows he was willing to let the other guy do the studying.

The point, though, was that the whole winter long he would have to take his ax and bust the water holes open every now and then or the idiot bovines would go gaunt and weak and pretty soon lie down and die.

Joe didn't so much give a damn about the beeves themselves, but old Mr. Schumacher somewhere back east and, closer to, his hey-boy Andy Plasser would not take kindly to a winterkill of half the herd or so. So the best thing to do was to go ahead and chop the damn water holes open now and then.

But it was a lousy job in this sort of weather, and that was the truth. Of course, come to think of it the only time you had to chop ice was in lousy weather. Otherwise there wouldn't be any of the crap to have to worry about, would there?

Proud of himself for having made that observation, Joe guided the grulla through the small herd of beeves—there were at least three of them wearing brands that had no business on this range, but he wasn't going to get all excited and make a push north for three lousy head—and on to a thin stand of winter-bare plums, where he dismounted and carefully tied the horse to a stout limb.

Funny thing how usually the half-wild range cattle would stay well clear of a man on horseback, but here beside the iced-over water hole they were willing to stand their ground and let him push clean through them without turning and running away. They were plenty thirsty, all right. Had it been more than three days since he'd last been here? He wasn't for sure about that. He shrugged. No sense worrying about it. He was here now. That was good enough.

He kept a wary eye on the beeves standing around him—more than one old boy had taken a horn in the back as the penalty for not paying attention; there is no gratitude in a stinking cow, after all—and lifted the ax out of its keeper.

The footing beside the creek was good, mostly because it was still so cold out. The rumpled, hoof-churned ground beside the creek was frozen in lumps and ridges from the cattle walking on it as it slowly froze over, so there was plenty of purchase underfoot. The creek bank would become treacherous again, oddly enough, when the sun got warm enough to turn this brown ice into snot-slick mud again. That was when he'd be in danger of taking a fall. And inviting a charge from one of those miserable cows. A man down is a man in trouble. Around cattle almost as bad as around hogs. Joe hated hogs and wouldn't have worked with them for twice the lousy pay a cowhand drew. You fall down in a hogpen and the sows will figure you for food. And if that isn't a scary thought then Joe Potter didn't know what one was.

Still keeping part of his attention on the thirsty cattle, he sidestepped down to the creek edge and whacked the yard-wide spot that he was keeping open.

It didn't take all that much. The ice probably wasn't a half-inch thick along the bank there where the cold creek water swirled and flowed through at a pretty good clip. It was plenty thick enough to discourage the beeves from drinking but not so thick it had to be really chopped up. A couple solid thumps with the top flat of the axhead and the ice busted into sheets and hunks and small slabs. Instant jigsaw puzzle, that's what it was.

Joe dabbed at the floating ice with the axhead a few times, inducing some of the sheets to slide underneath the thick skim of ice that covered the rest of the creek and prying up on some others so the current would help move them up on top of the mother ice.

Satisfied that there was a big enough hole for the cows to drink through, Joe used the ax like a cane to steady himself while he crabbed back up the steep creek bank to level ground above and went back to the grulla.

Cold? He reckoned. His ears stung and the tip of his nose was numb, and he had lost much of the feeling in his feet and some of it from his fingers.

One more lousy water hole and he'd head back to the shack, he decided. The hell with the rest of the cows. He'd get to them tomorrow.

3

Potter shivered and groaned. Jeez, it was about as cold indoors as it was out. He tossed one glove—but only one, the other was staying on his hand by damn—onto the table and scraped a match across the rough, rusty side of the iron stove. The sulfur head burst into bright flame, and he held it to a fat pine splinter, one of about a gallon of the things that he'd personally shaved off a pine chunk before coming out here. The pine caught, and he used it to touch off a pencil-thin stick of dry willow, which in turn lighted a small tepee of aspen splits and those soon got some cottonwood chunks to burning.

Satisfied that the shack would be toasty warm in a half hour or so—and feeling much warmer already himself even though there couldn't possibly have been any change in the temperature yet—Joe pulled off his other glove and unbuttoned his coat. He threw his blanket hood on the table with the gloves and used a slosh of water from the bucket to rinse out the pot he used to boil his coffee in. Funny thing, the water in the bucket not being frozen though he'd been gone most all day. He'd expected to have to wait for the water to thaw, but it was just fine. That was good. He tossed the morning's old grounds out the front door and poured a quart, quart and a half of fresh waster into the brown-stained old pot. He set that onto the stove and dumped an unmeasured spill of ready-ground coffee direct from the bag into the cold water. He would have added some eggshells. If he'd had any eggs. Which he didn't. Eggshell took the bitterness out of boiled coffee. That was gospel. But Joe hadn't seen an egg since he left the Zeke headquarters and likely wouldn't see another until spring or thereabouts.

Once his coffee was on the stove he pulled

the firebox door open, peered inside for a moment, and then added another couple lengths of split wood. The fire had caught and was drawing nicely. Joe turned the damper down to keep more of the heat inside now that the fire was well established, then gave some thought to supper.

He hated cooking and would have eaten all his meals out of cans if Andy Plasser and the Zeke weren't so cheap that they stocked his pantry more with dry staples than with canned goods, damn them.

Limited to what someone else thought he should have, he settled tonight for his old standby, johnnycakes. Johnnycakes aren't so bad. They are filling. And easy to make. A lot easier than beans, which you have to think about ahead of time so you can soak the things all day or the whole night before you want to go and cook them. That was the only thing Joe had against beans. He never thought to start the cooking process beforehand so that every time he thought it would be nice to have a pot of beans, maybe with some onion and bacon and molasses cooked in with them, it was too late to do anything about it. And why start soaking them one night when he might not feel like beans the next night and the soaked batch would just go to ruin waiting to be cooked? No, he wasn't all that fond of beans from a cook's point of view, even though he liked eating them well enough.

So usually he settled for the quick and easy johnnycakes that he could throw together at the last moment and not have to think about otherwise.

He got out the skillet that also served as a griddle and set it beside the pot with the coffee in it. While it started heating he sliced a thumb-sized piece off one of the slabs of bacon that he'd hung from the rafters over the unused bunk and tossed it into the skillet so the grease would leach out of it and keep the cakes from sticking to the iron.

Then he took a bowl and tossed in two handfuls of wheat flour and a palmful of saleratus. On top of that he added some salt and, his own invention, about as much sugar as he'd used saleratus. He stirred the dry ingredients together, then poured in enough water to mix into a runny, lumpy dough and added a hearty spoonful of lard, stirring and whipping the whole mess together one more time.

And that was all it needed.

Satisfied, Joe set the bowl aside so the stuff would sort of soak all together while the skillet was heating, then put his pokes and jars of ingredients back on the shelves where they belonged.

The bags of flour and sugar went on one shelf and the jar of saleratus on another along with the tin lard bucket. Joe put the lard in its place and then frowned. Something seemed out of place.

He wasn't sure what it was, but...

No, that was silly. What the hell could be out of place when the only one who was ever in here was him?

It was the sack of salt that he thought wasn't quite the way he left it.

So he'd bumped it when he picked up the

131

lard tin or maybe he hadn't put it back like he thought he did this morning or else there was some other simple explanation other than there being rats trying to carry the whole place away.

He went back to the stove and stuck a finger into the coffee water. It was still far from being hot, but he thought it'd begun to warm. A little.

And for sure there was a little grease seeping out of the piece of bacon to start coating the skillet for his johnnycakes.

Another five or ten minutes and he could start cooking supper, and by the time he was done with that the coffee should be boiling. Throw in a dollop of cold water to settle the grounds to the bottom of the pot, and he'd be all set for his night meal. Even the timing of it was working out all right this evening. Joe felt pretty pleased with himself as he pulled his gloves on again and, before it got dark and even colder, went out to refill the water bucket from the standpipe by the corral.

He had it, he figured, under control real nice.

WHITE SILENCE *surrounded him. He remembered. He had been here before, often. Misty white fog. Crusted white snow. Empty. Bleak.*

He could feel his heartbeat racing, pumping, pounding madly out of control beneath the black coat. The coat was really blue. He knew that. But if he were to look down it would appear to be black. He knew that, too. He did not look down. He was terrified of the lack of color he knew he would find there.

Did not look either at the rifle that he carried slanted at port arms. The rifle dragged at him. Its weight pulled at his arms and sapped his strength. The snow was as nothing to wade through, but the weight of the rifle was a burden beyond endurance. And yet he had to endure. He had to.

The mists eddied and spun. Gossamer film without substance. Enfolding. Entrapping. Terrifying.

He turned his head away, unwilling to breathe in the floating white mist, afraid of what would happen to him if he were to take the fog into himself. And yet there was no escape from the mists surrounding him. He could feel the chill sweat of fear form on his brow as he twisted his head first this way and then that. The mist enveloped him. Thin, wispy tendrils sought him out, a dread malevolence guised as pale innocence.

He squeezed his eyes tight closed, but even as he did so he plodded steadily, stolidly forward. The snow clung to his boots and clutched at his ankles and tried to hold him back. The weight of the rifle sheathed his aching legs as if in lead, making each succeeding pace more wearyingly difficult than the one before. But there was no halting, no turn-

ing back. Much though he longed to go back it was not possible. He had to move on carrying the burden of his soldierly weapon, always forward, never slowing, never stopping.

He felt the crunch of snow crust giving way beneath his boots but could not hear. It was as if the mist were soft white cotton that plugged his ears and filled his senses and would admit no sensations but those it chose to inflict on him.

Felt the stultifying fatigue and the beading of cold sweat and the laboring of his breathing, but he could hear nothing, not even the sound of his own gasping breaths. He could feel the pounding of his heart and the quick and ragged rise and fall of his chest but could hear nothing of the fog-laden air that gushed in and out of his aching lungs.

Tired. Lordy, he was so tired. He wanted nothing more than to lie down. Curl tight in the soft snow like a well-furred dog taking refuge from a storm.

But he dared not do that. If he did the mists would claim him evermore. He knew this with a complete certainty. The mists were beautiful, but their beauty hid an unspoken menace that he must avoid at all peril.

Forward. He continued to press forward one slow and weary step at a time. One and then another and then yet again, each footstep unbearably tiring.

And yet he endured. He had to. It was either that or allow the mists to enter him, and that he could not do.

He moved steadily ahead in the white and eerie silence, pressing through the snowflat and the fog into dull and deadly white emptiness. Into... something? A shape? Was there a half-seen, half-sensed black form ahead, lying asprawl on the snow?

A shape like... he did not want to think about it. Did not want to see it. Closed his eyes and marched on blindly into the white.

It was good not seeing.

But if he stepped on the form? If there was a form there. He could look. He knew he did not dare look. Because then he might see, and he could not bear the sight of the things he might see there. Better the deadly mist and ethereal fog than to risk seeing. Better...

He stopped. If he were to take one more step forward... But if he paused the mist would take him.

He could not go forward. He dared not delay for so much as a moment. No choices remained. No choice. No chance. He could not proceed. He must not pause.

No choices.

He tipped his head back, sweat running down his cheeks and into the stubble that darkened his neck and made the woolen collar chafe tender skin there.

Tipped his head far backward.

A scream ripped out of his throat. A scream of utter horror.

And yet... no sound. He screamed but still no sound was heard.

And all around him the white fog swirled and closed in tighter and tighter.

Chapter 5

1

Friday, December 3, 1909

Where the *hell* was that can of condensed milk? He'd put it... he thought... right there beside the honey jar. So where the hell was it? He needed it, dammit. Needed it to make the tea drinkable. Generally speaking Joe Potter hated tea. It was a sissified drink fit for the ladies' social circle or a bunch of queers or a Englishman, the last two of which amounted pretty much to the same thing so far as Potter was concerned.

But there were times, dammit, when tea was what was needed. Like when a man had a cold coming on and his chest was congested and he wanted to knock the stuff, whatever it was, before it turned into a fever or maybe something worse. Then a cup of tea was sovereign. Nothing else would quite do. Well, he had the tea itself, a fresh and never-before opened tin of the stuff from the Atlantic and Pacific Co., come all the way from the Orient if you could believe what they said painted onto the can. A blend of the finest teas from Ceylon and Assam. Which he assumed must be towns in China, since everybody knows that tea comes from China. That is where the phrase "all the tea in China" comes from, of course, referring to whatever things a fellow thinks are more valuable.

When he thought about it Joe decided that the phrase was probably as stupid as... well as stupid as tea itself was. After all, who the hell knew how much the tea in China was worth. Probably a whole lot if there were entire companies that did nothing but buy the stuff up and send it over the sea in a ship so wrinkly old women and cornholers and Englishmen could buy it here. At a profit to the Atlantic and Pacific Co., of course.

Still, tea had its place for medicinal purposes. Like right now, dammit. The tea was steeping in his cup, turning the boiled water dark. So where was his can of damn milk? The tea was no damn good without a stiff dose of condensed milk and a peck or so of sugar to go in with it. Vile, nasty, bitter stuff without those. So he had the tea, dammit, and he had the sack of sugar. Now where in hell was the milk?

He knew good and well he'd put it right here. Just last month that had been. He was sure he'd put it beside the honey.

Or was he disremembering about that? Dammit, why couldn't he think any better than this? You'd think it was his head that was clogged up and congested, not his chest.

Even so, he was sure he'd put the can of milk here.

Well, pretty sure. Could have been someplace else, he supposed. But if it was someplace else then where the hell was *that* place?

If only he could remember... he shook his

head, quite thoroughly annoyed with him-self now for forgetting where he'd put the stupid te—no, now, it was the milk he could-n't find, not the tea. The tea was already in his cup along with the water, and he had the sugar set out so it was only the canned milk he couldn't find. Right? Of course that was right. Had the tea, had the sugar, didn't have the milk.

Huh. Wasn't that a good one. Surrounded by cows. Hundreds of the damn things. Maybe thousands. And not a drop of milk. If that was-n't a kick in the ol' butt...

Frustration turning to anger, Joe gave the woodbox a kick that sent it skittering a good six or eight inches across the earthen floor—and wasn't that an accomplishment of the first order? You bet—at the cost of a howl and a severely painful big toe on his right foot. He happened to be wearing stockings at the moment but no boots.

Jeez, he thought. This morning was not getting him anywhere. Not anywhere at all.

What he needed, dammit, was some strong tea. With milk in it. Or barring that a couple belts of rye whiskey would help.

Whiskey. Jeez. That was better for a man than tea. Any day. Every day. All day. Damn right it was. That was what he would do, he decided.

The hell with the milk. He'd saddle his number one horse and take a little jaunt up to Peaker's store. He hadn't been up there yet, but he'd heard tell where it was. He could go up there. Get a few drinks on tick. If Peaker was a sport maybe Joe could even wrangle the use of one of Peaker's hoors on credit until payday. Likely not, but a man never knows. He was sure he could get the whiskey, though, and that was more important than some scabby woman right now.

Yeah, that sounded fine. Rye whiskey, hell any whiskey, beats tea anytime. Even tea with plenty of sugar and milk in it.

Yeah, he liked that idea just fine. He'd saddle that horse and go up to Peaker's... Andy wouldn't mind; Andy would understand that when a man felt a sickness coming on he had to do something about it... and get himself a couple drinks. Maybe a bottle or three to fetch back with him. Peaker should let him go a few bottles' worth on the tab. Hell, Joe worked for the Zeke, didn't he, and everybody in this country knew the Zeke. A couple lousy dollars' worth of whiskey wouldn't be anything.

Sure. Helluva good idea. Never mind the can of damn milk. He'd look for it later. When he was feeling better. Meantime he'd just pull on his boots and bundle up and go get that horse saddled, that's what he'd do.

This idea was sounding better to him all the time. The more he thought about it the better he liked it. Damn straight, he did.

Potter grunted and whirled around in search of his boots, swaying and almost losing his balance as a momentary haze of dizziness followed his abrupt turn.

That was all right, he told himself. He would be just fine once he had a couple drinks to kill off whatever cold was trying to settle in his lungs.

Three, four drinks and he would be right as rain.

He hastily pulled on the boots first, then his warm coat and woolen hood and finally the gauntleted gloves. It was still cold as a witch's tit out there. Hadn't broken once since the hard freeze set in and there were no signs that it was fixing to. No matter about that, though. He'd been told the way to Cam Peaker's hog ranch. There would be whiskey there and a crackling fire and maybe a friendly card game—hell, if he got lucky at the cards there was no doubt he'd take a close look at the women Peaker was running up there—and whatever else a man might want to see in the dead of winter in this miserable country.

Yeah, this was the best idea he'd had since he couldn't remember when.

He set the latch behind him and went out to the corral to saddle the horse. He had the best part of a day's ride ahead of him and if he didn't want to run out of daylight before he reached Peaker's would have to get a move on.

He hurt. Jeez, he hurt. Every muscle. Every bone and joint. His head throbbed and the pain down deep inside his chest was killing him. He was burning up. Just a little while ago he'd been wet and chilled, and now he was afire all over again.

Fever. He knew what it was. But the thoughts came dim and from a great distance. He was aware. He remembered. But only just.

He wasn't thinking straight. Funny how he would know that. A person would think if you could think well enough to know you weren't thinking right then your thinking

140

would be, well, all right. Wouldn't you think that?

But it didn't work like that. Because he did know. His mind was all muzzy and muddy and screwed over by the fevers, and there wasn't anything he could do about any of it. Nothing but huddle under the blankets and wait it out. First the fever and then the sweat when it broke and then more fever again.

He'd been sick before.

But never like this. Lord no, never ever like this before.

He shouldn't have gone to Peaker's.

That son of a bitch. No credit. Who ever heard of such a thing? No credit for a man the company thought high enough of to keep on for the winter. It was insulting.

There's been a time... Ah, but that time was not now. Not when a man felt like his gut was being burned up and the rest of him shaken clean to death.

Joe Potter lay in his sweat-sodden blankets alternately shivering and slow basting in his own foul juices.

He could not remember the ride back to the Zeke line cabin. Honestly could not recall hardly any of it.

He remembered getting pissed off at that miserable tightwad Peaker and telling the son of a bitch off. He remembered that, all right. That had felt pretty good. And if he ever got Peaker alone, well, they'd talk it over again, that was for sure.

But as it was there was a bunch of others there, all of them friends of the storekeep and strangers to Joe Potter. He knew better

141

than to trust them to keep their stinking mouths shut.

So he got onto the horse with his belly still warm from the bowl of greasy beans and one lousy on-the-house drink Peaker gave him after telling him there wouldn't be any drinking on tick, no sir, not for no stranger, not even if he did ride for Andy Plasser and the Zeke. A bowl of beans and one lousy drink. Then kick a man out into the cold.

Literally. Bad cold. Way the hell and gone below freezing. No telling how cold. Better, likely, that he didn't know anyway. It wasn't human to put a man out into cold like that.

So it was back onto the horse and down the trail again.

Except by then he was getting sick. Hadn't said anything about that to Peaker. Bastard wouldn't have believed him anyway. Back onto the horse and gone, that was all.

Fell off... jeez, he didn't know how many times. Last time he knew he wouldn't make it back onto the horse if he fell again. Used a piggin string to tie his own hands to the horn and dropped his reins.

He hadn't had any idea where he was by then.

Either the horse knew or they would both of them die.

The horse knew. It brought him back.

That had been... what? Two days ago? He thought maybe. He wasn't for sure. Two days. Three. What did it matter? He was here now and could be he was dying here.

If he didn't soon get well enough to get up and around he would either lay here and thirst to death—a couple lousy steps from a fine, sweet-flowing creek and a standpipe to boot but no water in reach—or else he would freeze to death before he had time enough to thirst to death.

Wouldn't starve, though. One of the others would get him before he could starve.

For a little while he amused himself by thinking about that. For a little while it seemed funny as hell, just about the funniest thing he'd ever in his whole life heard, that he might cheat death by starvation, if only because he would die of something else beforehand.

Yeah, that was funny all right. He'd laugh like hell about it. Just as quick as he felt up to laughing, that is.

He cried out, the sound like that of a mournful wolf alone in brittle cold moonlight, and rolled over in the damp blankets.

He ought to get up and put some wood on the fire. He would, too. Except there wasn't no more wood in the box. He'd looked. Just this very morning... he thought it was this morning... he'd looked. There wasn't nothing there. Not a stick. Not a sliver.

Now the coals were dying and the thick iron of the patent stove cooling off—he could hear the tick-tock of the joints contracting as the metal too-quickly cooled—and if he didn't go out and bring in some wood then pretty soon the stove would go completely cold and after that the freeze would be able to ease quiet and deadly inside the cabin.

Chill the wet blankets. Freeze them around him like a shroud. A shroud made out of ice.

A picture leapt into his mind. Was it imagination or memory? He could not be sure. He hoped it was imagination.

It was of a face. Frozen. Ice sealing the eyelashes closed. More ice caught, sparkling and slick and smooth, in the eyebrows. A dribble of spit frozen at the corner of the mouth. Skin all frosty and pale like the rime of a frozen fog caught on the needles of a spruce twig on a winter's morning.

He could end up like that. He could. He knew it and it scared him, and he did not know what to do about it.

He had to get up. Go outside. Get water and wood. Build up the fire. Make some coffee.

Coffee, that was what he needed. Needed more than anything right now. Fire and coffee.

All he had to do was to get up. Get the water. Get the wood. Just... get up.

He tried. He told himself how hard he was trying.

So then why in hell wasn't he moving? Why did he just lay there huddled deep inside the cold, wet blankets, shivering and crying out and waiting to die?

Rest. Just a few minutes of rest. Then he would get up. He'd be up to it then. A few more minutes. Close his eyes and just... sleep.

And when he woke up, why, he would fetch in the wood to build a fine fire and carry in water for his coffee, and everything would be all right again.

Yes. It would. Joe Potter told himself that. He even believed it.

Pretty much.

2

Dizzy. Jeez, he was dizzy. Felt ten feet tall and half an inch wide. The amazing thing was that he was upright. Holding on to the table for support but upright. That was good. That was fine. It was going to work out. A drink of water, a little wood, everything would be just fine again.

Water, though. He wanted water bad. He felt dried out. His throat hurt and he felt all swollen and lumpy in the cheeks, he was that dry. Or maybe it had something to do with the fever. Whatever, he wanted water. Bad.

He was purely desiccated inside and out.

Eyes burned. They felt like his eyeballs had been yanked out and replaced with hot coals shoved into the sockets instead.

Might as well have. He couldn't hardly see anything anyway. Everything was all misty-hazy, like the cabin was filled with smoke. Except that would almost have been welcome. Where there's smoke there's fire... that was a joke; well, sort of... and if there was anything he could use right now it was fire. Any kind of heat and warmth.

He knew that. But it was a head knowledge kind of thing. He no longer felt cold. Just hurting in his joints and down deep in his bones. Hurting in his throat whenever he tried to swallow. But he no longer felt cold. Not the least bit of it. If anything he felt a mite overwarm.

It was going to be a relief to get outside and get cooled off some after being so hot.

He let go of the edge of the table and took a step forward without support. Then another. He tried a third and began to topple but was far enough on by then that he fell against the front wall and had something to lean against. His knees buckled, but he didn't go down. He knew he dare not fall. He was sure he did not have strength enough to stand up again if ever he fell.

He moved hand over hand to his left, to the door, leaning against the wall the whole way so as to make sure he wouldn't fall.

He reached the door still standing. That was good. He managed a grin. It hurt his lips to grin. He was so parched the corners of his lips were cracked and likely bleeding. That was all right. All he needed was a little drink of water and he'd be just fine again. Little water, little rest, hell yes.

He pulled the door open. It was cooler when he did that but only a little. Funny how hot it was in the cabin with no fire. And funny, too, how it wasn't near so cold outside as he expected.

Was that a good thing or bad? He stood, weaving gently back and forth like a sapling in gusting breezes, and tried to decide. After a bit... he had no idea how long he stood there... he decided to work it out later after he got his drink and was well again.

Well? Was he sick? The thought surprised him. Then pleased him. It explained so much, didn't it? Of course, he was sick. But just a little. A drink of cold water was all he needed to wash the sickness down and away.

He let go of the frame of the doorway and

took a hesitant, careful step forward. Brought his body weight over that leg and stepped forward with the other foot. It was interesting to him, the process of walking. Why hadn't any of this caught his attention before now? It was a perfectly fascinating thing to do, and for several more paces Joe Potter concentrated very hard on the mechanics and the sensations of walking very slowly out into the yard and across it toward the corrals and the standpipe where water was flowing into the stock tank for the horses to use.

He was beginning to become cold now. Beginning to wish he had taken time to put boots on or a coat or something. That hadn't seemed important before, not when he was so overly hot with the fever that lay like stoked coals buried within his flesh.

Now that he'd been outdoors a little while...

He thought about going back inside. But if he turned around he was sure he wouldn't have strength enough to make another attempt.

He needed the water. Had to have it or he would die. He was certain of that. As certain of that basic fact as he was that... he was certain of it, that was all. Never mind as certain as what. That was his own damn business not even to be brought out into open thought, not even inside his own mind.

He felt a certain small sense of satisfaction at that rebellion against his own impulses. He was still in control, wasn't he? He was still Joseph Bascomb Potter, and he was still in control of himself. Yes!

He took two more steps, paused to gather strength and took two more. He was almost to the water now. Just a little way more. Just a little...

His feet slipped. He hit a slick patch where some of the water had been slopped over the side of the trough and froze on the already hard ground. The soles of his sock feet went out from under him without warning.

He felt himself going down.

Shouted, a reaction to the surprise of it all.

Hit the unyielding soil on his back. Hard.

The sound of his skull striking frozen earth was loud inside his head, loud and hollow like a melon thumped before it is fully ripe.

He felt nothing at all after that. Not pain, not cold, not thirst. A blackness, comforting and quite welcome, flowed over him and took him into itself and claimed him, and he left all care and sensation behind.

IT WAS HOT, *one of those heavy, humid, oppressively hot summer days when simply breathing is work enough to wear one out and the sweat runs so thick and sour that it makes the blue dyes run in any halfway new wool shirt and turns your underarms blue to match the uniform and mark you for the fresh fish you desperately do not want to seem.*

This was strange country, so very strange, but even a stranger to it could see—miles and countless miles away across the khaki-brown sunburnt grasses—that the distant thunderheads were mocking, not promising.

The clouds rose gray and moisture-laden far off to the north, but the cooling rain would not fall anywhere near. Perhaps would not begin to fall until the great and magnificent clouds had moved completely out of this country, for this was a dry and ugly stretch of earth. A place of waste and uselessness. Why else give it up to savages and soldiers? If it had been a place of any worth, better uses would have been found for it. Everyone understood that.

It was cold here in the winters. Or so they said. For certain sure it was hot here in late August.

Sunday afternoons were free time when vigorous youth could find outlets for tight-pent energies. Footraces, baseball games, wrestling matches, and such were encouraged. But on a day so hot? There were better possibilities.

The swimming hole in particular beckoned with its sluggish rill of lukewarm water collecting knee-deep at the lone shaded bend where a pair of trees with dusty foliage leaned out over the flow.

They collected there, the young ones, all pale skin and ladderwork ribs, knobbly joints and birdleg shanks, collected there to strip away the wool and jump splashing into the relative cool of the slowly moving water.

Laughed and shouted and made ribald remarks about things they did not yet fully understand.

A pair of dark-skinned young women carrying bundles of clothing came into view but did not tarry long. The more modest of the young men sank to the graveled streambed to cover themselves, but a few—always there were a few—hooted and waved and laughingly displayed themselves while they proferred suggested diversions to the visitors, who quickly blushed and ducked away.

More visitors came soon thereafter, but these were of a different sort. These were young boys, just as dark and no doubt not a whit more curious than the young women had been but not so inclined to run away. The small one with the huge eyes was one of them. Hanging at the rear of the pack, ready to smile or to duck as circumstances might require.

He recognized the child and, doing so, remembered the flavor of horehound that this memory called back to mind. He smiled. The boy smiled back, hesitantly at first but then easily, brightly.

The kid said something in that gobbledygook sequence of noises the savages took for language. He shrugged. The kid spoke again. He glanced briefly upstream—the young women and their laundry were long gone now, no longer a threat— and left the protection of the water to find his pale blue trousers and hold them up, pockets turned inside out so as to show there was no more horehound.

He had—no, they had between them, for in truth it had been a shared effort—already eaten it all. He shrugged and, smiling, shook his head.

The boy shook his as well and again said something that was incomprehensible to a civilized soul. Said something, then opened a small leather pouch at his waist and withdrew a dark, sticky pellet of some goo that looked like tar but for being more a purple hue than black. He offered it.

The boy's onetime benefactor held back.

The child said something, grinned, placed the gobbet of purple tar into his own mouth, and smacked his lips loudly. He reached into the pouch and brought out another misshapen lump of... whatever.

This time it was accepted. Tentatively licked, then placed upon the tongue. There was a heavy flavor to it like suet commencing to go rancid. But overlying that taste was another, this one sweet and mildly fruity. A primitive confection of some sort? An aboriginal candy perhaps? Berries, honey, and tallow perhaps? He could not be sure. But it was not an offensive blending of flavors. He could not claim it was good, exactly. But neither was it bad.

The point, truly, was not the object but the offer. The boy had been favored with the horehound. Now the favor was returned. The sharing was spontaneous and great-hearted and now was genuinely appreciated by the one who first was benefactor and now found himself as recipient.

The two boys, one near grown and the other only starting his journey, stood grinning at each other, differences in age and even larger differences in culture for that small moment unnoticed.

151

Someone in the water shouted a taunt and a challenge. Sides were being chosen. With a wink the tall, pale young man turned and leaped splashing into the creek to join the rough-and-tumble play.

When next he looked the kid was gone. That was all right. Perhaps he would see the child again sometime. Perhaps not. What mattered was that the day was hot and the shade-dappled water cool.

Someone, he did not see who, pinned his ankles and spilled him laughing into the water. His head went under while he laughed and the silted creek water filled his mouth. He came up spitting and still laughing, the aftertaste of the alien confection washed from his mouth and gone, a dim memory of no consequence. He shouted, grabbed up a sodden shirt, and flung it at the back of someone's head. The shirt became a ball and the throwing became a game. It was a brutally hot Sunday afternoon, but the creek was refreshing and the world was good. He could have asked for little more than this.

Chapter 6

1

Wednesday, December 8, 1909

Hot, so hot and wet. Dripping wet. But of course, it was a hot afternoon, an August Sunday and they'd been swimming. Except... that wasn't right. He was sure it was not. That had been... Jeez, twenty years? More? Somewhere around that long. In the past, that was for sure. So why was he hot and wet now?

Fever. His damn fever went and broke again. He was covered in so much blanket that his feet were held flat against the mattress, and he was soaking wet with his own foul sweat.

That explained everything, didn't it?

Except... hadn't he gone outside? He thought so. He thought he remembered getting up and going out for a drink of water and... he was pretty sure he remembered that... but nothing, not a single damn thing, after that.

Somehow he'd come back inside the line shack and put himself to bed and... the room was warm. Overly warm, really. He could feel that on the exposed skin of his forehead and cheeks. And it wasn't just the heat of fever he was feeling or the warmth of blankets. It was real stove heat. Hell, he could hear the fire now that he bothered to listen for it. The burning wood crackled and popped, and there was a hiss of steam from something sitting atop the stove, a pot or kettle or whatever.

Had he brought wood in and built up a good fire without remembering it? Could be, he conceded. Wood was one of the things he'd gone outside to get. Wood and a drink of water. He was sure... pretty sure... that was the way he remembered it. Except he didn't recall exactly doing either of those things. He thought... he was not positive about this but believed it was true... he thought he'd fallen down.

And that was the last thing he could recall with any degree of certainty.

So how the hell had he got back inside and how come the fire was burning so hot—a stove that hot had to be fed, regularly and damned often—and how come he no longer was so thirsty and how come... how come a lot of things, now that he thought on it? Just how the hell did all this happen and him not remember a lick of it?

He twisted and turned a bit under the weight of the blankets and moaned out loud just a little. He was weak and dizzy and disoriented. And he was imagining things, that was what he was doing.

He imagined he could see a woman with her shirt unbuttoned and pulled open so that her breast was hanging out for him to see. That tore it. If he'd needed any proof that he was imagining things, well, it couldn't get much more certain than that right there.

A woman just up and showing her tit to him? Joe Potter closed his eyes. If he was dying anyway he might just as well go ahead and get it over with.

2

He floated in and out of consciousness, never quite sure what was fantasy and what, if anything, was not. Reality proved to be elusive, no more substantial than a cobweb. And fantasy proved to be of much more pleasure and comfort than reality ever had.

In his fantasies Joe was young again. Strong and eager. And stupid. Ah, sometimes reality could intrude even into fantasy.

But fantasy was good. Fantasy was sometimes very good. In his mind a man could do... anything. It was all possible when reality would keep its stinking distance.

Reality was hunger and fatigue and cold through to the bone. Reality was balky horses, wet saddles, and hardly pay enough to buy a Saturday night on the town.

Fantasy was wide open women and liquor that never had to be paid for.

Reality was lousy. Fantasy was... fantasy was kind of like being chief of police.

Joe laughed about that. He was sound asleep and racked with a high fever, but he laughed about that half-formed thought until he damned near choked to death in his sleep.

3

He rolled onto his side, already groping, reaching out, feeling beneath the heavy blankets even before full wakefulness reached him.

There should be... no, of course not. That was stupid. That was the fever talking to him again, the crazy imaginings that had wandered through his sleep.

Still, he could almost believe that there was a lingering hint of warmth beside him there, underneath the blankets that were piled so thick and heavy atop him.

The dream, that particular one at least, was so strong that he could almost believe there had been someone, a woman, lying under the blankets beside him.

Jeez, he really had been out of his mind. A fellow had to watch out for craziness like that. A man living alone could go right round the bend. He'd heard of it happening but had had only contempt for anyone so weak as to let his mind give in to the lonely madness they so lightly and easily referred to as cabin fever.

Well this was no cabin fever. And he wasn't crazy. He was sick, that was all. And he wasn't going to let it get to him. He knew real from crazy. Damn right he did. Real was a hot fire and the smell of something steaming on the stove. Crazy was the thought that somebody had been in this here bed with him.

That'd be the damn day, wouldn't it? He was sick, but he wasn't so sick that the thought of a woman couldn't move him. Why, right now, just thinking about it...

He knew better but reached over to the side of the bed one more time, exploring the mattress ticking, finding it as empty as it ought to be.

Pity. But it proved that he wasn't crazy. It did prove that. Didn't it?

156

He blinked once and struggled in an attempt to sit upright on the line shack bed.

It was a battle. There were so many blankets on top of him that they weighted him down as good as an anvil. Good as a wagonload of anvils, almost. Why, there were blankets atop him that he didn't even remember ever seeing before now. Not only did he not remember crawling under the damn things, he didn't so much as recognize them.

That was... that was crazy, that's what that was.

The strange blankets. The insane lingering notion that he hadn't been alone here in this bed. A partial recollection of a woman... he couldn't recall what she looked like but he could remember something about her shirt being spread open so that he could see one tit.

Crazy. It was just plain crazy the things a fever could do to a man.

Smiling wryly at his own wild imaginings, Joe shoved and pushed and squirmed until he was sitting upright on the bed. Crazy. It sure was.

And then with a jolt that made his belly of a sudden feel all cold and empty it came back to him. He was alone here. Sick and weak and wiped out. Alone outside by the corral with no water and no wood and no real hope. Now... now here he was inside. In the cabin with a fire burning hot in the potbelly stove and a pot of soup bubbling over the heat and blankets, some he'd be willing to swear he never saw before, draped all over him. What in hell was going on here and why... ?

His gut rolled over with a lurch as the

metal-on-metal sound of the door latch jolted him.

The latch clattered, and the door pushed open.

Joe felt a chill that had nothing to do with the cold of the air that swirled into the cabin once the door was opened.

He looked in horrified disbelief and tried to bite back a scream that threatened to rip his throat out.

4

"You're dead! My God, go away. I killed you once already." Potter fell back trembling, the weight of the blankets trapping him in place and fear draining what little strength he had so that there was no possibility of escape from this apparition.

Half a heartbeat later he realized that this was not a ghost. Merely a woman. A no-account Indian woman. But a real woman nonetheless. It was, he realized, the woman whose tit he thought he imagined in his feverish maundering.

Potter felt foolish. And angry.

"What the hell are you doing here?" he demanded loudly.

She looked at him, her face unreadable, and did not answer.

Ugly sow, Potter thought. And in truth she was not physically beautiful. She had a flat face with cheekbones like the sharp angles at the corners of a spade. Her skin tone was dark, almost negroid, and her hair was twisted into thick, ropy braids that glistened with some sort of congealed, milky grease or animal fat. She was round and shapeless in a mass of rags and blanket scraps. She wore, he saw with fury, his own woolen helmet jammed atop her greasy hair and pulled tight over her ears.

At the moment she was carrying an armload of split firewood.

He suspected she was quite the ugliest human being he had ever in his life seen. And she was in *his* place, for God's sake, making herself free with *his* stuff.

"Get out of here, damn you," he demanded. "Get the hell out of here right now or I'll beat the shit out of you."

It did not occur to him that he was, physically, in no fit shape to accomplish his threat. There was no way he could have stood erect, much less inflicted any physical damage on her.

That did not occur to him, and apparently it did not occur to her either. Without speaking the Indian woman dropped her burden of wood into the box beside the stove, then obediently turned and departed the Zeke line shack where her presence was anything but welcome.

The woman came back in with another armload of wood. Put it in the box and went outside again.

"Get out, damn you," he hollered futilely at her broad, lumpy back. "Stay out."

She was back again a few minutes later with a third load of wood. After putting it into the now overflowing box she stoked the stove until the fire was a scarcely muted roar within the cast-iron device, then took up the bucket and carried it out.

Joe Potter had no choice but to lie fuming and furious beneath the load of blankets—which he now realized were not all his blankets to begin with—and watch the damn Indian act as free and cheeky here as a white human person.

She brought in the wood; she brought in water, and after a bit she went to the foot of the bed and leaned down toward the floor to where Joe couldn't see and this time when she came back into view she was holding some kind of bundle that she'd had stashed there.

The crazy Indian took off the scraps that she'd been wearing like a coat or cape or some damn thing and unbuttoned her shirt.

Joe couldn't believe it, never mind what he thought he'd seen or remembered that time a while back, but she did it. She really and truly did it. She unbuttoned her shirt and pulled it back to show one tit.

The woman was crazy, that was all. Stark, raving, out of her mind mad.

Except the bundle she was holding turned out to be a kid. A squat, fat-faced, dark Indian kid that she was keeping wrapped inside soft blankets.

That was what this stuff was all about. She held the kid against her belly, and next thing Joe could hear the little nit suck and gobble at its dam's pap.

He could hear it take the woman's milk right enough but hadn't heard a peep out of the miserable little thing when it was laying in its nest.

That puzzled him. But only for a minute. It came back to him then how it was with Indians. It wasn't like they were human or anything. He knew. Indians didn't think or feel like regular people did.

It was said that Indians always trained their kids to be quiet so they couldn't give the tribe away if there were enemies or like that creeping up on them. They trained the kids right from the first to never cry no matter what. Trained them by holding their hands over the kids' mouths and noses and blocking off the air if they tried to gulp in a mouthful so that they could bawl. It takes a lot of breath to bawl. You don't normally think about that but it's so. Every snot-nosed brat in the world has to drag in a big breath of fresh air before it can let out a howl. Indian kids, even though they are of a lower order, are the same that way. They got to breathe if they're gonna bawl. So their dams and sires close off their breathing to teach them to stay shut when a human kid would go ahead and yell its head off.

Indians, though, they didn't just get the point across and then quit. Joe had it on good authority that if the kid persisted in trying to cry the parents would go ahead and smother their own brats rather than let them learn to cry and maybe someday endanger the whole tribe.

Joe expected they still did that sort of cruel and heartless thing even though there wasn't no such thing as a warpath any more, the last of the Indians having been whipped—as Joe had reason to damn well know—almost twenty years back.

Officially there wasn't any such thing anymore as a frontier anywhere in the United States of America, and officially there wasn't any such thing as Indians and white men fighting any more.

Well, not officially. If sometimes a misunderstanding might occur out on the grass someplace where there was no one else around to see except the participants, well, that wasn't warfare and it didn't involve troops or anything like that. It was just another Indian lying dead on the ground someplace. And, hell, there wasn't anything wrong with that.

But regardless of things being peaceable now it was said that Indians still taught their kids to be silent or else pinched their noses closed and covered their mouths and smothered the louse-eaten pups with their own bloody hands.

Inhuman, that's what that was.

And now there was an Indian woman and an Indian brat right here in the Zeke line camp and not a stinking thing Joe Potter could do to stop it.

Not now. Not yet. But as soon as he got his strength back, well, he'd see about the two of them then, all right.

Kick their copper-colored asses right out into the snow, that's what he would do. Just as quick as he could get to his feet again.

He got over the amazement of seeing the homely Indian woman with the brat latched onto her dug and allowed himself to fall exhausted onto his bed again. Lordy, but he was tired. Wiped out just from trying to sit up and look around a bit.

He closed his eyes and tried to ignore the sloppy wet sounds, and after a couple minutes those noises and everything else just kind of faded quietly away.

THEY CAME OUT OF THE MIST, *surrounded by ghostly silence, mute and accusing with their eyes, eyes huge and wet and dark. They came one at a time, moving slow and solemn. They were walking, had to be walking, but he could not see their feet move. It was like they drifted a fraction of an inch above the snow. They were dark and ominous against the white of the snow and the white of the mist. They were faint shadows to begin with, then more substantial as they came nearer, and he could then see them clearly. Dark and menacing against the white. One by silent one. An old man the first in line. Then another man. A woman. Two kids wrapped tight in woolly robes so no more than their eyes and noses could be seen. No way to tell if they were boy children or girls. Not that it mattered. Two of those, then another man, a woman, two men, a woman carrying a child... they came on and on and on. All of them eerily silent. All of them accusing.*

They came drifting out of the mist and circled around him. He turned, trying to keep them from getting behind him, but there were too many. They kept on appearing. Moving. Circling. No sounds. No movement of limbs. No overt threats. But he knew. God, he knew.

Fear clamped hard round his heart, filling his chest until it near suffocated him. And still they came. Old men. Young. Shabby, ragged women. Children and young ones of all sizes and shapes.

All of them had the same look on them. All with those huge wet, accusing eyes.

They came from the mist like ghosts and formed a ring with him at the center. And still they came. Circling. Drifting. Not a single line now but two, three deep.

All of them faced inward. Took up their places and became as motionless as statues. And as pitiless.

Their eyes accused him.

There was no color to them, he saw. Stark black against the white of snow and mist. No color to their clothes, no color to their features. Only black and shades of black. Not gray. Shades of black.

And—the realization sent a chill into him as sharp and cold as a spear's point penetrating his breast—there was no puff of freezing breath hanging in the air. Not a one, not with any of them.

They stood there in the pale frigid light, and there was no smokelike pall of frozen exhalation in front of the least one of them.

He could sense—was not sure he could see, exactly, but without question knew—the white of his own frosty breath hanging before him. But none of his accusers betrayed breath in this freezing cold.

He felt a fresh chill of terror.

He knew them. He was sure he knew them. If not by name then at least by sight. Some of them he should know by name. He could not remember the names, though. Did not want to. If he named them he would have to... he dare not name them, that was all. Terrible things would happen if he named them. He knew it would. He did not know what, did not know how he knew. But he knew. Oh yes. He knew.

The huge eyes were fixed on him. The circle engulfed him. So many. In just the past few moments the numbers seemed to have increased. He did not know where they all came from. Had not seen them continue to materialize. One moment there was a circle, distinct but no more than three, four deep. Now of a sudden there was an endless vista of dark shapes and accusing eyes. One shape hardly differentiated from any other. Nor did it matter which shape was which. They were all the same. Man or woman, boychild or girl. They were all of a piece. All alike in their silent menace.

They surrounded him. Waiting. Waiting for what? He did not know, but not knowing he trembled and felt faint. Icy bands circled his heart as close and hard as these figures encircled him. Circled and constricted. It was difficult for him to breathe. Impossible for him to get away. He wanted to get away. Wanted that more than anything. More than he had ever before wanted anything his whole life long.

He turned. Whirled and spun. This way and then that. Everywhere they stood silently peering at him. Accusing him. Saying nothing. Dark and brooding. Implacable.

He whirled. Stumbled. His heart took a sudden leap. If he fell... He must not lose his balance. Dare not. If he fell then something terrible would happen. Something too terrible for him to allow himself to think about.

He caught himself. Stopped. Swayed just a little but managed to keep his feet. Great clouds of white exhalation hung in the air before him as the near panic quickened his heartbeat and the gasping for breath.

He stopped. Was fixed by a particular pair of those huge and awful eyes.

A boy. He could see only a runny nose and dark, chapped cheeks. And of course those eyes. Those terrible eyes. But he knew this one was a boychild.

166

He knew... no. He would not. Could not. No name must be put to this one. Not that.

But he knew.

And the boychild accused him. The eyes accused. The mere presence accused.

The mouth opened.

"No!"

"No!"

He was sitting up. Trembling and terrified. It was dark, black dark save for a red glow that showed through the cracks between the stove parts and around the rim of the firebox door.

The blankets smelled musty with old, sour sweat, and there was a warm, lumpy intrusion beside him.

The woman. Jeez, it was the lousy Indian woman. She was in the bed with him. The bitch had come into the bed with him.

Chapter 7

1

Friday, December 10, 1909

"I could have you arrested. Have your butt thrown in jail. Serve you right if I did, the way you been eating up my supplies. You think I didn't know?" Actually he hadn't known. He'd only figured out afterward, this morning in fact, that this Indian woman and her brat were the reason things sometimes seemed just the least bit out of kilter when he'd get back to the shack after being gone for the day. She'd been sneaking in and stealing from him for some time now. He was almost sure of that.

"I knew. Lousy thief, that's what you are. You're all thieves or worse. Slut." He grunted. "Prob'ly a whore. Of course you're a whore. Sell yourself for groceries. Well, you owe me. Don't you forget that. You owe me." He cackled. "You don't understand a damn word I say, do you. I can call you any damn thing I please. You won't know the difference. Whore."

The woman had been up early. Got the fire built back up so the place was almost too warm now. Brought in water. Fed the kid and washed herself. Stripped down naked to do it. Jeez. Joe had never in his life seen a woman in daylight who was actual, honest-to-God

168

naked. He had slept with women before. Lots of them. But he'd never before seen a grown woman all the way naked. The kind of women he was used to, they kept their smallclothes on and the guy, hell, he usually kept his boots on. Once—that was a very long time ago—he'd had a girlfriend. Not a hired woman but an actual lady friend who'd liked him. She gave him what he wanted—free, too; he hadn't paid her a penny—but she always had her nightdress on when they went off together or just pulled up the bottom of her skirts if it was a quickie, like on a picnic or something. Ankle length, it was, every damn thing she ever wore, day or night. He had no idea what she'd looked like under the clothes. Nor any of the whores he'd been with, white or red or brown they none of them ever bothered to get all the way naked for a man. That would've taken too much time. With them it was get on, get off, and go away. Quick and efficient.

This Indian whore, though, she got herself all the way naked so she could wash. It got Joe kind of excited even if she was a lousy Indian. She wasn't fat like he'd thought at first. That was only the bunch of rags she'd been wearing that made her look fat. In fact her body wasn't all that bad to look at. Her face was flat, but everything else looked interesting enough. More than interesting. If it hadn't been daylight he might've wanted to do something about that. But not, well, not the way it was. Tonight, maybe, but not now.

That, of course, was earlier. She washed herself while the coffee was heating atop the stove and by the time she was done with herself she had a pot of water hot, and she'd used that to wash him!

Jesus God, who'd have thought it. He'd put up a fight. Hell, there hadn't been a woman seen him all the way naked since he was old enough to dress himself, but this Indian bitch was stronger than she looked. And he was still a damn sight weaker than he ought to be. So weak he could hardly manage to stand on his own hind legs without support. He hadn't been able to put up much resistance if the truth be known. The stinking Indian pulled all his damn clothes off and washed him all over—*all* over—and dried him and then put clean clothes onto him.

The clean clothes felt and smelled a whole heap better than the old, sour nasty ones had. That was true enough. And maybe he felt better after the bath, too.

But it was damn well humiliating to have a woman, and a lousy Indian woman at that, see his body and wash him like that. Like he was some kind of damn baby.

That point was made all the clearer in that once she was done washing him and getting him dressed in fresh things and helping him to a seat, a real sitting-up seat, at the table, she'd gone and bathed the kid, laid it on a piece of sacking atop the table and washed it in a basin and dried it all off and wrapped it up fresh with a wad of dried grass stuffed around its butt to keep it from soiling itself or its blanket so bad. He hadn't thought Indians would be smart enough to think of anything like that. Which he told her, although of course she couldn't understand what he was saying.

She gave him coffee and mixed up some dough in a bowl and commenced cooking once she had a greased pan hot to cook in. What she made wasn't like flannel cakes exactly. It wasn't sweet like flannel or johnnycakes are. More like a pan bread. But good. He had to say that. Whatever it was it tasted all right. She poured a thick dollop of molasses all over it before she gave it to him, and it didn't taste all that bad.

She gave the kid a little molasses on a fingertip and ate some of the pan bread herself, drizzling it all over with the thick, dark molasses, too.

"You eat all that up I won't have any more, damn you. Stupid bitch. Don't you have sense enough to not eat everything up like that? Those are my supplies you're s' damn free with, you know. But you don't care about that, do you? Whatever you can get your filthy hands on you'll steal. You're all like that, aren't you? Every one of you. Sell your soul for a drink of whiskey and half a cup of sugar. If you had a soul, that is. Which you don't. I asked a preacher about that one time. He said Indians are... what did he call them? I forget. He had a word for it. Big long word, it was. His point was that Indians aren't like regular people. Indians aren't kin to God. That's what he meant. You never heard of Cain, o' course. He was the son of Adam and Eve. Had him a brother, but Abel got killed. Later on, or maybe it was before, I disremember, later on Cain needed him a wife. Couldn't marry his own sister even if he had one. Which he didn't. Not that girl babies are worth a shit, but the Bible, it never

171

mentioned anything about Cain having a sister. But he went out and took a wife. Now where would a guy who was practically the only human person on earth go and find himself a wife? From the natural, animal, godless tribes. That's where. That's what this preacher explained to me that time. Godless and not human. Animals in human shape. Like you Indians. Animals. Savages. That's what you are. Not really human though you look like the folks that God made. Same shape anyhow. But different, too. That's why you're colored all wrong. Indians, niggers, I guess there's all kinds of human-looking animals. But none of you got souls, see. That's what the difference really is. White humans have souls. Savages don't. I expect that's why you can't talk right neither. Just make those grunts and growling noises instead of real words. Give me some more of that pan bread, will you? And don't go light on the molasses neither. It's my damn molasses, I expect I can have as much of it as I want."

He held his plate out and mimed refilling it and pouring molasses over the cakes.

The woman silently and obediently went to do his bidding.

2

It was terrible how weak he was. Disgusting. He really ought to throw the Indian and her brat out. Serve them right if he did. But... not right now.

The woman was hell for hard work. He had to say that much. She didn't lay about.

172

She put more water on the stove to heat and commenced to doing laundry. Shaved soap into one pot and heated up rinse water in another and brought in more water that she left cold for a final rinse.

She washed Joe's clothes and the kid's stuff and then laid into the thinner, and the sweatier, of the blankets off the bed.

Pretty soon the inside of the cabin looked more like a Chinese laundry than a respectable line shack. It was a good thing there were no neighbors around to see. Joe would have been positively embarrassed for a white person to witness this.

Everything smelled of suds and hot water and clammy, drippy cloth.

The woman had used the bale of brand new hemp, left there by the Zeke in case any of the hands needed to cut new catch-ropes off the big spool of manila, to make clothesline. Clothesline, for God's sake! Perfectly good catch-rope turned into damn clothesline. It was humiliating. Or would have been if there'd been any people around to see.

After lunch she put Joe to bed. He would have objected just on the principle of the thing, him preferring to make up his own mind what he would do and when he would damn well do it. Except by then he really needed to lay down again. So simple a thing as sitting up at the table had him worn down and reeling. And the rest of the truth was that he needed help making it the few steps from the stool over to the bed. Sitting up for several hours was enough to use him up completely.

She helped him over to the bed and laid him in it, covering him over with what of the blankets she hadn't thought sweaty enough to need washing right away, and the last thing he knew she was busy at the table kneading some kind of dough while the kid laid in a sort of sling nursing and snorting while its dam kept up her work.

Joe wasn't sure he could trust an Indian not to do something—knife him or steal something or who knows what—while he slept.

He considered staying awake to keep a sharp eye on her. But while he was thinking about the need to do that he kind of drifted off.

3

Bacon and beans. Bacon and beans. Breakfasts in hell must be bacon and beans.

Half... no, dammit, three-fourths of the meals Joe had eaten in his life were bacon and beans. Maybe more than that. Now here this Indian bitch was feeding him more bacon and beans.

He grunted his dissatisfaction. And took another huge, dripping spoonful. If a man had to eat bacon and beans, these here were better than most. He admitted that.

She had gone and put something in with the beans. Molasses. He recognized that all right. Probably some other stuff, too, though he couldn't be sure what all it might have been. And the bacon was cooked in with the beans so that the smoky flavor of the bacon got into

174

the beans along with the molasses and what-ever else.

All in all it wasn't that bad. For bacon and beans.

He held his half-empty plate out and motioned for her to spoon some more onto it, and she did.

She was kind of standing over him while he sat at the table—she'd helped him to it, although after resting most of the afternoon he thought he could have made it on his own if he'd really wanted to—holding the kid in the crook of one arm and a big serving spoon in her free hand. She smiled when she ladled the second serving onto his plate.

"Don't you get to feeling proud of yourself," he told her pleasantly. "You and that kid are still gonna be outside freezing your red asses off just as quick as I'm on my feet and right again." He pointed to the kid and gave the woman a big grin and nodded, like as if he was saying something sticky-sweet and nice. "That kid there has to be the ugliest excuse for a whelp I ever in my life seen. Except maybe you're ugli-er even than it is." He cackled and laughed and bobbed his head like he'd made a joke to add to the compliment, and the woman cackled and nodded right along with him. "I swear, you're as dumb as you are ugly, aren't you?" He grinned and nodded, and she nodded back at him, and that got him tickled and he com-menced to laughing for real and pretty soon she was laughing along with him. The kid peered all big-eyed and intent from one of them to the other.

When he stopped laughing and his sides

weren't aching any more he sighed and pulled the plate of beans to him. "Look, I don't like it when somebody watches me so close. You know? Hell, what am I saying? Of course you don't know. You Indians are too damn stupid to know anything. Shoo! G'wan now, shoo." He motioned the woman off toward the stove. "Get away from me, dammit," he warned, raising a fist toward her, the laughter of a moment ago forgotten now in a surge of anger that this unwanted woman would hang over him like that. "Get!"

The woman remained where she was for a moment, a puzzled expression on her flat, dark face.

Joe brandished his fist again, and she turned soundlessly away, taking the kid with her and going over to the stove where she had water heating. Not that her watching it was likely to help it get hot. But she stood with her back to Joe, pretending to attend to the pot of hot water while he finished the bacon and beans she'd cooked for their supper.

4

He whacked her one on the hip, hard, to get her attention and pointed first to the kid lying snug and warm against her belly, then down toward the foot of the bed where the kid's box was. Just to make sure she understood what he wanted, he concluded the gesture by reaching between her legs and taking a grip on a handful of flesh there, squeezing and pulling at her until she winced. Then he let go.

The woman got up, taking the kid with her, and took a couple minutes to settle the kid in the box. It was a regular wooden crate, Joe had noticed earlier, one that his supplies had been carried in, that she lined first with some old sacking cloth and then with some Indian crap that looked like thistledown sewn together like a quilt. Anyway it looked soft and warm enough. She put the kid into the box and covered it and while she was up took time to replenish the wood in the stove.

"Hurry up, dammit," Joe snarled. She acted like she hadn't heard. He knew good and well she heard and figured she should understand the tone of voice even if she didn't know the actual words.

The woman used a coal shovel to carefully position the embers that were pulsing a bright red inside the firebox, then clanged the door closed and came back to bed, stripping her dress over her head before she crawled in at his side.

Joe grunted his satisfaction and took a firm grip on her flesh, like grabbing a saddle horn to help secure a firm seat in anticipation of a hard ride, then on an impulse squeezed so hard that sweat popped out cold and shiny on her forehead and upper lip.

He couldn't make her cry out, though. No matter how hard he tried.

"It must be true," he observed. "It's only human beings that have real feelings."

That lack, however, did not keep him from pleasuring himself within her flesh.

THE LITTLE BOY LAUGHED *and said something. At least it looked like he was speaking. Of course he was speaking. How odd that no sound came from his mouth. He could see the mouth move, the tongue, the teeth so white against the dark of skin. Could see the wrinkling at the eyes as laughter tugged at the corners of them. Such immense eyes. Huge and bright with the laughter. And the mouth moved again, repeating the word.*

He did not need to hear to know what the word was. After all, the kid only knew one lone word of American. That and the gutrumble of his own savage tongue. But of American just the one word, and it was easy enough to read without it being heard. Although it was indeed very strange that the kid should speak and no sound be issued. So odd.

The kid said the magic word and laughed again and turned. So slow. Like he was underwater almost. More, in fact, like he was submerged in something thicker than water. Molasses as clear as water, clear as air. That was how slow and deliberate the boy moved. Turned. Pointed. Out over the grass. Summer grass, he saw with unexpected relief. Why was that important? He could not remember. But it was. It was the brown grass of summer and that was good. It was the stark dark and white of winter that he hated and feared. Although he could not remember why he should feel that way. There was something... he did not know. In summer he did not care. But of course it was summer. The boy was dressed lightly. Old pair of breeches cut off at what had been the knees but on him came to his grubby, dusty ankles. Piece of webbing strap for a belt. Old discarded bit of webbing, but he loved it because his friend Joe took and cut it to fit and fancied it with a piece of brass bent and formed to act like a collar button and make a proper belt of the length of old haversack webbing. Stupid old thing like that and you would have thought it was a lord's sash complete with jewels and tassels the way the kid fussed and preened and showed the gift off for all his little friends to see and envy.

The kid said the one word he knew and pointed, laughing, happy.

He turned back, still so slow, and came bounding forward. Floating. Silent. The laughter and the joy bright in his eyes. Huge eyes. Unnatural. Bright. Shining. Alive.

The mouth moved again. The one lone word. "Joe!"

Laughing. Light. Happy.

Oh, Jesus. Jesus, God!

If only...

———•◦•———

Chapter 8

1

Wednesday, December 15, 1909

Potter bent low to tug his boot on, then snapped into an upright position on the side of the bed, deliberately quick about it as if trying to trick his body into a betrayal. But there was no hint of dizziness, no discomfort, no loss of his senses whatsoever.

He was, he told himself, quite fully recovered from the dark fevers and soul-sapping illness that almost claimed him.

Today he no longer needed the Indian and her ugly little get.

"Reckon I can throw you the hell out of here now," he said as he stood and stamped his feet to settle them inside the boots that he hadn't had on his feet in so awful long now. "You're nothing but in the way here. Eating up all my damn food. That's what you damn Indians are like though. Ain't it? All of you. Take anything you can put your hands on, damn you. Can't trust you while I'm gone working. Like as not you'd steal me blind. Take everything and go off somewhere with it. I leave you alone here, there won't be a damn thing inside these walls to come back to at night. Huh. Don't tell me. I know. I know you damn Indians. Seen a heap of you. Not a one any damn good. I know."

The woman was at the stove. That was one thing you could say about her, though. She could cook. Damn, she could make some eatable stuff out of the few miserable things the Zeke left here for him. If she went... that is to say, when she went... he would miss the cooking.

Huh. Miss something else, too. Sick or no, he'd gotten kind of used to having it regular. And discovered that he liked it. He'd never before had a regular supply like that. Payday and maybe a couple nights afterward if he was lucky and didn't lose it all right away. Or over the winters in Denver he got it once a week whether he needed it or not. Would have liked to have it more often, but a man making it through the winter on the autumn payout couldn't afford to blow all his poke poking the hoors regular.

But this, this was something else again. Regular as could be, any time he wanted it. Twice a day if he wanted it. Which he'd discovered he sometimes did.

Damn Indian didn't care. Just an animal anyhow. Didn't mean a thing to her.

But, oh, he did like it just fine. The truth was that he would miss that more than he would miss the cooking.

Damn her anyway for coming in here uninvited and making him get used to having a woman. And one who could cook at that.

"If you could talk American I'd explain all this to you," he told her. "As it is I'll just have to put you out. Kick your butt if you give me any trouble. You think I won't do it, you just try me. Knock you down and stomp you

181

and that brat of yours, too. Just see if I won't."

He found his coat and gloves and muffler and a scarf to tie over his ears. It was witch-tit cold outside. And still no snow on the ground. That was the crazy thing. This time of year you'd think the country would be ass deep on a tall horseman. But there wasn't anything on the ground and rarely so much as a flake in the air. But that didn't keep the water from freezing over, and old Andy Plasser would have a fit—and likely fire Joe's butt to boot—if ever he found out Joe'd been sick and hadn't been out in better than a week to chop the ice out of those water holes. By now half the Zeke cows could be dead or dying. Well, they weren't Joe's damn cows, were they? It would be a shame. Sort of. But better those cows croak than he kill himself trying to keep them alive.

"Go on now. Get your crap together. Time for you and that nit to get outta here. Go on." He sighed and gestured in an attempt to get the message across. She caught on quick enough and began packing her things, what few of them there were, into a willow basket that had straps rigged on it so it was like a great huge knapsack.

She put her stuff into the basket and put the kid into a sling arrangement under the blanket cape she had, then hefted the basket onto her back and hustled out the door ahead of Joe's prompting.

"Go on, dammit. And stay out, mind. I got work to do. I can't be worried are you gonna keep sneaking around. If I find you are, I'll have to do something serious. You hear me? No? Well,

182

you best figure it out, that's all I got to say. Damn shame you don't talk American so I could warn you. But you best get the idea. You come back around here, I won't be responsible for whatever happens to you." He gave her a hard look of warning and pointed off toward the horizon, hoping she would get the idea. Not that it mattered if there was another one or two Indians alive somewhere. Wouldn't mean a thing to him if he had to rub out this woman and her brat. But, hell, this one time he kind of thought he would rather not. "Go on now. Get outta my sight while I'm still feeling softheaded, you ugly damn sow. Take off."

Without waiting to see the Indian and her kid leave he turned and headed for the corral to saddle up and get off on his rounds. It was just a good thing Andy didn't know about all this. Just a damn good thing.

2

Thieving damn red-butted bitch. He was right. You couldn't turn your back on one. Not on any one of them. Indians are all alike. Blink too slow and they'll have stole you blind, he told himself in helpless rage.

Three days in a row he came back to the damn shack to find she'd been in and helped herself to his food.

Three days. That wasn't the worst of it. It would have been one thing if she'd come in and stolen a full sack of groceries. Hell, he could almost understand that, her with a kid sucking on her and everything.

But no, what she did, she came in and fixed for herself and the damn kid. *And left supper hot on the damn stove for him to find when he got back!!!*

That was what was so damn insulting about it. Not only did she steal from him, she was rubbing his damn nose in it, too.

But with no snow on the ground to track her by, there was not a damn thing he could do about it. Joseph Potter had no illusions about his abilities to track a woman afoot on frozen ground. Hell, he was no tracker. That's what you hired savages for. Even the damn army hired Indians when they wanted something tracked. Why, Joe couldn't track a cow in a mud bog. He knew that of himself. He admitted it right out. Nobody ever hired him for his tracking. Nobody ever would. And in country like this and weather like this and trying to catch up with one small woman traveling on foot? No damn way. No way in hell. She could hide herself and that kid behind a foot-tall clump of sage on bare prairie and he'd never find them.

Damn her. Smartass Indian. Uppity, she was. Cheeky. Sneaky, too. But most of all cheeky. Come in and cook for him and then disappear.

Dammit, if he was going to have to put up with losing his stuff he at least ought to get something out of the deal. Like having her back in the bed with him at night. She was a lying, stealing, lowlife, but she was a female and there was something to be said for that. He'd gotten right used to it when he was sick and sharing the bed with her, like for warmth there to begin with and then for more interesting purposes.

But this... this was just a crock, that's what this was. This was no damn good at all.

He stomped around the cabin and cussed some more and threw a few things—nothing breakable—and after a bit he settled down some and sat at the table and ate the supper she'd left for him.

Damn woman could cook, now that was the truth of the matter. She could take a moldy potato and a can that the label had come off of so that she didn't even know what she was starting out with and she could turn it into something that a man would eat for the pleasure of it and not just to get something warm into his belly.

Miserable damn Indian!

3

He cut his day short. Didn't hurry to get everything done particularly, just turned back toward the line shack shortly after nooning at the Y where Evans Creek and the rill they called Cowfoot joined together. There had been seventy-some bawling, unhappy head of cattle waiting there for him to open the water to them. Most of the cows wore the Zeke brand, but there were a dozen or more showing the marks of outfits to the north. Eventually he figured he would have to get around to pushing those back where they belonged. But not this day.

Instead of continuing to make the east and south swing from Cowfoot he calculated where he was in relation to the cabin and made a beeline across country for it.

Didn't miss the shack by more than half a mile either, which he thought was plenty good, considering.

Instead of riding straight into the yard, though, he stopped down along the creek and tied his horse there, walking the last little way so he wouldn't make any noise about it.

Just as he'd expected—and hoped—there was smoke lifting from the stovepipe at the roof. That damn female and her brat were trapped inside. They wouldn't get away from him this time. He might be no good at finding them out in the brush, but he was damned if they could hide from him inside his own damn place.

Damn woman didn't even have the decency to act ashamed of herself when he walked in on her. Didn't look much surprised either.

She was standing by the stove. The kid was lying all bundled up on the bed—*his* bed, dammit—instead of being in the box where it should have been. Well, the box wasn't at the foot of the bed anymore, of course. He had moved it back along the wall where she'd found it to start with. And of course there was no sacking or thistledown padding or any of that other stuff in it now. But still and all, it purely was not right that she go and make use of his bed like that.

When she saw him the woman waved him toward a seat at the table and took up a cup and the pan of coffee, like as if to pour hot coffee for him.

That tore it. The fury he'd been feeling boiled over and spilled out all over the place. All over her is more like it.

He didn't even think what he was going to do, really. He crossed the room in a couple quick paces and lashed out at her.

She was trying to hand the coffee to him, and his blow ran into the tin cup more or less without plan, knocking the cup back and splattering the boiling hot coffee all over her front.

She cried out and raised both hands and for half a second there he thought she was trying to hit him or something.

That was all it took. More than enough.

He hunched his shoulder and whipped a hard, low, underhand right square into the pit of her stomach, doubling her over right quick. He followed that with a clubbed fist that slashed down over her left ear, splitting the skin open and driving her to her knees. Served her right, damn her.

She fell, rolling away from him, and he followed behind her, kicking and yelling. He wasn't exactly sure what all he was saying to her. Didn't matter anyway.

He kicked her in the ribs, not doing any serious harm as she still had her coat on. The place wasn't all that warm yet so she must not have started the fire very long ago. Long enough to get coffee hot but not long enough to take all the chill out of the corners. Damn her. He wished she didn't have that coat on still.

She twisted and curled herself into a hard, tight, bony ball as he rained punches onto her butt and back until he began to wear out. He wasn't all that strong yet after being sick and didn't have the stamina he used to possess.

He stopped, bent half over and gulping for breath.

The place was a mess. The table had gotten knocked over somehow, and a bowl of mush or something that had been on it was splashed across the floor now.

The kid was bawling and carrying on like a white child. Lousy Indian brats not supposed to cry? This one for sure didn't know that. Not right now, it didn't.

Joe's coffee cup was lying on the floor all covered with dirt and crud. And the place was turning cold again because he hadn't had time to shut the damn door before all this got started.

He was pretty well disgusted.

He clomped over toward where the kid was yammering, thinking to see could he do something to shut the thing up. He hadn't hardly more than taken two steps before the woman jumped him from behind, the treacherous bitch. She grabbed his legs, wrapping herself around him and sobbing and screeching and carrying on.

At first he took it that she was attacking him and kneed her in the face. Then he realized she was only trying to hold on to him, to keep him from beating up on the kid.

Dumb damn thing. He reached down and gave her a sweeping backhand that sent her flying and got her off him. Then with a snort he kicked the door shut and stalked over to the bed, plopping down on the edge of it beside the kid, which was slowly quieting, kind of like a bell-alarm clock that has about run its spring down so that it isn't quite so noisy as it was to start with.

The woman came to her knees. She wasn't pretty. But then, hell, she hadn't been that to start with. She was running blood from that one ear and from her nose and one side of her mouth. Both her eyes began to swell, and a mouse the size of a turnip rose high on her cheek.

She said something to him in that stupid language of hers and came wobbling onto her feet. First thing she did was come over and check to see the brat was all right.

"I haven't touched the damn thing," he told her. "Yet. That's what I ought to do, though. Next time you get out of line I ought to see how high I can kick that stinking kid of yours. Bet I could get it into the rafters. Hah? What d'you say to that, eh? Kick the damn thing right up there into the rafters." He made a gesture as if he was kicking something and pointed toward the ceiling and laughed.

"I am a Christian lady but as God is my witness, if you ever touch my baby you will be dead the next time you fall to sleep. Yes."

4

"You... what'd you say?"

The woman ignored him, grabbing up the kid and holding it tight to her breast.

"You lying damn bitch, you. You speak English. Been knowing it all this time and never let on, didn't you?"

She continued to ignore him, hunching over the kid and kind of rocking it and crooning to it, half humming and half singing some sort of

189

lullaby thing that sounded about half-familiar to Joe yet not really. It was like he had heard the tune before but not the words. Whatever they were. He listened close for a moment until he realized the lullaby was being sung in whatever passed for words among stupid damn Indians.

The woman made sure the kid was calm and all right, then laid it back down on the bed at Joe's side and without so much as a look in his direction—or so much as wiping the blood off her face—went to tidying up the cabin, picking up and straightening all the stuff that had been knocked around and getting the fire built higher in the stove and wiping off his coffee cup and stuff like that.

Joe didn't particularly like having the Indian here. But then it was better that she clean up this mess than he have to do it himself.

Besides, he was plenty horny again.

While he sat there watching her work he decided he would keep her around for a couple more days. If the bitch was going to sneak in and eat his food anyhow she ought to pay. One way or another. And he could sure think of a suitable method of repayment.

"Put the kid in the box, dammit. Then come over here an' lay down."

The woman did what he said.

5

"My name is Mary. I am Lakota. What you would call Sioux. This child is Sarah, named for the wife of Abraham and the mother of nations."

190

"No shit," Joe said dully. He had thought the kid was a boy. But then he hadn't really looked all that close. Didn't particularly care, really. The point was that the kid was a lousy Indian. That was the part that mattered.

"You have seen the marks on the little one's cheeks and body, yes?"

In fact, he had not. Who the hell cared?

"This child was sick. The pox, they said. Once long ago a sickness like this killed, oh, so very many of our enemy. The Mandan and the Ree, they are gone now, all of them dead. They are no more because of this sickness. The ones you call Blackfoot were once strong but no more. The sickness laid them low."

Good for the sickness, Joe was thinking, although he didn't bother to say it aloud. By all means, let's hear it for the ol' sickness.

"Many of my people died, too. Many and many. So when this child has the spots they tell me I must take my child and leave else the sickness will spread through our houses and our clans will be no more. That is how we come to be here, Sarah and me. We cannot return to our home, such as it is. My man the father of this baby, he is dead more than a year, yes. He had a sickness and his belly swelled up like he was with child and then he died. There is no one to attend to us, to make meat for us and to sing prayers over us. That is why Sarah and me, we come to this place. In years gone my husband and his brothers sometimes came here. Traded a little of this for something of that. It is known the man who lived here alone in the winters is a good man. I do not think this man of the past was you.

191

It is no matter. You have given food. I have given back to you what you require. This child is alive. It is enough. Yes."

Joe scowled at her. He rolled over on the narrow bunk, turning his back to her. She acted like she expected him to say something. The hell with her and all her wants and wishes. As for the kid, who the hell cared about it anyway? Let them both go out and freeze to death or starve if that's what they wanted to do. He wouldn't care. In the meantime, well, in the meantime he'd take what he wanted of her. She was a female. There was that as could be said about her. She was a female and a place to put it, and if she was gonna eat his food then it was only fair she pay her way. One way or another.

He felt the rope-sprung mattress wriggle and move a little as her weight shifted on it and she got up from beside him, taking care to not jostle or disturb him overmuch.

"Sleep now," she said. "I will have food ready when you wake."

THE WOMAN EMERGED *from the eerie mists at a run. And yet she came on slowly. He knew she was running. He could see it in the way her hair streamed back from her face. In the way the flesh of her seamed and filthy cheeks sagged and bounded with each syrup-slow footstep. In the tug and pull of speed at the loose, capelike rags that covered her against the cold. The haphazard garments fluttered and flapped behind her like the windblown bunting of some obscene flag. A colorless flag, for the scene before him was starkly black on dull white with no relieving color anywhere in sight.*

Behind her the mists. Around her the fields of snow.

And beneath her feet… he did not look down to see what it was she leaped over in her frantic efforts to reach him.

He knew what it was, but he would not acknowledge what he knew. Not to her. Not to himself. Better not to know, better never to see, than to look or to admit or to sorrow.

He kept his eyes straight forward. Peered in horror at the apparition that slowly, so slowly, ran at him.

The woman's hands were extended, talonlike, clawing. Reaching for his throat. Oh, he knew. He knew.

If she touched him those awful nails would pierce his flesh. Dig deep beneath the skin to rip and rend. Tear out meat and cartilage, sinew and vein.

He watched her come on. Would have turned to flee but could not. Knew with a sure and certain knowledge that if he turned his back on this

193

woman she would overtake him. She would slay him. Her claws would slash deep to flay him open. She wanted his blood. He knew she did. If he turned his back she would run him down and rip his back asunder. She would reach into the steaming heat of his living flesh. She would take handfuls of lung and liver and rake them out onto the ground where snow and dirt would foul them.

And he would die.

If he turned his back on this woman he would die. He knew that for a certainty.

He dare not run and he dare not let her touch him. Either of those would be death.

And death... no. The consequences of death were more terrible than death alone. They were... unimaginable. Worse than that, they were imaginable. And he knew he could not bear to imagine them.

He shuddered. Braced himself.

She came on. Leaping. Flapping. Hands extended. Hate gleaming in those obsidian eyes.

Leaping over the thing that lay in the snow.

Mouth opening now in a wordless, soundless cry of fury and, yes, he knew, of anguish. The fury he could see on her straining features. The anguish he would not confess. Could not. Dare not. But it was there. Oh yes, it was there. He knew it. Could feel it. Could never admit to it.

Damn her. Damn her to hell.

She was coming closer. Closer. Reaching. Clawing. Wanting his blood, his flesh, his life. Wanting... he could not finish. He knew. But not openly. Never to be admitted. Never.

She reached out for him.

He raised his hands to fend off her attack.

The rifle—where had that come from? Oh yes,

in his hands; he had been holding it unnoticed and forgotten for all this time and now there it was, as starkly black against white as the figure of the woman who was attacking him—the rifle came up. Steady. Poised. Slim, wicked steel of bayonet spike extended.

The woman floated slowly, slowly into the air. Soundless shrieks preceded her. He could hear nothing. He knew everything.

He stood as if at a distance and watched.

Slowly she rose into the air in one high, convulsive leap.

Slowly she came forward.

The bayonet held steady. He braced himself for the impact but when it came he felt nothing.

It was as if he, the rifle, the bayonet, were forged of cold bronze. Parts of a statue erected to all the futilities of mankind.

He held firm, held the bayonet firm.

The woman's leap cast her breast onto the sharpened tip of the bayonet.

Steel burst through skin and cartilage and soft organs alike. Steel pierced living flesh and drove deep into the woman's body.

Her own actions impaled her. He was innocent of her blood. She did this to herself. He swore that this was so.

She leaped upon his bayonet and perished there, the look on her face, the hatred in those dark, accusing eyes unchanged from moment of living to moment of dying. And beyond.

She died. She fell away.

No matter. He could see her there before him still. Could fell the malevolence of her charge against him. No matter that she was dead and gone. She remained. Her spirit remained where the body was not.

He could feel the wickedness of her hate.

He could not acknowledge why she should have felt such. He could only know that it was so.

The woman was dead, her threat removed.

He looked down, saw the black, colorless blood dripping from the shaft of his bayonet. Sensed without seeing the dark, ugly lumps of death in the snow before his numbed feet.

He turned away. Weary and sobbing, partially grateful to be alive. And partially not.

He turned. Tried to step forward. Would have stepped forward.

Except... before him. The mist swirled slowly, a curtain briefly parting, and a dark and shadowy form took shape. Moved silent and wraithlike toward him. Assumed form and substance.

No! Dear God, no.

The woman.

Dark and silent.

The woman emerged from the eerie mists at a run. And yet she came on slowly. He knew she was running. He could see it in the way her hair streamed back from her face. In the way the flesh of her seamed and filthy cheeks sagged and bounded with each syrup-slow footstep. In the tug and pull of speed at the loose, capelike rags that covered her against the cold. The haphazard garments fluttered and flapped behind her like the windblown bunting of some obscene flag....

Chapter 9

1

Friday, February 18, 1910

God, it was cold. Joe's feet felt like a pair of wood stumps. He might as well have lost them for all the good they were doing him right now. A damned peg leg, that's what he felt like after a day in the saddle chasing after somebody else's stupid cows.

Still, this was better than starving. He supposed. A little bit better.

The brown horse crested the last ridge and picked its way slow and careful down the other slope, moving one cautious foot at a time and swiveling its narrow butt first one way and then the other the way the miserable beasts will do when they're going downhill. Joe did his part by standing in the stirrups—that was why he was so sure his feet were gone, the last of the feeling leaving him sometime since the last downhill section over on the north side of this drainage—and leaning back against the cantle.

The ground wasn't so slick except in patches here and there, but it was hell for solid. Frozen hard as ice even if it wasn't slippery as, and any bit of gravel atop such hard ground made the footing as bad as if it'd been ice they were covering. The horse had slipped and faltered more than once already today and was

197

about worn out to begin with, so it was moving slow and careful and Joe had no desire to make it get along any faster. He was as anxious as anyone might expect to get inside next to the fire but not so anxious that he wanted to risk going down with half a ton of horse laying on top of him just so he could save a minute here or thirty seconds someplace else. No, he'd as soon the horse take it nice and slow.

They reached the thin, winter-gray brush that lined the creek bank and turned up it.

Off in the distance a little way he could see smoke rising up from the line shack roof, the smoke pale and almost indistinguishable against the gray of an overcast sky.

It didn't take much, though, to make for a welcome on a day like this. The thought of a fire was good to look forward to. The thought of supper and coffee even more so.

If the Indian had supper and coffee ready, that is. She'd better, that was all. He would thump hell out of her if she didn't.

Not that there was much to worry about that way. She'd only missed having his supper ready once, and that was about a month ago when he got so cold he cut the day short—the hell with a bunch of stupid cattle; they weren't near so important to him as losing his toes would've been—and came in three, four hours early. She'd learned her lesson that time though, b'damn. He'd taken a chunk of harness strapping and like to wore it out on that woman's broad ass. She was welted up and bruised all black and purple.

That was all the lesson she needed, though. She hadn't messed up on him since.

He guided the horse up along the creek, frozen over except for here and there some open patches of dark, colder-than-ice water where the water was moving too fast to freeze, and out into the open below the corral.

The other horses and the woman were all standing there looking his way. Damned if he could figure that out, but it was so most every time he rode in.

Oh, the horses he could understand. They were outdoors anyhow and could hear better than any human person. But the Indian, how the hell did she always know he was on his way in?

He was sure she would spend near all her time inside close to the fire and her damn kid. And while she wasn't exactly human she wasn't a horse or dog or coyote either to have hearing like a wild creature. So how did she always know to be there waiting for him?

He couldn't figure it, especially as it didn't seem to matter what direction he came in from. A couple times he'd even swung wide around and come up from the south, where he had no business riding, and there she was, standing at the corral gate wanting to pull the bars down and let him in.

Just another proof that Indians aren't the same as people, he supposed, and therefore not worth worrying about.

The point was that his supper would be ready and his coffee and whatever else he needed to warm up and get the feeling back in his feet.

He heeled the brown into a trot for the last few rods and hauled it to a stop, sliding off his saddle and tossing the rein ends to the woman. Let her unsaddle and see to the horse. She hadn't been out in the cold all the day long.

"Your food is on the table," she said.

He grunted an acknowledgment and stumped his way across the hard-frozen yard to the cabin door and inside where the heat washed over him like water closing in all around. Thin, tiny tendrils of steam or condensation or whatever lifted off his clothes as the heat sank into the fabric.

He sat on the side of the bed and kicked futilely at the heel of first one boot and then the other. Between his lack of coordination after being half-froze for so long and the slickness of cold leather he was still sitting there trying to get his icy feet out of the damn boots when the woman came in from tending to the horse. She had a bucket of water with her and didn't even carry it to the stove but just set it down beside the door and hurried over to him, dropping to her knees and taking first one boot and then the other tight between her thighs so she could wrestle the things off him.

"Stay," she said, turning to take the boots away and set them into a box where they wouldn't drool all over the place as they warmed up, then bringing him a cup of steaming hot coffee. She gave him the cup and went down onto her knees again on the hard floor, this time taking his feet and unwrapping the rags he customarily wore wound tight around them.

She commenced massaging his feet then, rubbing the balls of each foot hard with the bony pads of her thumbs. It should have hurt, he supposed, but in fact felt plenty good and pretty soon the feeling began to return, the prickly tingle of the returning blood flow moderated and made more bearable by the massage that she kept up.

He frowned down at her and looked away, his glance falling on the fat kid that was standing big-eyed and quiet in its box. Damn kid was most too big to stay in the box anymore. And if she let it out it was able to walk some nowadays. The nit was growing into a louse, all right, and too quick for his taste.

"No, damn you, this other one now. You been messing with that one long enough."

"As you say, yes." She placed the foot she'd been rubbing onto the floor and took the other one into her lap, the rhythm of her movement scarcely interrupted as she continued to massage warmth and feeling back into his flesh.

2

"You're crazy as hell if you think I'm gonna wear some stupid contraption like that," he told her.

"Please. Try. One time is all. You will see."

"Bullshit."

"I ask you. Please."

"That ain't proper footgear. Not for a white man."

"There is no one to see. You try it. Please."

He shook his head doubtfully. Crazy damn Indian. The only thing she was right about was that there wasn't anybody else around to see if he did decide to go ahead and make a complete fool of himself.

He'd wondered why she had been gathering rabbit skins for the past couple months, practically since she'd first moved in.

Practically ever since then she'd been setting snares along the brush in the creek bottom, ranging way the hell up and down the creek bed to set and watch her string traps.

He'd figured she was adding to their meat. And of course she was. Stewed rabbit is about as good as it gets, and he'd welcomed whatever she caught. Had wondered, though, about the hides she scraped out so careful each time and then tacked to the north wall of the shack where they could cure out of the direct rays of what little sun there was.

That had been going on for some time, first drying out the flimsy skins and then stinking up the place to rough tan them inside where they wouldn't freeze. He had no idea what all she did to them then, what all kind of shit she put on them. Whatever it was it stunk. He knew that for certain sure. Let her know about it, too. After that she brought the skins in when he rode out each morning to chop ice or to push the neighbors' cows back off Zeke range. Crazy woman would bring the rabbit hides inside then and take them back out once he got back in the evenings. The place still smelled of the stuff she put on the skins, but it wasn't so awful bad so long as he didn't have to put up with the skins being inside while he was to home, so he let her get away with it.

Now he found out what she'd been up to.

She'd taken the poorer skins and the scraps of otherwise unused fur and, not tanning those pieces, cut them into narrow strips of rabbit hide. When those dried, the skin part kind of shrank so that what had been flat pieces curled in on themselves to form rope-like pieces covered all around with fur. She'd woven those together so they were like stockings except made of soft fur instead of thin yarn and bulky, real bulky. They would have been grand stockings except, of course, they were much too big and fluffy to fit inside any boot.

Which was where the tanned rabbit skins came in. Out of those the woman had sewn together what looked like boots, soft ones, of course, except real big. Big enough that the rabbit-fur socks could fit inside with room left over.

Crazy damn arrangement, he thought. Crazy.

"Try them. Just one day. The stirrup, it is big enough. I made sure of this. Wear these. They are very warm. Better, your foot can move inside. Not like a hard boot. The foot does not move inside the boot. It gets cold and cannot move to help the blood to flow. Then the foot freezes. You see? You cannot feel, maybe get the…" She paused for a moment to search for the word she wanted. "…frostbite. Yes, frostbite. The foot does not move and sometimes there is the frostbite. With these, the foot moves. Blood flows. There is no frostbite. Cold maybe but you never lose feeling. Stand in the stirrup. Move around some. You will be warm. Much better. Try it one time. Please."

"Crazy Indian bitch."

But he gave in. He didn't know why he'd go and do something like that, but shit, anything to shut the dumb bitch up. If he kicked her in the face today, tomorrow she'd be back asking him to try the stupid rabbit-skin boots. It was easier, he figured, to go ahead and wear them just this one time and get it the hell over with. Then tomorrow if he wanted to he could kick her ass and tell her to throw the lousy things in the fire. Today he'd wear them.

Not that it would do any good, but what the hell.

Joe stepped down off the horse and threw the reins to the woman.

No way in hell he would give her the satisfaction of knowing it, but for the first time in months he could still feel his toes at the end of a long day's work.

The loose, floppy, stupid rabbit-skin boots—if that is what they could be called; they looked more like furry bags than proper boots—were as effective as they were ugly. Well, almost so. Nothing could really be that effective, because for damn sure nothing else could possibly be that ugly and dumb looking.

Still and all, the point was that the things were warm. Daylong warm. And in weather like this, that was going plenty far and then some.

He was pleased. Didn't tell the Indian that, of course. It wouldn't pay to let her think she was putting something over on him. Or whatever. But, well, he was pleased.

He let her take the horse off to water and feed it and brush it down while he walked inside, not stumbling or staggering or anything like that, and helped himself to a cup of steaming coffee out of the pan atop the stove.

Over in its box the kid looked at him with those black, oversize eyes and chortled and cooed even though he hadn't done a damn thing amusing.

Joe scowled at the kid, but all it did was chuckle back at him.

3

Jeez, he was commencing to hate snow. Three solid days of it now. Three days and three nights and no letup in sight. Wind blowing it sideways so you couldn't see from the front door to the empty, leafless trees alongside the creek.

The woman long since strung stout rope from one tiedown to another so there was a safety line to hang on to. One running straight out from the cabin to the corral, another branching off from the corral to the haystack, a third going from the side of the cabin back to the outhouse. Pretty much wherever a body might need to go there was a line to help get them there and back again.

The woman was somewhere in the white-out now, gone out to see there was water in the trough and hay in the bunk. Gone out to see to the horses. It was just as well she was there to do that, for Joe damn sure wasn't interested in risking freezing his butt for the sake of a horse.

The woman, though, she bundled up and

got out there twice a day regardless of the weather. Joe supposed a thing like that would've been admirable if it was a regular person putting himself out to do what was right. But, hell, Indians weren't regular people. He wasn't even sure they felt pain the same as white folks. For sure the woman didn't react much when he had to slap her around or punch her or boot her one in the belly, whatever.

It was like she didn't have the same capacity to feel. Not pain, not emotion, not anything so far as he could tell.

Damn Indians. They looked most human. But who knew? Who the hell really knew?

He sighed and rolled onto his side, deliberately rubbing himself on the blanket that covered him in an effort to get rid of some of the sticky dampness that clung to him.

That was one good thing about having a woman in the place even if she was an Indian. She was useful. Not pretty. Not by any stretch. But she was damn sure useful. And never complained or said no, no matter what he wanted or when he wanted it.

He yawned and let his mind wander, conjuring up remembered images of a blond doxy with big tits that he saw in Cheyenne a couple years back. It was funny, but he could remember that woman better than most others he'd seen in the past. And that one he'd never had. Someone else had got to her before him and bought her out for the whole damn weekend. He remembered that all right. Couldn't call a thing to mind about the whore he'd ended up with instead of that blonde. But it was the blonde he could as good as see in his mind's eye to this very day.

He thought about that a mite and pictured the blonde inside his head.

He would have visualized plenty more, playing an old game that involved figuring out what the blonde would have looked like without clothes although even if he'd had her that weekend he knew he never would have seen her actually naked, which did nothing to negate the pleasures of the game. But even that was cut short by an interruption.

Craziest damn thing.

First off he felt a warmth. Just a hint of warmth encircling one of his fingers. Just one of them. The third finger on his right hand, it was. Nothing but this little bit of warm feeling. Then the warmth got tighter and more insistent.

He opened his eyes.

Found himself face-to-face and nose-to-nose with the kid. Huge black eyes smack in front of him so close he couldn't hardly focus on them until he pulled back a couple inches.

Damn kid got out of its box somehow and held on to the side of the bed while it walked and wobbled up from the foot to the side where Joe was flopped out resting and trying to get himself a little after-nooky nap.

Took hold of his finger with one fat little hand.

It wasn't pulling or really doing anything. Just kind of standing there holding on to his finger with one hand and looking at him and grinning that mindless babble-grin that kids have. Stood looking at him for the longest damn time after he went and opened his eyes and looked back at it.

And then be damned if the kid didn't shriek out a yelp and a laugh and put its head back and say a word. An English word at that.

Joe heard the kid speak and felt a chill run clean through him.

"Da," the stinking kid said. "Da-da."

He snatched his hand away from it and rolled over to present his back. But it was too late. The damage was already done.

Stupid damn kid to say a thing like that. Jeez!

He GAVE THE BOY *a horehound candy and got a grin back in return. Fair exchange, that. If anything he figured he'd gotten the better of it.*

The boy laughed and they didn't need a language in common for him to know that the kid, like himself, was thinking back to the suety stuff the boy once gave him. He could still as good as taste it, as if the heavy, almost smoky, afterflavor was a memory residing on his tongue for all time. The stuff hadn't been bad. Not good either, of course, but not bad. Not nearly so good as the sharper, cleaner taste of this horehound.

He thought back to that other time and knew the boy was, too, and they laughed together.

That had been back in summer. Late summer? He couldn't remember for sure. They had been at the swimming hole, him and a bunch of the other fresh fish—that kind of fit, didn't it? fresh fish at the swimming hole; yeah, that was kind of funny—him and a bunch of other raw recruits not long off the farm. Or wherever each of them actually came from. It didn't matter, of course, what had been before. Once they got here it was all the same. There wasn't any past nor any future either, just right now, right here, living through bad weather and boredom, no more spice to life than there was spice on the mess table. Bland and boring with an occasional payday to put some salt on things.

It wasn't all bad, though. Not all. A guy—he supposed he should call himself a man, at least in the privacy of his own thoughts, but he couldn't quite bring himself to do it, not quite; he was grown and a soldier wearing the proud blue, but

209

*he still couldn't think of himself as a man; call him-
self that out loud maybe... but not deep inside his
own head—a guy, a man, who-the-hell-ever had
his moments. Friends. Good times. A little play-
ful cutting up now and then. And, like, this big-
eyed little boy here.*

*The kid was always around. Not just on pay-
days either. He wasn't looking just for handouts
of the horehound candy. No, he was a really good
kid, and for some reason there was something
between them. A friendship you could say, except
of course one of them didn't understand a damn
word the other said.*

Except that never seemed to mean much.

*It wasn't something he could explain to the other
guys. Some of them teased him. Hell, some of
them had taken to calling the kid Joey. Joe and
Joey. Except during duty hours where you seen—
saw—one, you seen the other. Saw the other. He
knew the difference. Not that he had to mind his
grammar now. There wasn't anybody setting out
to put a grade on it. But he knew the difference.
He was proud of that, too, proud of knowing
right from wrong in grammar. And in other ways.*

He wasn't no—he wasn't any*—hellion. He
was just a guy... all right, a man... trying to get
along. Trying to do his duty and not get in any trouble and do what was right.*

*It wasn't right to get drunk or lay with painted
women. It wasn't right to lie or to cheat or to steal.
He didn't do any of those things. And if some of
the other guys wanted to make fun of him for not
running wild, well, that was their nevermind, their
own problem, not his. He would just go right
along doing what he thought was best and the hell*

with trying to keep up with what everybody else thought.

Right? Damn right!

It was all right to cuss a little now and then, though, wasn't it? He expected likely it was. Like putting a little salt into your words, same as a body needed now and then to put a bit of salt into his life. So cussing was okay. In moderation, that is.

He thought about this stuff lazily, enjoying the free time after getting paid, and gave his little buddy another black sugar-coated lump of horehound. The Indian kid giggled and said something to him, and Joe laughed. It was perfectly all right that he didn't know what little Joey was saying. He didn't need to.

Yeah, this was a good day. Crisp and cool, the heat of last summer broken and the leaves a bright, golden yellow along the meandering creek banks, the rolling grasses pale brown so that in some places, in some light, the grass looked about as yellow as the fall foliage on the trees.

It was good here, Joe thought. Good country. Not near so bleak and empty as he'd thought when he first saw it.

It was really good here.

The kid said something and laughed and Joe, not knowing what he said, laughed with him and reached out to ruffle his unkempt mop of thick, shiny hair.

Yeah, Joe thought, it was good here, all right.

Chapter 10

1

Tuesday, March 8, 1910

He came inside stamping his feet to knock the wet, clinging snow off his rabbit-skin boots—he damn sure preferred to think of them as boots instead of some kind of over-grown moccasin—and immediately tipped his head back and wrinkled his nose like as if he was smelling of a fresh breeze.

Except what he was smelling was supper. The aroma of it was enough to set his mouth to salivating so hard he had to swallow a couple times to get it all down.

He hadn't smelled anything like that in... never mind how damn long it had been. Or where. He didn't want to start thinking about that. Not after all these years, he didn't.

He kicked the boots off and dropped his coat onto the floor as he was already in motion headed for the stove and the source of that rich, heavy odor.

There it was, all right. The biggest pot they had and a lid over top of it and the aromatic steam escaping from around the rim of the lid.

He found a towel draped over the edge of the woodbox and used it to protect himself from a scalding so he could lift the lid off the pot and peep inside. He couldn't help grinning just a little at what he saw there.

A pot roast, by damn. An actual, honest-to-God pot roast. There were even potatoes nested around the brown, peppered lump of meat. Potatoes and onions and some other sort of tuber that he didn't recognize. No matter. The point was that there was a pot roast cooking. Had been cooking probably all the day long to judge by the yellow-pale globules of fat floating on the water it was cooking in. No, much better than water at this point. Meat juices. Potlikker. Pot liquor? He wasn't sure which it ought to be. Didn't much care either. Lordy, he could remember how good potlikker tastes. That was what mattered here.

Still grinning he found a spoon and used it to dip up some of the light brown juice. He blew on it—not long enough to cool it, he was too impatient to wait that long, but long enough that he could stand the heat of it on his tongue—and sipped at the fine, fine likker.

Jeez! It was every bit as good as his memory told him it ought to be.

Who the hell would've thought?

He slurped up the rest of that spoonful and had another and then a third. This was fine.

He heard the door creak open and felt a chill against the back of his neck, then heard the thump of the door closing and the softer thumps of the woman's footfalls as she crossed the room. She'd been lagging behind to tend to the horse, of course, as had become her habit and in fact her job.

"Hey, this here is good," he exclaimed right out loud. "Damn good."

The woman beamed. It was, what the hell, it was the first compliment he'd ever given her.

213

Damned if she didn't take on like it was something special.

"What for meat is it?" It hadn't occurred to him before this moment, but they hadn't seen any fresh meat—except now and then a rabbit, and those fatless bits of stringy meat didn't hardly count—since last fall sometime.

Yet now here was a whole pot roast bubbling away in its own fine juices. Helluva thing once a fellow thought on it.

"Deer meat," the woman said, stooping to pick up first his boots and then his coat. She hung the coat on a peg against the front wall and started in cleaning and drying the fur boots.

"Deer meat. Where the hell'd we get deer meat?" Damn woman didn't have a gun he didn't know about, did she? He wouldn't like that. Not that he thought it possible. But still...

"The uncle of my dead husband. He came by today early. Wanted to see how Sarah and me are. Wanted to see if we want to come home yet."

Joe frowned. "There was some strange Indian here while I was gone?"

"Not a stranger, Joe Potter. The uncle of my dead husband. It is all right. He is family."

"Not my family, he ain't, damn him."

"He brought us this meat. There is more. Under the cloth there. A rear haunch and some neck meat. The neck meat will make a fine broth. I will cook you a stew. Very good. You will like it."

"I'll decide what I like or what I don't, damn you. You let that Indian inside the house?"

"Yes."

"'Don't be doing that again. I don't want no stinking Indians in my place. You hear me?"

"Yes, Joe Potter, I hear."

"An' that's another thing. Why are you calling me by name all of a sudden?"

"It is your name, yes?"

"Yeah, but I don't recollect ever telling it to you. Never seemed to come up. You know?"

"The uncle of my dead husband, he saw you when you left this morning. He told me your name."

"He seen me?"

"Yes. He was across the creek. Watching. He saw you leave. When he comes to visit he tells me who you are. Is this not correct?"

"Sneaking son of a bitch was hiding in the brush and seen me leave?"

"I did not say he hid there. Only that he watched. Very sensible to know who is in a house before one approaches. It is not for harm that he watches. He would do no harm here. This I tell you is true. He is a good man, the uncle of my husband. He has no little girls of his own. Sarah is what is called an apple in his eye. He is very fond of this baby. I told him... I told him you are, too, Joe Potter. He liked that. He said he will bring more meat if he comes this way again and if he has meat then."

Joe scowled. Jeez, he didn't like that. Sneaky son of a bitch of an Indian spying on him like that. And him never knowing it. That was maybe the worst part. Damn Indian could be out there in the brush right now and he wouldn't know.

God, Indians gave him the shivers. He hated them. Every louse-ridden one of them. Hated the bastards.

"Put supper on the table, bitch. I'm hungry."

She nodded a silent acquiescence and laid the fur boots down carefully so she could begin setting food before the man of the house.

2

Something was wrong with the tail hairs the woman plucked and brought in for him. If the hairs were better he'd be able to do this, dammit.

He was trying to plait some horsehair string that he could then braid into a horsehair halter. They could be pretty damn things, especially if you had some interesting colors of hair to work with. Braiding gear was probably the second most common bunkhouse activity, coming in right behind lying as an evening pastime. But it was something Joe never had got the hang of. Not like the boys who considered themselves to be actual cowhands. Which Joe himself never did. He was an old soldier and a damn fine officer of the law. The job of being a cowhand to him was just that: a job. A way to keep the damn wolf from howling at the door too often or too loud. It was allright work for a man, but it wasn't what he thought of himself as being. Maybe that was why braiding horsehair crap wasn't important to him like it was to those poor, stupid bastards who thought of such a lousy job as being their special calling. Or something. Bunch of fools with numb heads and boils on their butts was the way he saw them.

Still, there wasn't anything better to do of a cold evening than braid horsehair. Hell, he might've enjoyed it if he could make anything that a disinterested observer would recognize as what he'd intended it to be. Never mind pretty. He would have settled for merely recognizable.

"Hey."

"Yes, Joe Potter?" She looked up. She was sitting across the table from him, both of them sharing the one light, while she picked rags apart to make thread. God only knew what she might want the thread for. She was constantly making one thing or another, sometimes for him, sometimes for the kid.

"This hair isn't worth shit. Didn't I tell you to get me good tail hair?"

"It is hair of the tail, every piece."

"Looks like some mane hair mixed in. You been cheating on what I told you, haven't you?"

"I take only from the horse tails, just as you say."

"And I'm telling you some of this looks like mane hair to me."

"Yes, Joe Potter. I am sorry. I will be very careful from now on."

He glared at her, feeling mildly cheated for some reason.

How the hell d'you work up a good mad-on with somebody that all the damn time accepts whatever blame you want to throw and

217

even apologizes for it? Thinking about that maddening trait was in itself enough to fuel a small fury to heat his bowels and tighten his scalp.

"Slut," he snarled, shoving the mess that was supposed to have been a halter into the box where he kept it.

"Yes," she said, eyes down and hands dropping quietly to her lap.

He swung his legs around, intending to get up and go over there and work off some frustration by thumping on the woman. But when he swung around like that he bumped into the damn kid. It was toddling his way from over by the bed where it generally hung out now that the damn box wouldn't contain it any longer.

He bumped it and it went sprawling onto its butt.

Joe frowned. Miserable little shit!

Damn kid got up cackling and grinning and ran to throw its arms around the knee that'd just bopped it. Reached around his leg and hung on like it was hugging him or something and all the while laughing and saying something.

He thought about giving it a kick to send it flying.

But he didn't.

Not that he was afraid. Hell no. But he hadn't forgotten what the crazy Indian bitch said that one time neither. And, hell, she was nuts enough, all Indians were nuts enough, that you never knew what one of them might do. Any damn thing, that was what an Indian could do.

Knife a fellow in his sleep, that's what an Indian might do. You just never knew. Act so nice you'd think butter wouldn't melt in their mouth. Lay down and spread their legs for a fellow. Then soon as he falls to sleep haul out a knife and slip it between his ribs while he dreamed and snored.

You just never knew.

Joe had taken—she didn't know about it and wasn't damn likely to—he'd taken to looking under the mattress every now and then. Just to make sure there wasn't a knife or something hidden there.

And just because he hadn't found anything so far didn't mean there wouldn't be something there sometime.

No, he wasn't afraid of the bitch. And he'd kick hell out of the kid if ever he took a mind to. But right now he just didn't feel like it.

Instead he reached down and disengaged himself from the kid's hugging and hanging on. The kid looked at him and laughed some more, those damn eyes big and dark and trusting. It needed to learn better. He would teach it to learn better than that. Damn right he would, and soon.

He thought again about going around and giving the woman a reminder to mind herself when she spoke to him. And to do what he told her to from now on. Be a lesson for her and a lesson for the kid, too. Keep the both of them in line if he did that.

But he didn't. Not right now, he decided.

The stupid kid ran forward and flung itself onto his leg again, gabbling and cooing and hugging herself to him as hard as ever she could cling.

Damn her. Damn the both of them.

3

He grunted, lips drawn back in a rictus of pleasure that could easily have been mistaken for pain. He cried out as he spent himself in the woman. After a moment he sighed and relaxed the tight-pent muscles so that his entire weight was on her. She didn't seem to mind. In fact she reached around to stroke his shoulders and the small of his back and then up again to knead and lightly massage the back of his neck.

Nice. That was damn nice, all right. He kind of liked it. She'd never done anything like that before. He wondered if she...

Joe scowled. Stupid damn Indian. Not smart enough to know he couldn't stand her. Too damn dumb to know her place. Keep up like this and she'd go to getting uppity. Count on it. He knew. Damn right he knew. He'd seen it before. Let an Indian go to thinking it was as good as white human people and you had trouble every time.

This one wouldn't be any different. Not a lick of it. It was the old saying all over again. Give an Indian an inch, they'd take a mile.

No good. They weren't any of them any good.

He lay where he was, letting her stroke and please him, while he worked up a good strong hate for her and every one like her.

Damn this one anyhow.

Ought to kick her and the kid out, the both of them.

He would, too, except for the one thing she was able to provide him that he couldn't do for himself.

With a grunt of annoyance he pulled away from the gentle touching and rolled off her, thoroughly pissed off now although he wasn't quite sure at what.

4

Joe felt pretty damn good. His belly was full, warmed by the thick stew she'd made with the last of the deer meat. She'd flavored it with wild onion that she'd dug somewhere not too far off. The wild onions had a thicker, heavier, almost smoky taste compared with regular onions. Those were pretty much gone anyhow, dark and slimy and sprouting pale, ugly, unhealthy-looking growths that hadn't ought to be there. The wild ones were a nice change from what was left of the staples the Zeke had laid in for him. The onions were most gone and the potatoes rotting. There was some rice left and some beans but not much else. Not much to work with, that was for sure.

Damn woman could cook. He had to give her that. She was ugly as a sin. And an Indian. But she could cook. Little as there was to cook with, he wasn't going hungry and wasn't finding reason to complain about what was put onto the table neither. Yeah, the woman could cook.

Not worth a shit except for that, of course. But it wasn't all bad. Everything considered.

He stretched out on the bed, enjoying the warmth of the meal that spread through his belly. The woman, crazy thing, came over—not seeming to rush about it or make a big deal of it exactly but moving swift and sure and smiling—to pull his dirty socks off and replace them with some loose, floppy slippers she'd made for him out of scraps of rabbit fur.

She wasn't really thinking of him, he knew. She was worried lest he get something onto the sheet she used to cover the mattress. She might want him to think she was worrying over him, but he knew better. It was the sheet she was thinking of, not him. Hell, if anything he was too hot with the slippers on. The weather had broken and started to warm already—it could change back in a heartbeat; he knew better than to trust it this early—and they scarcely needed the stove now even at night. A little fire early in the evening and then bank what coals were formed, that was all that was needed. That and fire to cook with.

By this time he rarely found any ice to break open, and mostly when he rode out he was looking for strange beeves to push off the Zeke grass and back toward wherever they belonged.

This was a pretty fat time of year, actually, with nobody around to tell a body what to do. And with a woman in the place so he was getting it regular and had good eats at the same time. Hell, this wasn't half bad really.

He stretched again and partially stifled a yawn, then closed his eyes and listened to the distant, half-heard sound of somebody snoring.

After a bit he felt something warm and soft tucked in close against his breast and a faint, gentle touch along his cheek and the side of his neck.

Funniest thing, that. Soft as goose down, it was. Kind of tickled, too, but not in a way that a fellow could mind. If anything it was sort of nice.

His lips fluttered just a bit, and he found himself snorting.

His eyes came open.

And came up facing another set of eyes. Huge. Dark. Moist.

It was the damn kid. She'd crawled up onto the bed somehow and tucked herself in close against his chest, with her face square in front of his and her chubby hand touching him here and there as if exploring. Checking the whisker stubble on his cheek and neck, lightly twitching the hairs that grew out of his nose—damn if *that* didn't tickle plenty—and in general examining whatever she could find.

"Da," she chortled. Then drew back from him an inch or two and laughed like hell.

Joe felt something twist and burn inside. It felt like something there was curling into tight, hard knots and threatened to choke him. Or something.

He should pick the stinking brat up and throw it across the room. He knew he should.

He would have, too, except for the damn kid's mother. That was the only reason he didn't. Only reason in the whole damn world why he didn't.

As it was he settled for pretending none of this was happening. That he was still asleep and didn't even know about it.

The kid patted his cheek and poked a finger inside his ear and made a happy, gobbling sort of sound.

Joe let his eyes drag shut again.

And after a bit he was no longer pretending.

IT WASN'T LIKE *it was any big deal. Just an old horse blanket. Not the kind that goes underneath a saddle but the kind worn by fancy horses so their hair would not be too coarse and so they would not catch cold. This particular blanket had been the property of the regimental adjutant. The cavalry regiment, that is, those preening, prancing poppinjays. Silly sons of bitches, as any good infantryman soon enough learned. Easy prey, too. The cavalry liked to strut and swagger in front of the ladies, right enough, but when it came time to brawl it was the infantry having the better of it, all the silly horse soldiers being little bitty bastards. There was even a rule about it. Horses being of more importance than a trooper, the army wouldn't make a full-sized man into a horse soldier, no sirree. A hundred forty pounds was the absolute limit, and they wouldn't recruit any that big if there was a choice in the matter. A hundred thirty pounds was what they liked when they could get it. An infantryman, though, who marched with all his kit on his own strong back was wanted big and muscular, and so it was the darkleg foot soldier who had the edge on a raucous payday night.*

Silly damn troopers not only could be whipped easy, it seemed a good many of them could be gulled just as easy. Something else that was quickly learned by every infantryman, that was.

Which was how he'd come into possession of a perfectly good, extrafancy quilted horse blanket that used to belong to that major—whatever his name was—who kept the pack of wolfhounds and a pair of hot-blooded, skinny-necked fancy horses to run over the prairie after them chasing coyotes, which some called prairie wolves. Or maybe that was a different animal. Not that it mattered. What mattered was the blanket. Fine piece of work, it was, and no doubt the major was unhappy when he was told how his fancy horse got itself into a storm inside its stall and ripped the blanket all up.

Tore the blanket up, hell.

Dumb, gullible trooper on stable detail made the mistake of wagering the major's blanket on a footrace, that was the truth of it. Dumb bastard thought just because he was little he'd be quick as well, and wasn't that a mistake?

It turned out the blanket didn't cost a cent, so he had cash money to pay to the Mexican laundress—one of the few times a post laundress ever earned anything without having to lay down on her back—to take all that fine material and turn it into a capote.

He paid her fifty cents in coin and she got to keep all the straps, buckles, and scraps that were left over. Which amounted to plenty of bright red cloth, since the capote itself was so small.

The laundress did a good job of it. He had to say that about it. The capote was a cunning nice garment when she was done with it. No way anyone could ever guess the hooded cape/coat thing was ever once a horse blanket—and a mighty good thing for that, too, since the major thought his ruined horse blanket was thrown out in the garbage pit.

Even the size, guesswork though that had been, proved to be just right, b'damn.

Joey's eyes got even bigger when he first saw the capote Joe had had made up for him.

Joe wouldn't have thought it possible for those huge, wet eyes to get any bigger than they already were. But this time they did.

The way the kid took on, grinning and dashing around to show his new capote to first this person and then that one, a body would think Joe'd gone and given him a robe set with jewels and trimmed in ermine and not some dumb old capote made out of a horse blanket.

Why, Joey acted like it was the finest thing anybody ever did for him. And come to think of it, maybe it was. Maybe it just dang well was.

Whatever, the pleasure on the little guy's face when he first tried on his new red capote was recompense in full and ten times over. Worth way the hell more than the little Joe laid out to get the thing for him.

Darned old capote wasn't such-a-much, after all. And every kid needs something to keep him warm when the cold of winter is coming on.

No big deal at all, no sirree.

But Joe sure got an awful lot out of watching Joey's pleasure in it. He surely did that.

Chapter 11

1

Thursday, April 21, 1910

The thin, pale string of smoke lifting into the still air drew him like a cat to a yarn end. Certain sure even if he pretended otherwise.

He topped the ridgeline and stopped there, making damn sure him and the horse were silhouetted hard against the blue of the sky behind. Making damn sure they couldn't miss seeing him from down below.

Took them long enough to spot him. They were lazing through the nooning, not paying attention to what was going on, and for a while he thought he was going to have to ride down uninvited.

He would have done that if they hadn't got around to seeing him but eventually they did. One of the fellows leaning forward to reach for the coffeepot glanced up and spotted him and said something to the other two.

The one on the left looked around and didn't hesitate a bit but stood and waved him in.

That one looked kinda familiar, and as he came closer Joe saw it was that cheeky fellow... it took him a minute to call the name back to mind now... McCarthy, foreman of the 23 Bar, whose cows he'd been pushing off Zeke graze for the whole winter past.

228

"Step down and join us, Potter." McCarthy grinned. "If you've a mind to take me up on that offer I made you a while back."

"The coffee I'll take; the makings I still don't need," Joe said, proving to the man that he could remember things as good as anybody.

"Light and welcome then. Potter, this here is Jeremy Jones—or so he claims to be—and that one over there is Bob-White Quayle. We're out making a tally so we can get a handle on what to expect come the spring working. Seen any of our beeves lately?"

Joe stepped down from his saddle with a grunt and a sigh and hobbled the horse before stripping its bridle, loosening the cinch and turning the animal free to crop at the grass. "Ayuh," he said, limping over to the fire, "I ran some back up this way just this morning. Took them up the draw over yander and turned them loose up near that little creek... I don't know the name of it...."

"That bottom underneath a rock wall and some runty, twisty little cedars over on the other side?"

"That's the place."

"Lemon Creek, that one is."

"Yeah, well, I put fourteen head of your stuff on that bottom just a little while ago. Nine cows there were, three calves, and a pair of steers with more horn and legs on them than beef."

McCarthy nodded and pulled a notebook out of one pocket and a stub of pencil from another. He jotted down the figures Joe gave him and made a notation beside it, presumably the location of where those cows could be found. "Thanks."

Joe hunkered beside the fire and helped himself to some coffee once the 23 Bar hand called Jones gave him a tin cup to use.

"Damn, this coffee smells fine. I run out two, three weeks ago. You wouldn't have any tinned milk to go in, would you? And maybe some sugar?"

"I thought the Zeke fed good."

"Aw, it does really. It's just that I eat even bigger than the Zeke feeds." He didn't want to get into the reasons why his stuff was running short. It wasn't anybody's business but his own.

"To tell you the truth, Potter, I figured you'd have pulled it in before now and been back on the Zeke range. Not that I'm complaining, mind. It's a big help to us to have you down there moving our stock back where they belong. I'm just surprised is all."

"Yeah, well, I expect it's about time, all right. I've been busy, that's all."

Reluctant to give up all the free lays, that was the truth of it. He'd got so used to having it regular that he'd come to like it and kind of expect it, and he wasn't going to enjoy having to give that up now.

"The milk and sugar are in that sack over there. Help yourself. How about some biscuits to dunk in the coffee?"

"Biscuits? You're shitting me."

"No. They aren't two days old neither. Cook made them before we took out yesterday morning. Have some."

The biscuits were soft and crumbly and tasted absolutely marvelous. Wheat flour was something else they'd run out of at the Zeke shack.

"A man forgets, sometimes, what things oughta taste like."

The one called Bob-White laughed. "If I ever had to eat my own cooking I bet I'd starve clean to death."

"That may be so, but I expect your horse would appreciate it if you'd at least gaunt down some."

"If he don't say so how'm I to know it? Say, Potter, while you're in that sack whyn't you hand me a couple of those biscuits. I purely hate to see a man eat alone. It ain't polite."

It was kind of nice for a change to have white men for company, Joe admitted to himself.

And it was for damn sure nice to have coffee again and with milk and sugar to go into it.

He sat and jawed with the men from the 23 Bar for a while, then helped them kick dirt over their fire and pulled his cinches tight again.

He even remembered to thank McCarthy for the hospitality.

2

The woman came out to take the horse and tend to it. Like always. And the damn kid came out to grab on to him. Like always.

Ever since it started warming up good—and the kid started walking good—the woman had let the kid outside to run around and get dirty whenever she was outside, too.

Somehow—he hadn't ever quite figured out exactly how or when—it had gotten to be a part of the routine of things that when he rode in of an evening the woman would come out to unsaddle and curry and feed whatever horse he was riding that day and the damn kid would scramble along after her but instead of going into the corral, where it wasn't allowed for fear some horse would step on it or something, it would come wobbling over and grab hold of Joe's leg. Whatever leg was handy, it didn't seem to matter which. Grab on just about knee level, which was pretty much as high as short stuff could reach. Wrap its fat arms around him and grin and hang on.

Well, shit, what could he do? If he kept on walking with a damn kid stuck to his shin he'd end up kicking the thing into the dirt. He didn't want to do that, particularly.

So in self damn defense he did about the only thing he could do and that was to reach down and pick the damn thing up and cart it along with him.

First thing you knew, the kid seemed to've taken to that as an evening playtime. Or whatever. Seemed to expect it, anyhow. Stupid damn Indian kid. They were all of them dumb. He knew that.

So he'd pick the dumb thing up and cart it on into the house with him and light for a minute at the table while he had a cup of coffee. If he tried putting the kid down it'd just latch onto his leg again and there was no point in that so he'd got sort of in the habit of letting it set in his lap while he drank his coffee.

Then after that he liked to lay down on the bed for a bit while the woman finished up the chores and came inside to get supper ready.

First damn thing he knew the kid was after him to let it lie down next to him on the bed. So it sort of got to be another habit lately that after drinking his coffee him and the damn kid would lay down together for a short nap while the woman was seeing to the household crap.

The kid would curl up in front of his chest and maybe mess with his whiskers or poke around inside his ear for a couple minutes, but pretty soon it would settle down and go to sleep and then he could catch a wink or three himself.

It was a stupid damn kid but, hell, you couldn't hardly blame a dummy for being dumb. He could put up with it a little while longer.

This particular evening, though, he wasn't in any mood to mess with any Indian brat. The woman should've known that.

This particular evening the damn kid came running to him—it was no damn wonder kids run so slow; mostly they seem to wobble side to side instead of coming on when they try to run—and tripped just about the time it went to grab hold of him.

It went down on its face and got scraped up some. Not hurt, hell no, but startled. That was all it was was startled. Scared, like. He knew that. The woman should've known it, too, damn her.

She'd just taken the reins of the horse and was turning to lead it into the corral when she

233

heard the thump of the kid hitting the dirt and then a short, frightened bawl as the kid tried to figure out what had just happened.

The woman jerked back around to see what was what and that spooked the damn horse and then of a sudden there was a helluva storm going on.

Kid crying. Woman shouting. Horse trying to turn around inside its own skin. Dust and gravel flying.

The horse kicked and damn near knocked the kid in the head, and the woman shouted some more. Which wasn't doing nobody any good.

Joe threw a shoulder into the horse's near flank and knocked it off balance, which kept it from kicking out again but didn't do a thing to improve its humor so he kept on after it, pushing and shoving, grabbing the reins from the woman, who seemed too surprised to know what the hell to do next, snatching the horse's head around and smashing his weight into its shoulder so the animal toppled clean off its feet and went down onto its right side. Hard.

Behind him the woman finally woke up to the fact that something was happening here. She gave Joe a wide-eyed look and dived for the kid, which was sitting cross-legged on the ground with tears washing tracks in the dirt on its cheeks.

The woman grabbed up the kid and went skittering away with it clutched to her chest like she was having to protect it from *him*, for Christ sake.

Joe was pretty thoroughly pissed. He didn't

stop to figure out what he was pissed at. He just knew he was truly and properly pissed off.

He hauled the horse's head around and gave it a boot in the stomach. It lurched once and then again and finally made it back onto its feet. After a couple seconds of shivering and looking around it seemed to decide there wasn't anything wrong after all and calmed right down again.

Joe took the horse into the corral and turned loose of it there—if the damn thing wanted to step on the rein ends and bust them it was welcome to try; those working reins were an inch-wide strip of good thick latigo, and the horse was like to tear its mouth up before those reins would pop—and went to dragging the poles back where they belonged.

The woman, over her fright as much as the horse was or so it looked like, went over to the shack and put the kid inside, closing the door on it so it couldn't come out again.

Damn her anyhow. Damn the horse. And damn that stupid kid, too.

The woman came over, probably to unsaddle for him and finish tending to the horse; he didn't wait to see.

Soon as she came near enough he reached out and socked her one. Hard. He then backhanded her and drew blood from her nose and the corner of her mouth.

"Don't you never," he hissed. "Don't you *never*!"

He honest to God didn't know himself what it was he was warning her to never do. But he was so blind-furious mad that he was shaking from it, trembling head to toe.

The woman closed her eyes and hunched her shoulders and stood there waiting for the next blow to fall.

Joe bunched his fist tight and drew back. Then, all the madder, he let out a loud snort and spun away without hitting her again. God, he hated Indians. Every lousy one of them.

He stalked across the yard and into the cabin. Damn her.

The kid was there. And the coffee filling the place with its smell. Damn kid latched hold on his right leg just about knee high like as if nothing at all unusual had happened.

He like to kicked out to shake it off but didn't. After a second or two he shuddered and bent down, taking hold of the miserable tyke and lifting it up so he could carry it over to the table and do all the shit that it expected. Coffee, nap, all that stuff.

Dammit, anyway.

3

"It's time," he said.

"Yes."

"Got to go back to the damn Zeke. Should've gone a week, two weeks ago. They'll be wondering."

"Yes."

"About outta food here anyway."

"Yes."

"I won't need none for the ride back. You and the kid, you take whatever's left. If it's left here the mice will just get it. No point to that."

"No."

"It don't mean anything to me. You know that."

"Yes."

"Yeah, well... pack my stuff for me and get the horses ready. And mind you do it right. No laying around, hear? If I'm going then I expect I'd best get moving."

"Yes, Joseph Potter."

"And quit calling me that, dammit." He was starting to feel anger bubble up somewhere about gut level. Starting to feel that tightening in his belly and across the back of his shoulders, starting to feel the hairs rise on his neck. He didn't know if the hairs on the back of a man's neck will actually, truly, for sure stand up like they do on the back of a feisty dog's neck... but the feeling was damn sure there and he wouldn't have been real surprised to learn that there was physical movement to go along with the feeling.

Whatever, he was commencing to feel it now.

He was getting downright good and pissed with the woman again. He wasn't real sure why, but he could feel it coming on.

"Get on now, damn you. And be quick about it." He balled his hand into a fist but didn't lift it or anything. He was just kind of letting her know.

"Yes, as you say." She bobbed her head, looking like she halfway expected to be punched but not flinching away from it. Making herself ready, just in case.

He unclenched the fist and turned his back on her.

Joe sat at the table and had another cup while

237

the woman went about the packing. Not that there was so much of it to be done. He didn't own all that much to start with. A rolled-up canvas bed. Poke of clothes and stuff. And of course the little trunk. He was never without that small trunk of stuff.

He ignored her while she worked at getting his things together and carrying it all outside.

The kid was harder to ignore. It came galloping over to him quick as he sat down and tried to climb into his lap. Stupid thing wasn't big enough to make it but it didn't know that and kept on trying, grabbing onto his pant legs and trying to pull itself up and slipping back down again because it wasn't strong enough to come up like that.

After a bit, just to make it stop being so stupid, he reached down and took hold of the back of the wad of coarse cloth that passed for a diaper and gave a little tug to help boost it the rest of the way up. It settled onto his lap and leaned back against his belly and sat there looking around.

Black coffee is supposed to be bad for a kid, but what the hell did he care? He gave it a sip out of his cup and had a hard time keeping from busting out laughing at the sour face he got back. Kid probably thought it was getting a sweet, but they'd run out of sugar ages ago and there was no kind of sweetener in the coffee. Not even the molasses that he'd been using lately. The kid's eyes went all wide when the bitter flavor of the straight coffee hit its tongue, and then its face scrunched up so for a minute he thought it was going to cry. Instead it just looked startled for a few seconds there. And then damn if it didn't reach out for his cup wanting another taste. Which he gave it. What the hell. It wasn't his kid, so what should he care if its growth got stunted? Or whatever it was coffee was supposed to do to a youngun, which he didn't particularly believe to begin with.

He and the kid were on their second cup when the woman came back inside.

"Everything is ready now."

"Yeah, well..." He stood up, taking the kid with him in the crook of one arm like a puppy that'd been sleeping on his lap.

He felt... awkward. Dammit, he didn't owe her any parting words. She was just a lousy Indian and there was no reason in hell why he should have to say good-bye or any sentimental shit like that.

"Here." He held the kid out to her. She bobbed her head and took it.

"Next year," she said.

"Yeah?"

"I will come to you here when the leaves fall from the trees."

"You don't have to do that. If you don't want."

She gave him a funny sort of look. "I am your woman now, no?"

"Hell no," he said forcefully.

Still looking at him like that, she shrugged and said, "It is right that you think what you do. It is right that I think what I do. I am a Christian woman, Joseph Potter. I do not lie with every man who wants to push my legs apart. I prayed about this, you know. Long time back. There is no preacher to read over us, but

239

in the sight of the one above I give myself as your woman. This is to make right the things you have me do. You think what you like. I will be here when the leaves are gone from the trees. If you are here, good. If the other man, *the kind man*, is here again I will go home to my people. You do what you think is right." She lifted her chin in a gesture that was very nearly defiant, and her eyes met his without flinching. *"I, too, do what I believe is good."*

He grunted once and headed for the door.

He did not tell her any stupid good-byes and did not look back at the damn kid either. The hell with the both of them. He wouldn't see them again. Ever. Not either one of them.

Still full of the rage that of a sudden had come over him he mounted the horse she'd saddled and took up the lead rope that the others were following. He threw the steel to the saddle horse and got the hell out of there in a hurry as if to outrun the anger that churned inside him.

HE RAN KNEE DEEP *in snow, the pull of it against his ankles adding to his fatigue and making him stumble.*

If he fell... He was terrified of falling. He did not know what would happen to him if he went down. He only knew the consequence would be more awesomely terrifying than he could endure. Whatever it might be.

His chest ached from drawing the subzero cold into his lungs as he ran, and his feet were numbed and near frozen so that he could scarcely feel the footing beneath the snow and that made it all the more difficult to run without falling.

Clouds of white, smokelike condensation huffed out of his mouth and streamed back from his nostrils.

He gulped at the brittle-cold air and snuffled and snorted as he ran.

He knew this was so. He could feel it.

But he could hear... nothing.

All about him was silence.

He felt the crunch of the snow crust breaking under his feet, but he could not hear it.

He felt the gasping, rasping breaths that rushed in and out of his lungs, but he could hear nothing of the effort of that labored breathing.

He felt the panic that seized him but could hear nothing of the thin, whimpering whine he could feel escaping from drawn lips.

What should have been sound, the sense of sound, the ability to comprehend sound, was occupied and filled to overflowing with a vast, empty echoing of some previous sound. A roaring sound. He knew this to be so although he did not under-

stand how he came by the knowledge. He was sure, though, that it was so.

It was as if he retained a memory of having heard this... something... but without being able to recall what that sound had been.

He found that odd. But only distantly so.

After all, he hadn't time to ponder imponderables.

Right now all he could concentrate on was... running.

Fleeing.

Getting away from... something. The source of that great roaring that had so numbed his sensibilities? Perhaps. Or perhaps it was something else entirely. He neither knew nor cared. He only knew that he had to run.

Through the snow. Over and around the dark, still lumps that littered the snowfield where he ran. Dark, elongated, grotesquely twisted shapes.

It was not those shapes he was frightened of, though. Those shapes were silent and still and could no longer do him harm. Those shapes were dead.

But behind him... ah, behind him was dread. Something awful. Something truly terrifying.

Behind him was the source of that immense, echoed roaring that would overtake and overwhelm him if ever once he looked back, if ever once his footing was lost, if ever once he went down.

He dare not fall and he dare not slow and if ever he looked back he would be like Lot's wife, stricken lifeless and immobile, she a pillar of salt and he perhaps a spire of pale ice given manshape but empty of life, devoid of soul.

He knew this. Knew he must outrun whatever evil it was that pursued him. Knew... but felt *his strength flagging, his thighs trembling, his muscles turning to jelly.*

And behind him the great, awesome roaring swept relentlessly on. Overtaking him. Coming nearer and ever nearer.

Chapter 12

1

Lusk, Wyoming
Sunday, July 3, 1910

Joe was extra careful, at great pains to ensure he did not spill any of the liquor as he refilled his glass from one of the bottles—at this point no one could possible figure out who paid for what bottle, nor did it really matter now—and just as carefully lifted the glass to his mouth. Quite thoroughly satisfied with his own exquisite control, he tossed the drink back in one quick gulp.

Whiskey that was raw at the neck of the bottle seemed mellow and sweet closer to the bottom.

Funny how that worked.

Of course he was mighty well along to being drunk. Hell, he knew that. That's why he was being so careful. A man got drunk, he could get sloppy, too. Spill some whiskey. Damn shame to spill whiskey. Criminal. Ha! Ought to lock up any son of a bitch sorry enough to spill good whiskey. And this whiskey was good. No doubt about that. This whiskey was *fine*.

Joe could sure feel it now. His nose was numb and his cheeks and lips were growing slightly stiff so that he had to take care when he attempted to enunciate a word.

Not that he was much interested in talking. Tomorrow would be the time for talking. Or anyhow time for some serious listening.

Tomorrow there'd be speeches the whole afternoon and kegs of free beer brought out by the fancy-dan politicians who were giving those speeches and one helluva barbecue. They'd started the cooking already. He'd seen it. Hell, he'd smelled it. Already smelled good enough to break out the plates and the pickles if only somebody would.

Why, there was a whole steer, donated by the Rafter J. It was trussed up and hanging on a steel beam that was serving as a spit, the contraption being turned by a family of Mexicans hired in for the occasion. They'd turn the beef slow and steady the whole night through and half of tomorrow until the thing was cooked and ready to serve.

Word among the boys was that the beef was donated by the Rafter J. But it was actually provided by the Pinetree outfit. It was just that the Pinetree didn't know how generous they had been. That was common knowledge *except* among the managers and foremen and such.

In addition to the beef there were a pair of hogs—Joe got to thinking about that: hogs; why, if there were hogs around then there must also be a hog ranch; a real one; helluva notion, that; who'd have ever thought it? The idea put him into a fit of laughter that lasted until his belly ached so bad it took the fun out of the merriment and he quit laughing again—and huge washtubs that'd been scrubbed out and filled with beans that were cooking all fixed up with molasses and bacon and onion and stuff and another tub they'd boil sausage in but of course that wouldn't be started until morning as it didn't take as long to cook as the other stuff.

Why, just thinking about all that was enough to make a man hungry.

Joe felt the hunger roil inside his stomach and helped himself to another drink to quell the sensation. This time he forgot to be so careful, and he spilled about as much as he got into the glass. He got enough poured—inside the glass, that is—to make a drink, however, and drank it. He remembered to take care getting the glass from the table to his mouth and this time did not spill any.

Yeah, that was better. That was making the ol' hunger go away all right.

He reached for the nearest bottle about the same time Raymond Veile did. Raymond was one of the new hands. A fair number of last year's crew hadn't come back to the Zeke this spring. But then that happened every year. It wasn't anything unusual. Just a nuisance having to put up with a bunch of damn strangers all the time. Seemed there was always some asshole wanting to be everybody's buddy. If there was anything Joe did not need, or want, it was a damn pal. Screw all of 'em. Except the ones that would spring for the price of a bottle. This Veile now, he was kind of all right. Poured his own glass full and emptied the rest of what was left in the bottle into Joe's glass and waved to the barman for a replacement, which he paid for out of his own pocket. Now that was all right. Raymond Veile, he was a regular gent, he was.

Have another drink, Joe, Joe told himself inside his head. Thank you, reckon I will, he answered, again in silence.

Ah, there was nothing like a holiday. Not a thing could beat it, not by half.

2

Jeez, he was horny. Going to pop the buttons right off his fly if he didn't get some soon. And that was a fact. A purantee, certified fact.

He left the bar and, using the banister for a mite of support and guidance, made his way up to the big room at the top of the stairs, the ones where the ladies waited for the menfolk to come along.

This was a strictly honest joint. You had to say that about it. No women allowed in the bar. Not like those places where the ladies came around interfering with a man's drinking and trying to get a fellow to buy them cold tea at whiskey prices. No sir, there was none of that going on here. Strictly straight and honest, this joint was. Joe liked that.

He reached the top of the stairs and paused a moment to steady himself. Took two steps forward and half a step back. Stopped again and shook his head. Sheesh, he was fuzzy. But that was all right. All part of the fun. Damn right.

He let himself into the room and blinked. Not much light in there. Only one lamp burning and it was turned low. What he could see looked all right, though. There were two sofas in the room, one directly in front of him and the other to his left. The one facing held three women and another pair sat on the divan on his left. Five whores to choose from and all of them plump and powdered.

Joe grinned and two of the whores smiled back. The other three pretended they weren't paying any attention to him at all.

There were three blondes, one woman with henna-red hair, and one with long, thick black hair.

Joe belched and swayed a little, reached out for the doorjamb to steady himself, then pointed to the one with the dark hair.

"Come here, honey."

"My, ain't you the handsome one?" the black-haired whore cooed with a big smile. She got up, adjusted a shoulder strap that was falling down off the flimsy garment—he had no idea what a contraption like that might be called—she was wearing and came sashaying over to him with a broadly exaggerated swing of her hips. He liked that. He was already in the mood, but if he hadn't been that damn sure would have put him into the mood for it quick enough.

"Got your dollar, honey?" she asked, her voice all syrup sweet.

He grinned again and winked at her. "In that pocket right there."

The whore laughed and dug her hand down inside his jeans, taking time to feel of him while she was in there. Yeah, this one was all right. He liked her just fine.

"What's your name, darlin'?" she asked as she extracted the coin, holding it up so he could see it was a silver dollar she was taking, nothing more.

"Does it matter?"

"Not if you don't want it to, honey."

"Let's go," he ordered gruffly. For some damn reason his mood was changing. He didn't know why, but he was starting to get pissed off. "Now."

"Sure, honey. Whatever you say." She smiled and took his arm, tucking in close at his side. She smelled of toilet water and scented powder and old sweat. "This way, sweetie. Right over here."

Joe swallowed back an impulse to puke and followed the whore out of the room and on down the corridor.

The woman screamed and threw her arms over her head, trying to protect her face behind a wall of elbows and forearms and blind hope.

"Jesus God, mister, don't hit me no more."

He backed up and swung a roundhouse right that landed on the point of her shoulder. He could feel the jolt of it all the way up into his own shoulder, and in fact the punch probably hurt him more than it did her.

He blinked, threw a punch, and felt it whip wildly and inaccurately past her bloody face.

That wasn't right, dammit. He'd had good aim. He tried again, only to have the same thing happen all over.

Scowling, he tried to step in closer and only then realized that something was holding him back.

He jabbed back, hard, with the point of an

elbow to try and make whoever it was let go. He heard a grunt of pain and felt a momentary loosening of restraint and took that opportunity to move ahead and punch the whore a couple more good shots square in her ugly face.

"Dammit, Potter."

He felt arms wrap around him from behind. More than one set of arms, he was pretty sure. He didn't know who they were and didn't care. Bastards were holding him back, that was the thing. They oughtn't to do that.

He tried to hit the woman again and couldn't. Tried to wheel around and hit whoever was holding him. Couldn't do that either.

There were two, three, who the hell knew how many? Too many. He didn't give a damn. He'd fight them all if he had to. Sons of bitches.

He felt a flailing hand connect with something. Felt one of their blows thump against the side of his head. Felt or more accurately heard the blow, for it seemed he could hear the sound of it much more clearly than he could feel it. He was kind of numb all over and particularly from the neck up. Damned if that wasn't the truth. He was numb but that wasn't going to stop him now that he was on the prod. Take them all on. Whoever the hell they were. Take them on and all their kith and kin to boot.

Boot. Damn right. The whore was just coming up off the bed, trying to get clear of the fight. Joe kicked her in the stomach, doubling her over. He kicked her again and someone pulled him over backward, a bunch of them swarming over top of him so that he couldn't reach the whore anymore. That made him right thoroughly mad.

"Dammit, Potter, she's gone. Now hold still, will you?"

He looked. Andy Plasser was holding him with some kind of wrestling lock around the neck. That Veile bastard had one of his arms and some fellow Joe'd never seen before had the other.

"What's got into you, Potter?"

Joe blinked. "Hey, Andy. What're you doing here?"

"You like to killed that woman, Potter. What'd she do to you?"

"Damn Indian, Andy. That's all. They're no damn good. None of them."

"That whore is no Indian, Potter."

"The hell you say."

"The hell I don't."

Joe began to laugh. "Damn. Now ain't that a joke on me."

Plasser gave him a funny look and after a moment let go the hold on Joe's neck. "Are you all right now?"

"Sure. Just fine. Why?"

"How much pay you got left on you, Potter?"

Joe shrugged.

"Whatever it is, damn you, hand it over. We'll see will they take that and call things square. Otherwise I'm thinking you'll be needing it for a lawyer."

"Lawyer? What the hell for, Andy? It was just a damn Indian I was showing who's boss."

"I told you, Potter, that woman is no Indian. Honest."

251

"You sure, Andy?"

"Real sure."

"I'll be damned."

"Yes, I expect you will be. Now hand over whatever you got left in your pockets. I'll get a couple of the boys to take you back to the Zeke."

"But what about...?"

"Never you mind what about. You get on back to the Zeke and stay there else you wind up in jail. If you do that, damn it, I got to find another man, and that wouldn't be so easy this time of year."

"Whatever you say, Andy." Joe grinned. "You know me, Andy. Never no trouble."

"You know, Potter, I never can figure out what all you believe of the things you say. It can't be very many, but sometimes I swear I think you believe at least some of them."

"Why, thank you, Andy. That's real nice of you to say so."

"It was not a compliment, Potter."

"No? You sure?"

The Zeke foreman gave Joe a look of sheer exasperation and shook his head slowly back and forth.

Joe grinned at him. And passed out.

THE BAYONET DROVE IN *deep. It slid into the flesh easily. Much easier than he would have guessed. You would think it would be hard to push even that sharp a splinter of steel into human flesh. There was bone in there, after all, and cartilage.*

Why, you could feel how hard the human chest was if you thumped yourself on the breastbone. A person would think that would be awfully difficult to penetrate.

But it wasn't.

In point of fact, the bayonet went in with surprising ease.

Went in seven, eight inches or maybe more.

Went in and then... stuck.

Stuck there like it had gone and taken root.

He couldn't push it in any deeper and couldn't pull it out.

Oh, he tried. He wrenched and twisted, waggled the rifle back and forth. Yanked it fore and back again.

The bayonet was just right properly stuck in place, that was all. And the skinny woman on the other end of the thing was still alive.

That was the awful thing about it. The woman was alive and looking at him whilst he killed her with his bayonet.

Her eyes were large and... not so much angry as they were sad. He could have accepted fury. Could have understood it. But not this quiet, solemn sadness.

That somehow made it all the worse.

He pulled and tugged some more, but it was no good. The bayonet was stuck and might stay there for all time yet to come, at least judging from the way it felt right at that exact moment.

But he would get in trouble with the quartermaster if he lost his bayonet or, worse yet, the rifle it was attached to.

He had to bring them back with him. He just had to. He had to get his bayonet and rifle out of the damned woman's chest.

If he could just... she went down, her strength beginning to ebb. She dropped down to her knees and reached up and wrapped both hands lightly around the forearm of the rifle stock, held on to the barrel and stock just a couple inches in front of the second iron band that held stock and action together.

He pulled and it was like she was pulling back against him. Like she was trying to hang on to the thing that pierced her body and was killing her. Maybe to hold it still. Maybe it hurt when the bayonet moved. Inside her there. Jesus!

He felt sick. And frantic with worry. He had to get his rifle and bayonet back. He really did have to.

It occurred to him that there was a way. Some of the older fellows had told him about it. He'd always thought they were just lying to him, making up whoppers and war stories about stuff like that. But maybe they hadn't been. Maybe they'd been telling him the truth at least some of the time.

He almost hated to try what they'd said. But what choice did he have?

The rifle was empty. He'd already fired it and not reloaded. He was pretty sure of that.

The woman was on her knees, her eyes big. She was watching him while he clung to the rifle with his left hand and with his right reached down and tripped the catch that let the trapdoor pop open. An empty cartridge case jumped partway out of the breach, and he pried it out with a thumbnail and tossed it on the ground.

The woman watched the glittering brass cylinder fall into the snow between them, then her eyes returned to him.

She watched him fumble in the black leather box at his waist while he found a fresh cartridge and shoved it into the chamber of the rifle.

She watched him push the trapdoor down until it snapped shut with a distinct click.

Watched him drag the big, heavy hammer back to cock the piece.

Did not close her eyes even when his right hand wrapped around the grip of the rifle and his glove-clumsy finger sought and found the trigger.

She knew. He would swear that she knew exactly what he was doing. And why.

Even then she did not close her eyes. She knelt in the snow watching while he yanked hard on the trigger.

The rifle bucked and something, the recoil of the gun or maybe the shock of the bullet passing within fractions of an inch of the steel bayonet, something about firing the rifle was enough to jar the bayonet free of the woman's flesh.

He had his rifle back in his hands, and the woman was no longer attached to the front of it.

She lay on her back now in the red-streaked snow.

Lay unmoving. No longer looking at him, although her eyes remained wide open. Not staring now, though. Not seeing anything now.

And on her breast the cloth of her clothes and blanket burned with a small, bright flame ignited by the gunpowder.

He turned away gagging and dropped to his knees, spewing his vomit onto the churned and already soiled snow there.

Chapter 13

1

ZK Ranch headquarters
Saturday, September 24, 1910

"Come in. Oh, it's you, Potter." The foreman's voice was neutral, neither particularly welcoming nor particularly annoyed. Joe had always preferred dealing with people he could read. He could fool Andy Plasser most of the time, but he could damn seldom figure him out.

When Joe came in Plasser had been bent over some tally books laid out on the open surface of the big rolltop. The front room of the main house had been made over into an office where the foreman spent much of his time. Comfortable place, too. Andy wasn't shy about spending for a few comforts. Not when they were his own. Own comforts, that is. The money to provide for them would have come off the company's books. There was even a Gramophone and box full of cylinders for it. Pretty dandy. Over in the working hands' bunkhouse they were lucky if they could find somebody with a mouth organ that hadn't been stepped on.

Now the foreman swung his oak swivel chair around to face the door. He pointed a finger toward one of the slick-seat straight-back chairs across the way. Joe grunted and took the weight off.

"What can I do for you, Potter?"

"It's about what you asked me the other day."

"Staying over for the winter, you mean?"

"That's right."

"I take it you've thought it over?"

"Yeah, I expect I have."

The foreman smiled. "Which wins out, Potter? That fat little old gal in Denver or some winter pay?"

Joe was surprised. He might have mentioned something about his Denver plans once before. But that would have been the better part of a year back. He was sure he hadn't said anything about Denver the other day when Plasser asked him about his plans for this year. Damn foreman never forgot anything, it seemed. But then he supposed that was what foremen were supposed to do. Officious bookkeepers with overlong memories, that's what they were. Bury themselves in musty ledgers and have to keep up with the wee tiniest detail. That wasn't Joe's idea of how authority should be put to use. But then he'd never been a dry, civilian foreman himself and wasn't ever likely to be. Didn't want to be, when it came right down to the truth of it.

"I expect I'll stay over," he said.

"All right, Potter, that takes care of that." Once again Joe could not tell if Plasser was pleased with the information. Or if he didn't especially give a damn.

The foreman turned his chair around with a squeaky creak of protest from the springs underneath it and leaned forward to rummage through the row of pigeonholes built over top of the leather-covered writing surface. It occurred to Joe that that desk was probably worth more than an ordinary cowhand earned in a full season of hard work. Owners and bosses, they always had it good.

Plasser found what he was looking for, shoved the rest of that particular bunch of papers back into their slot, and swung back to face Joe again, holding the sheet out for him to take.

"This is a copy of the list of supplies we generally lay in for the line shack. It's a standing order. Coosie will pick everything up when he goes in to buy the things he needs to stock the cook wagon for the fall roundup. He'll have Benny swing by and drop your stuff off at the cabin, then circle down again to join us at the working."

Joe nodded, glancing at the list. It was long. And contained a dozen or more things that he never would have thought of if he'd had a month and a half to plan all his winter supplies.

"I want you to go over that, Potter, and add anything else you want. Anything short of whiskey, that is. You'll see we provide you one quart of rye. Past that it's up to you if you want to pack in more. You're an old enough hand that I won't insult you with any lectures on that subject. I'll expect you to handle yourself with the outfit's best interests in mind."

Joe grunted and managed somehow to keep from laughing in the foreman's face. If that wasn't a line of bullshit he didn't know what was. Telling him how he wasn't going to get a lecture was just a left-handed way of giving him the damn lecture without having to come out and say any of it. Hell, he knew that. Who'd Plasser think he was dealing with here anyhow? Some wet-behind-the-ears kid on his first job? Joe Potter'd had authority, too, dammit. And hired men. Deputies, night patrolmen, Joe knew what it was to handle men.

"I appreciate you being that way about it, Andy, I surely do," Joe said smoothly, his face a study in true and humble sincerity.

"Anyway, Potter, look it over this weekend. Add whatever you think you'll want additional. Coosie will see that it's there when you get to the line camp after roundup."

"Hay and cordwood already laid in, are they?" Joe asked.

"The haying crew says you're all full up. There was some old hay left over from last year, they said. Not much. They hauled it out in the clear and burned it. Said there was some mold down inside it. No good for feeding anymore, so they got rid of it. Everything that's there now is fresh and bright. Good crop, they said. I haven't seen it myself, but I trust Hector Apolliano. He's the one who was in charge of the hayers this year. Good man, Hector."

"Absolutely," Joe agreed. Huh! Hector was a Mex.

"Turn that list back to me Sunday night or first thing Monday morning, Potter, so we'll have time to get it all laid in for you."

"I'll do that, Andy. Thank you." Joe stood, smiling on the surface, and carefully folded the list and buttoned it inside his shirt pocket where it couldn't get lost or too badly soiled.

2

Joe went out the back way and across the alley to the crapper. Damn beer got to him. Sometimes he would have sworn that he pissed more out than he drank in. Not bad stuff, though. And it didn't cloud the thinking as bad as whiskey does. At least not so quick. Better to stick with the beer when a man was playing cards.

He finished his business in the outhouse and let the spring-loaded door slap shut behind him as, still stooped over to finish buttoning his fly, he ambled back the way he'd come.

He heard something and caught some moving around over to his left in the shadows. He thought he recognized the voice and slowed a mite to listen in. After a moment he scowled and altered direction.

"Dammit, Hostin, what d'you think you're doing?"

"Gonna get me a little, Potter. What's it to you anyhow?"

Emil was young and dumb and generally easy to get along with but this evening he'd been drinking some. And maybe thinking about proving himself all grown up, too. Joe could remember how that was, the biggest problem with it being that a yonker who was still worrying about being grown most likely wasn't.

Stupid youngun had a girl caught in a corner where the back of Jelliman's Saloon met up with the side wall of the hardware store next door.

There wasn't anything wrong with that except for the girl not being more than eleven or twelve years old. She didn't more than come up to Hostin's shirt pockets, and she was so skinny and scrawny she looked like she ought to be staked out in a corn patch. More to the point, though, she was not at all interested in selling what Emil wanted to buy. When he reached down to grope and feel of her she tried to twist away and started to cry some. She would have run except that Hostin had his other hand tight around her upper arm.

"Leave her be, Hostin. She don't want your money. And hell, you don't want to go around messing with some kid too little to have hair. That's a bad habit. Get people to talking nasty about you if you do like that. You wouldn't want that, man."

The girl looked at Emil and then at Joe and then she busted out in a rapid flow of gobbledygook noises that Joe couldn't understand and he was sure Hostin couldn't either.

Joe cussed more than a little bit then. Damn kid was an Indian. He hadn't been able to see that in the bad light, just how little she was. Now he'd gone and done it.

"You telling me what to do, Potter?" Hostin asked belligerently.

"Hell no, Emil."

"That's better."

"I'm telling you what *not* to do."

"What?"

"Leave her be, Emil. She's just a kid. Damn Indian kid at that. Likely already got diseases that'd shrivel a fellow's wonker and make him useless. Maybe make the damn

262

thing curl up and fall right off. You'd be in a helluva fix then. Have to squat to pee. And I want you to know, Emil, when all the rest of the boys tell me you already squat to pee, I tell them they're wrong. I always tell them you don't have to do that. It's just you *prefer* peeing that way."

Hostin laughed, his mood lightening considerably. After all, Potter was one of the senior hands. And not much given to horse-play like the younger fellows were.

"Look, Joe, I'm just wanting to get me a little. You know?"

"Of course I know, kid. Just don't force it on some baby that don't want to play. Take it upstairs. There's grown women up there as know what to do when they get a hold of a man's tool. Let one of them fix you up. Go on now. All it takes in there is a Yankee dollar and the nerve to walk up them stairs. Kid like this, she's like to scream and carry on. Then where would you be? Have to pay off her old man. Maybe get a doctor for her. Shit, Emil, you'd end up spending five, ten times what it'll cost you inside. And those hoors in there know how to please. Little bitty thing like this wouldn't know what to do with it anyhow. Go on now." Joe slapped Hostin on the shoulder and added, "When you're done come back downstairs and I'll buy you a beer. How's that?"

"You serious, Joe?"

"Hell, yes, I'm serious. Go on now."

Hostin grinned and went inside.

Joe lingered behind for a moment, scowling again, peering down at the Indian kid that was still backed tight into the corner and acting like she wasn't sure but what she'd traded one threat for another when Hostin left and Potter stayed behind.

Ugly, Joe thought. He couldn't see why Emil would have wanted any of that to start with, never mind her being just a kid. They weren't any one of them worth a healthy crap.

The girl said something to him, the incomprehensible words soft and shy.

Potter frowned. He didn't want the little bitch thinking she had anything to be grateful to him about.

He turned his head and spat, making it about as cold and as rude as he could manage so that the stinking kid wouldn't mistake his intent, then spun around and stomped indoors, leaving the girl child in the shadows behind Jelliman's place.

3

"Come in, Potter."

The foreman was again—or for all Joe knew was still—seated in front of the rolltop with a bunch of books and papers to work on. Lousy job, the way Joe saw it.

"Is that the list? Good." Plasser took the paper from him and motioned for him to sit.

Joe crossed his legs and leaned back. He was tired. Sometimes a man needed a week of hard work just so he could get some rest. This looked to be one of those times.

Of course he better rest fast if he wanted to get the job done. Come Thursday morning they were supposed to pull out for the roundup.

Meet up with the reps and the hands from all the other outfits on Friday evening and start the fall working come first light Saturday.

The fur would be flying—and a helluva lot of dust along with it—from then straight on until the last cow was counted and the last calf earmarked and branded and the last culls put aside to be shipped.

It was always a gamble whether to ship and sell in the fall market or risk winterkill and whatever else to wait on the spring prices. And a man never knew whether the prices would go up in the next six months or turn around and plummet. All of that depended on market conditions in Chicago and Kansas City and far-off places like that. Joe didn't understand all that market stuff and didn't want to. Wouldn't want to be the one, like Andy Plasser, who had to guess what a bunch of crazy city people were going to do come next year.

Andy grunted.

"Say what?"

"You added an awful lot of tinned milk and sugar and molasses to the list."

"If you got a problem with how I like my coffee, Andy, speak right up and tell me you want me to change. I can try and take it black. I'm not sure how that'd work out, but I expect I can try if you want."

"You can't... no of course you aren't serious. And that isn't at all what I'm saying. Naturally we'll lay in whatever you think you need. I just never noticed you using so much of the stuff. I don't mind it. Just kind of was surprised. But it's no problem, Potter, and I'm not telling you how to take your coffee." He spun his chair to face the desk and took up a pen, one of those fancy patented fountain pens with a gold nib and a rubber reservoir of ink carried right inside it. Nothing but the best for the bosses, no sir. The foreman uncapped the pen and put a quickly scrawled set of initials onto the revised list. "Take this to Coosie and tell him he's to make sure he gets the items you added. And if you have any special instructions on where you want things put or how they ought to be packed, this is the time to pass them along."

"No special deal, Andy. I know it will all be done just fine." Joe held his hat in both hands and gave the foreman a boyishly inoffensive grin. "I know you got everything under control. You always do."

Plasser gave him a look that said the foreman suspected he was being buttered up. But there was no way he could prove that and for sure no way the man could object to a touch of flattery. Joe felt like busting out laughing except of course he didn't dare. Not where Andy Plasser could see, he couldn't.

"Is there anything else, Potter?"

"No, Andy, I don't reckon there is."

"Take this to Coosie then."

"I'll do that right this minute."

"Oh, and Potter."

"Yes?"

"Tell Coosie to send over a pot of coffee for me, will you?" The foreman frowned. "I'm afraid this is going to be a long night."

"I'll fetch it along myself if he's too busy, Andy."

Again there was that look of mild skepticism.

Then the foreman turned back to his desk, and Joe let himself out into the ranch yard.

He was whistling as he ambled across the yard toward the cookhouse.

THE TREES WERE BARE *of leaves, the pale limbs and myriad twigs combining to present an appearance of soft, lifeless gray that filled the bottoms along the watercourses and from a distance looked amazingly like mist or smoke.*

On the plains and the barren hillsides the grasses were an equally pale tan, dry and colorless and empty.

In the villages the lodge walls were all rolled down to meet the ground instead of being tied high to allow for the circulation of cooling air. Now the need was for warmth, and the insulating wall liners had been put into place, dangling from the lodgepoles and forming a skirt around the interior of the conical lodges—the mobile skin structures he once thought were called tepees—so heat would be trapped inside and the soon-to-come winds of winter be handily excluded.

It amazed him how efficient, seemingly simple but not so much so as they first looked, these tall and really quite immense native tents could be.

He had been shy the first time he was invited into a lodge. Shy and, indeed, quite honored. Boys in blue wool sometimes pushed inside the lodges. But in arrogance that was, with rifles in hand and frowns on their faces, and not by smiling invitation of the owners of the lodges that were so invaded. He did not know anyone else who was ever made welcome, and it pleased him to be singled out and made much of in this way.

That first time he had been led by the hand— quite literally so, since there was no language in common among them—and led around the rim of the lodge, keeping well back so that he was not allowed to walk between his hosts and the firepit in the center, and taken to a seat of honor with a hair-filled pad for a chair and a cunningly woven willow backrest to lounge against.

It was all quite fascinating to him. The bags and bundles and leather pouches hung from the poles around the walls and the robes and blankets and more boxes or bundles piled here and there to form beds and partitions and even, more or less, areas of some small degree of privacy. For after all, a very large family lived here, and there were no interior walls nor any visual partitioning to keep any one person from watching what all the others were about.

Odd, he thought, his first question—unasked and unaskable—being how a couple ever managed to have a second child. Or for that matter a first one, since each lodge seemed to hold many more adults than the single, basic pairing one would expect. He was not sure who all the extras might be. Uncles, perhaps, and aunts and grandparents and cousins and... there was no telling the extent to which that could be taken.

There was so much he did not know. But it was all thrilling. Mysterious and exotic and deliciously foreign.

He was seated, smiled at, waited upon. He was given coffee, bitter with acids and gritty with grounds and no small amount of sand as well, but welcome for its intent if not for its excellence.

Several adult males, probably with some relationship to Joey but he was not entirely sure about that, were seated in the circle immediately about him, as were a number of women. Those, however, came and went without seeming purpose, sitting for a while and then either moving elsewhere

269

within the lodge or slipping quietly out into the evening air.

Off to one side—there were no corners to banish them to or likely that would have been done—a gaggle of small children grinned and giggled shyly from behind upraised hands that were held between him and themselves like small shields, showing only their huge, laugh-crinkled eyes above.

The one exception to this separation of grown-ups and children was Joey who, presumably as a special treat for this auspicious occasion only, was given a seat immediately to the right of his friend and mentor, provider and sometime protector.

From that place of honor Joey altered between mugging for his young chums and contemporaries and preening with self-important puffery before his elders.

He did seem proud of himself that day.

Once the ritual of the coffee was ended, a meal was served. A thick and savory stew served in a tin bowl—he had expected something considerably less mundane and ordinary than that—that contained hunks of unidentifiable meat that he hoped was ordinary and mundane along with common vegetables like potato and carrot and turnip, the whole dipped up with a nearly flat horn spoon that proved something of a challenge when it came to the juices. The stew was palatable if bland. The only disconcerting part of the meal was that he seemed to be the only one partaking of it. The others, male and female, adult or otherwise, sat in wide-eyed silence and stared at him while he ate. That had the effect, intentional or otherwise, of making his meal a brief one. He finished quickly, wiped his mouth ostentatiously on his sleeve, and loudly thanked his hosts for their hospitality in a language none of them understood in the least.

Language, however, was unnecessary. Communication could be had by other means, and broadly exaggerated gestures were enough to bring huge smiles onto the dark faces that surrounded him.

After that—he was amazed to realize it was still daylight outside even though he felt like hours had passed since he was brought here—Joey stood and took him by the hand and led him out.

They were followed by every man, woman, and child who had been so engrossed in observing his eating habits. They lined up, the men first, and one by one filed past to vigorously shake his hand and say something, he had no idea what, in their own tongue.

He thanked, bowed, shook hands until he was sure there could be no doubting his gratitude for the occasion.

Then Joey took him by the hand and, strutting and preening once more, led him to the edge of the encampment.

There were other visits after that and other lodges, but none ever made such a memorable impression as that one.

Chapter 14

1

ZK Ranch line shack
Wednesday, October 19, 1910

He saw the thin plume of smoke pale against the intense blue of the sky even before he topped the last rise. He grunted aloud, causing his horse's ears to twitch and rotate in response to the unaccustomed sound of a man-voice, for unlike some this was not a rider given to talking to his mount.

He rode slowly down the final slope and into the bare yard, leading his short string of circle horses.

The woman came out to take the horses from him, her appearance as common and as ordinary as if it had been happening each evening at this hour the whole summer long.

His face remained set and without expression, showing neither greeting nor pleasure. He simply swung out of the saddle and handed the reins to her, turning his back and walking away to leave her to the work of unsaddling and grooming and feeding the stock.

The cabin door—he noted from the sound that it was spring-loaded now; someone had gone to the trouble of mounting a keeper on it although whether that was Apolliano or the woman he did not know and was unlikely to ask—pushed open and the kid came rushing out to greet him.

Sarah had grown half a foot since he last saw her. Looked like that much anyhow. And she was much steadier on her feet now. But no more reserved than when she'd last come running to him. She came at full tilt, grinning hugely, arms lifted high and small legs churning.

"Daddy." She was a-bubble with joy at the sight of him.

He bent and in self-defense lest she knock his pins out from under him and bowl him clean over snatched her up, using the momentum of her own headlong charge to carry her high overhead, swinging her into the air as she shivered with the pleasure of it all, then dropping her into the crook of an arm while she flung her own chubby arms around his neck and squeezed with all her tiny might.

She planted a wet, sloppy kiss on his cheek, the moisture cold in the chill autumn air, and squealed her joy.

"Come on, dammit, you don't have your coat on. You ought to know better than to come outside this time of year without a coat." He had no idea if she could understand him or not. When they were here her mother mostly talked English to her. But the rest of the year she likely heard that Indian crap all the time, so there was some doubt about what she could figure out and what was just so much noise to her.

Besides, how much does any damn kid know when they were this small? Joe had no experience with children. Didn't want any

273

for that matter. Damn nuisances. They would all be better off drowned.

"Come on, then, before you catch cold."

Sarah squealed louder than ever, bouncing and squirming within his grasp, and gave him a kiss even wetter than the first had been.

He lengthened his pace and hurried to get the damn kid inside and away from the cold.

2

There was coffee ready on the stove—and a real coffeepot this time instead of the battered pan that had been used for one before; damn woman must have thought to bring it along, for that hadn't been on the list, and Apolliano wouldn't have given a shit about it—and a bowl of sugar and a yet-to-be-opened tin of milk on the table beside the heavy, crockery cup—another thing new this fall—set out for him.

The shelves and bins and floor space close to the stove were all bulging full of the supplies the Zeke sent up. Joe supposed he should take an inventory of it all to see that Coosie's halfwit helper Benny hadn't stolen him blind when he hauled everything in last month. He supposed he should, but he knew he wouldn't likely ever get around to it. That was one of those things that are shot full of good intentions but never really happen.

The important thing was that there was plenty enough to eat. This year there wouldn't be any running out of milk and sugar and things like that. Wouldn't be or else there would be hell to pay with the woman for being wasteful, damn her.

Joe set Sarah down and poured himself a cup of the coffee even before he took his coat off and tossed it in the general direction of the door where the woman would find it and take care of it when she came in.

He admired the new coffeepot for a moment, then set it back onto the stovetop and carried his cup to the table. He spooned in plenty of sugar and used the foldout awl point from his pocketknife—first wiping the thing on the leg of his britches, for that was the same point he always used for cleaning horses' hoofs—to poke a couple holes in the milk can. The coffee was just exactly the way he liked it best, light brown and syrupy and with a brisk, rich flavor to it. Just right. With a sigh he settled onto a chair at the table there.

More than half expecting Sarah to join him for a swallow of the thick, sweetened coffee—and maybe half disappointed when she didn't—he looked around.

The kid was over by the foot of the bed leaning down and messing inside the sleeping box there.

Joe frowned. That was odd now that he thought of it. Sarah had pretty much outgrown her box last spring. And she was a damn sight bigger now than she'd been then. So what. . . ?

He thought about that for just a bit and then realized. What with Sarah getting bigger and likely to pay more attention to what was going on around her now, the woman was probably thinking about the kid looking on and seeing what him and her mother did in the evenings. And for that matter sometimes in the early mornings, too. And wasn't he damn sure ready for some of that again. All he wanted and not having to pay for it piece by piece. Damn right he was ready for it. And yeah, maybe he could see that Sarah shouldn't be watching.

But sticking a kid her size into a box like some kind of kitten or puppy or something, that wasn't right. Never mind that she was only an Indian, shit, he didn't particularly want that.

He'd speak to the woman about it. Maybe get her to hang a blanket for a partition and sort of wall off the other bed over in the empty front corner.

He looked over there. And frowned.

The second bed was made up. The ticking had been stuffed and laid out on the ropes—new ropes, too, judging by the light yellow color instead of the gray and withered old ones—and blankets and a pillow laid ready.

If that Indian thought she was going to stay over there by herself he'd thump that notion out of her right quick. She would do what he damn well told her, or she'd have the bruises to convince her otherwise.

"Daddy."

"I'm not your da… I'm not your daddy, kid."

She was grinning like hell and acted like she didn't understand a word he was saying. And, hell, probably she didn't.

"Yeah, all right, I'm coming."

He set his cup onto the table and, groaning from the effort of moving again after the long ride up from the Zeke, came to his feet.

Damn kid seemed almighty interested in the

sleeping box, he thought. Likely had a new corn-husk dolly or some such to show off to him there.

Well, what the hell. It couldn't hurt for him to take a look at it. He stifled a yawn and shuffled over to the box at the foot of the bed.

Joe slapped the woman. Hard. She gasped and closed her eyes but didn't try to turn away, didn't try to run. She held herself stiff, head down and eyes squeezed tightly shut but her hands kept at waist level. She made no move to block his blow or to defend herself.

He slapped her again, a backhanded swipe this time. Her head jerked. A thin, dilute stream of blood and spittle trickled out of the right corner of her mouth and down her chin.

He raised his fist as if to club her to her knees, hesitated, and instead reached out to grab a handful of hair at the back of her head very much like one would take hold of a dog—in this case a bitch—to pick it up.

Just as rough and painfully as he could he yanked her around and pushed her across the floor until she was standing over the box.

"How dare you," he told her. "How damn dare you. Bad enough you bring the first brat. Now another one, too? Damn you."

Sarah, wide-eyed and frightened now, began to cry. That woke the baby that was sleeping in the box, and it began to cry, too.

The woman stood silent while Joe shook her like a terrier shakes a rat, doing his best to rattle the brains, what she had of them, clean out of her head.

"Bitch," he told her.

Sarah, still crying, took hold of his leg with one arm and pummeled him on the thigh with her other hand.

He wasn't angry with her about that. Any kid will defend its dam. That was only right and proper. Besides, she didn't know his reasons. She was too little to understand.

But the woman. That was another story. She should have left the kid, the new one, or hell the both of them, Sarah and this other one, too, back on the stinking reservation for somebody to take care of. If there is one thing a lousy Indian always has it's a bunch of relatives. Bunch of animals, all of them. Swarm like cockroaches. And about as useful as a nest of roaches.

"Well?" he demanded. He shook her again.

Her eyes remained tight shut and he thought he saw the glint of tears in the corners of her eyes. Served her right, damn her. He hoped he hurt her bad enough to make her cry. She would be damn lucky if that's all he did.

He let go of her so he could punch her one on the side of the head with the heel of his hand—he knew better than to hit an Indian on the head with his knuckles; do that and he'd wind up busting his hand; thickheaded sons of bitches every one of them—and looked down to see was there anything he could do to make Sarah quit beating on him. It wasn't bothering him so much except that, shit, he'd as soon she calmed down now.

Quick as he turned his attention off her the woman bent down and picked up the bawling infant. Picked it up out of the box and pulled her dress open and offered it a tit.

"What are you, some kind of damn cow? Every time I see you you're dripping milk," he complained.

At least it was quieter with the kid, the baby one that is, sucking. And once the little one quit bawling so did Sarah. Joe leaned down and picked her up, thinking maybe that would keep her from starting in to bellowing again.

The woman looked over to him and Sarah, then down again to the one that was sucking at her dug.

"This baby is named Joseph."

"What the hell is...?"

"This baby is your baby."

"You expect me to believe that?"

"I do not neither expect or don't expect. It does not matter to me what you believe, Joseph Potter. This baby is your son. I told you before, I am a Christian woman. I was with my husband dead all this long time. I was with you. There was no other. It is too long for this baby to be the child of my dead husband. But you believe what you want to believe. I only tell you what is true. You decide what you want to think. Not me." She hunched her shoulders and transferred the kid to her other arm, switching it to the other tit when she did so.

"You're a liar," he said.

The woman shrugged and turned away. Holding the infant nested in her arm, she went to the stove and began setting pans out ready for making supper.

Sarah touched him on the cheek and he looked at her. She probably needed some reassurance.

But he did not know how to give it.

He carried her back to the table and sat down with her in his lap. When he picked up his coffee cup she reached for it, and he let her have a swallow, taking that as a sign that she was over being upset.

3

"Joseph Daniel Potter. That is what I name him. Do you know of Daniel?"

"Who?"

"Daniel of the den of lions. In the Bible, yes. He walked with the lions but they did not bite him because his faith was strong. A child with the name of Daniel will not be bitten by the evil around him when his faith is strong."

Joe grunted and kept his eyes averted from the sight of the kid—swarthy little son of a bitch—noisily sucking. Greedy, strong little bastard, it was.

"I still say it isn't mine."

The woman said nothing.

It was at least five minutes later that he looked over at her—the kid was done eating; now it was sprawled on her belly sound asleep—and frowned just a little. "You naming him Daniel and that stuff about him being in a den of evil lions... that shit have anything to do with me?"

"Why would you think a thing like that, Joseph Potter?"

He scowled some more. But did not answer. Damn woman didn't say anything more either, and he decided it might be best to just let it be.

HE WAS IN A FIELD *white, snowy white, smooth and virginal snow, walking among bright and brilliant blossoms. Gold and yellow and red blossoms of quick-growing, short-lived eruptions.*

He watched with acute interest as shells from the Hotchkiss guns floated in amongst the people.

The shells landed on the snow-covered field and grew into blossoms there, first the petals of fire spreading, sending up leaves of flying snow and frozen earth around them.

And spreading their pollen amid the people.

Pollen of hot, jagged steel. Splinters of shrapnel.

The pollen from these flowers sought all flesh without regard to age or gender.

This pollen was cleansing. But it did not give new life, oh no.

He watched, absorbed in the many sights.

Watched the sharp steel pollen spread out from each new blossom.

Watched the splinters cut and tear. A woman's flesh entered here, a man's there.

Saw babies ripped and children shredded.

Viewed with intense fascination the sight of a shard of twisted steel eviscerate an old man who looked dumbly down at the moist, glistening, red and white and gray of his intestines as they spilled out of his belly and coiled on the frozen ground. The old man tried to wlk away, dragging the tangled mass behind him, leaving a red-smeared track in the white of the snow.

Saw a woman's throat open up to spill bright blood over her child, the hot blood steaming in the bitter cold so that for a time it looked as if the child were emitting smoke or was giving off some ghastly mist.

Watched the shells blossom and soon fade again.

Watched the people scream and watched the people die.

And all of it in a slow silence.

There should be noises. He knew there should be noises. No sound reached him.

No feeling reached him.

Not sound. Not cold. Not pity.

He was numb to all he saw. He was no part of it. Held himself aloof from it. Saw it all as if from a distance. Watched with the idle disdain of a spectator. Was not touched, could not be touched by anything that happened here.

Wondered idly, disinterested yet mildly curious, about an infant whose head was missing. Not mangled, not crushed, but simply... gone. And apart from that not so much as a bruise. Curious. So curious.

Later, when the civilian gravediggers came, hired at day wage to dig the hard-frozen soil and cover over the many interesting sights, then he asked. And they, too, were curious. Everyone he spoke to had seen or at the very least heard of the child whose skull was gone. No one remembered finding a head that lacked a body.

That was funny, he thought.

Surely they would have remembered a thing like that. Surely someone would have mentioned it.

Or would they?

He did not know.

Not anymore.

There was much that he was unsure of now.

Chapter 15

1

Tuesday, November 29, 1910

The woman washed Daniel's butt—he had put his foot down about that; she could think of the kid as being Joseph if she wanted to, but they would call him Daniel, not Joseph—and made up a fresh wad of the soft, compacted fluff from some tree bark or whatever, packed that around him, and then tied his diaper back in place.

She kept Daniel clean, he would say that for her. And well fed. Damn woman made milk like a dairy cow. There was enough for all of them to share if that was what was wanted. Which it was not.

She finished with Daniel and laid him back into his box. Sarah wiggled off the side of the bed, abandoning Joe in favor of her baby brother, and went over to peer into the box and assure herself that Daniel was all right.

She was a solicitous little nit, Sarah was. Practically a second mother to the little guy.

And Daniel, he really wasn't much of a nuisance. As babies go, that is.

Eat, sleep, belch, and shit, that was about all he was good for. But he was most always in a good humor, laughing and cooing and trying to pull Sarah's hair.

He wasn't so damn dark either. The woman

284

was practically as black as a nigger. And Sarah was pretty dark, too, although not as bad as her mother. Her color was closer to that of a Mexican but with a hint of copper in it instead of just being brown. Daniel, though, it would be hard to figure out what he was just from looking. There was no telling how that would go for him when he got grown. Of course it was too soon to tell anything, really, about what he would look like then. He might darken up considerable. Might end up looking Indian through and through.

Not that it mattered. Joe didn't figure he would ever know anyway.

Another season or two, he'd be getting too stiff and stove up to spend his winters riding line through this cold, miserable country.

He'd go south then. Stay south. Maybe even see could he find work as a cop again. He would like that. It would feel good to walk tall and cocky again with a pistol on his hip and a brass shield shiny on his chest. It could happen again.

Go to Arizona Territory, say. It was supposed to be warm there. And no one knew him in that country. He could go down where it was warm the whole year around and get a completely fresh start. He wouldn't have to tell anybody anything more than he wanted them to know. It wasn't anybody's damn business what he'd done in the past anyway.

The past didn't matter to anybody.

Not even to him.

"Give me some coffee," he told the woman. "And put some apple butter on some of that pan bread you got left over from breakfast. Make some for Sarah, too, while you're about it."

"As you say, yes."

2

The woman came in from tending to his horse. It was still fairly early. The water holes hadn't started to freeze over yet, so all he had to do was make sure the graze was clear of everything except Zeke beeves. And that wasn't difficult yet either, since the snows they'd had so far were all light, none of it the deep, windblown stuff that would start the cattle drifting.

This was a fat time of year, the work easy and the days short.

Joe had Daniel on his left arm and Sarah perched on his right knee. She was busy trying to sneak a sip of sweetened, milk-laden coffee to her brother while Joe was just as busy trying, without words, to discourage her from that abuse. It seemed to have become more of a game with her than any serious inclination to pour coffee into the little guy.

The woman took Daniel from him and fed the kid, then changed him and returned him to Joe. She set a cutting board onto the table and brought out her best knife, then unwrapped a bundle that she took down from a high shelf. The bundle turned out to be a dark red haunch.

"Deer meat?"

"Yes."

"Your uncle been here again?"

"The uncle of my dead husband, he was here."

286

"You gonna do that thing with the fresh deer meat? You know, how you cut it up in the little pieces and flour and fry it?"

"That is the way you like it, yes?"

"Damn right it is."

"Damn right," Sarah mimicked.

The woman gave him a hard look. Well, shit, maybe he earned that one, he conceded. But not out loud.

Maybe he'd ought to watch his words from now on. Around the place anyhow. He could cuss outside. Damn horse wouldn't mind. But it wasn't right for a little girl, even an Indian little girl, to be hearing talk like that.

"I will cook the meat the way you like it."

"Good," Joe said, feeling virtuous about not adding any emphasis to the statement, anything of the sort that Sarah and for that matter Daniel shouldn't hear.

The woman was busy stripping long pieces of meat off the venison haunch, pulling with the lie of the muscle and separating the pieces into inch-wide strips, then laying the slender strips of fresh meat on the cutting board and slicing them into small cubes that she would dredge in salted flour and deep-fry in tallow. Based on past experience the result would be about the tenderest and most tasty meat Joe ever put a tooth to. He was looking forward to it.

"Aiyee." She stopped what she was doing and slapped the flat of her hand to her forehead.

"What was that about?"

"I forgot. Sorry."

"Forgot what?"

She held a finger up to tell him to wait, then left the table and got a small, oilcloth packet from a shelf. "The uncle of my dead husband said I should give you this."

"Yeah? What the he—what is it?"

"It is not for me. I do not know what is inside. Open. You will see then."

"I'll be da—uh—arned."

He put his coffee cup down—out of Sarah's reach lest she try to put one by him—and dragged the packet closer. "You want to help me open this?"

Sarah understood some English or else managed to get the general drift of things from his tone of voice, for she didn't waste any time peeling the oilcloth back.

What came to light was a black, gooey lump of something that looked pretty much like tar.

Except it wasn't tar. Not hardly.

Joe hadn't seen anything like that in... in an awfully long time. Hadn't ever expected to see any ever again neither.

The woman looked puzzled.

"You know what this stuff is?" he asked her.

"Yes, of course." She said something, he supposed the name of the stuff, in her own tongue. "You know?"

"Yeah. Sort of."

She raised an eyebrow but did not question him. Instead she observed, "It has been many years since I have tasted this. Many years since anyone I know of makes it."

Hesitantly, almost reluctantly, Joe reached out and took a dab of the goo onto a fingertip.

The flavor came rushing back to him almost before the native candy—or whatever—touched his tongue.

It was as he remembered. Suety, almost smoky but lightly sweet with the bright, sharp flavor of berries. He remembered it all right.

He took another, somewhat larger portion onto his fingertip and fed that to Sarah and then—he more than half expected a protest from the woman although none came—to Daniel.

Damn stuff was likely spoiled, though. Or else maybe it was going down wrong. He felt it clog up in his throat and for a moment thought he would choke.

He grabbed his coffee cup and took a deep gulp of the hot stuff, and that seemed to help.

"You are all right?"

"I'm fine, dammit," he snapped, hardly aware that the cuss word had jumped out before he had time to think. Well, damn kid was bound to hear a little something every now and then. It wouldn't do any real harm, dammit.

"Go ahead," he said. "Have some if you want."

The woman nodded and took a taste, smiling after she did so and bobbing her head. "Very good. The wife of my dead husband's uncle made this. You like?"

He shrugged, unwilling to say that he liked it.

For that matter, dammit, he wasn't entirely sure that he did.

The time he had had it before... it had been too long. And too much had happened since then.

"I don't want no more of it," Joe said. "You can give the rest of it to the kids. They seem to like it pretty good."

"Yes. As you say."

He did not ask why in hell her uncle—all right, her dead husband's damned uncle— would have sent any of this to him.

Nor did she ask him either.

3

If the woman said anything, if she uttered the first damn word, he was going to punch her right in the mouth. He surely would.

He'd seen it coming but too late to do anything about.

By accident she'd opened the wrong side of his saddlebags. She had his lunch wrapped in a bit of cloth and was going to put it into the saddlebag pocket like she did every damn morning, but today the bags had been hung on the peg wrongside-to and she opened the other pouch, the one where he kept his tools, his wire cutters and fence pliers and staples and such, and so she went and saw what he kept hidden there.

She looked in, saw, but didn't say anything.

Lucky for her.

She would go and spoil everything if she opened her stupid mouth, but she held back and the moment passed and then it was all right. He sat back and let the tension drain out of him.

She turned the saddlebags around the way

they should be, put his lunch inside, and then fastened both pouches shut again.

"Do you want me to saddle the horse now?"

"Yeah, you do that. I'll want the grulla today. The sorrel was limping last time I used it. I want to let it rest another couple days before I take it again."

"The grulla, yes."

"I'll finish this and be along in a minute."

"I will have the horse ready."

Joe drained his coffee near to the bottom but not quite and gave the last, sugary swallow to Sarah.

He ruffled her hair, turned her in the direction of Daniel's box, and gave her a pat on the backside. "Watch out for your brother now. Your mama will be back soon."

She grinned at him and went scampering off to do what she was told. At least that's what he assumed she was doing. If she understood any of the words. He still wasn't sure about that.

He took his coat down and got into it but left the ax where it was. There was still no need for it, nor for the rabbit-skin boots and heavy muffler. He wouldn't have to resort to those until the hard cold set in. And he was willing to wait for that along until next July or thereabouts. It wouldn't hurt his feelings any if the winter proved mild.

He checked on Daniel while he buttoned his coat, winked at Sarah, and went on out.

The grulla was saddled and waiting for him, the woman standing there holding it.

He swung onto the saddle, shrugged, and reined away, walking the horse only a short way and then bumping it into a lope. The horse hadn't warmed up yet and he shouldn't use it at more than a walk for very long until it did. But then he had no intention of going far just yet.

Soon as he was out of sight of the cabin he stopped and turned around sideways—the grulla, thank goodness, would stand idle without a body having to fret with it all the damn time—so he could unbuckle the straps on the saddlebag pouch.

He knew the woman hadn't messed with anything. But he wanted to see that for himself. He reached down into the pouch and pushed aside the greasy cloth that he wrapped his things in. Including the short, stubby, exceptionally sharp knife he carried there.

Yeah, there it was, dammit.

He pulled the thing out and turned it over in his hand.

Damn thing didn't look like much. Not yet. But it would. He was no great shakes as a craftsman and couldn't make horsehair gear worth a shit. But if he did say so he was a fair hand at carving wood.

Rough as it still was, the shape of the head and the outline of the face were coming along pretty good. Finish this head, he figured, and make a couple hands and a couple feet, then all he'd need would be some cloth and stuffing and he'd have a pretty damn decent doll for Sarah's Christmas. Get that out of the way and he could make a gourd rattle—he figured he would carve some pretty designs on the outside of the thing so it wouldn't seem too plain next to Sarah's dolly—for Daniel.

It was going to be all right, he supposed, but he felt sort of uncomfortable knowing the woman was aware now of what he was doing. It wasn't that he was ashamed of it exactly. Just that he never in his life did anything like this before.

It felt more than a little strange to him now.

THE RED CAPOTE *provided the only color to be found
in any direction. Any. From horizon to horizon
there were only the white of the snow and the black
of the lumps lying immobile on it. No hue or tint
or relieving color.*

Except for the crimson capote.

*It, too, lay on the snow. Crumpled. Abandoned.
Forlorn.*

*He stared at it from a distance, then circled wide
around so as to view it from all sides. He could
hear his footsteps crunching in the snow crust. He
moved slowly and very smoothly in a perfect circle with the red capote in its middle and yet the
sounds of the footsteps were quick and slightly errat-
ic, as of someone running over uneven ground.*

*It was really quite odd that movement and
sound failed to blend, but this puzzlement was not
disturbing, merely noted as from a distance.*

*And still all about, in every direction, there was
no color save that of the brilliant red capote.
White of snow. Black of fallen objects. And the stark,
eye-jolting red of the capote.*

*He viewed it with curiosity. A complete circle
around it in a counterclockwise direction, then
reversing to make another turnabout in the other.*

No other color, no other sound.

*He moved, drifting effortlessly a few inches above
the snow surface like a moth fluttering over the
unblemished sheen of a pond in the morning's still-
ness, moved closer to the capote, closer and closer still.*

*He could see it better now. The color as before
but now the texture as well. It was a fine capote,
a garment its owner could wear with pride.*

*Yet it lay here in disarray, abandoned and...
empty? Not empty. He was near enough now to
see that something small lay half hidden beneath
the rumpled folds of fallen cloth.*

Something small and pale and still.

*A sense of unease washed through him, filling
his breast with dread that had neither form nor
apparent cause although he could not deny its presence. It brought his breath up short and set his pulse
to racing.*

*Whatever lay within the capote... he did not
want to see, did not want to know.*

Against his volition he came nearer, nearer.

*Found himself looking down upon the bright
red cloth.*

*Realized that not all the red was that of the cloth.
There was the scarlet of blood as well. Scarlet capote.
Bloodstained garment.*

*And within it, imperfectly hidden... he tried to
close his eyes. Did not want to see. The vision
remained before him no matter that he labored to
squeeze his eyelids shut.*

*Inside the capote like the pale center of a scar-
let flower, a tiny face was lifted to his view. A small
face that was pale with death, pale with a rime
of ice crystals in the cold, a small face with pale
lips and sightless eyes staring into the empty cold
of a bleak eternity.*

*He knew the face. Child's face. Beloved face.
He leaned closer.*

And recoiled in horror.

*The face was not the one he expected there. Was
not Joey.*

Daniel. It was Daniel he saw there.

Lying in the folds of the red capote.

Daniel.

295

He came awake with a start. Found himself sitting upright on the hard bed. His heart pounded and his breath was coming in fast, labored gasps. A cold, greasy sweat gathered on his forehead, and he felt a sickness in the pit of his stomach.

A nightmare. That's what it must have been. Damn nightmare.

That was all it was. Whatever it was. He could not remember what had startled him so. In truth he did not want to remember. Not something that made him feel this anxious and afraid.

Just a damn nightmare.

He reached out to the sleeping woman, took the hem of her nightdress and yanked it to her waist, then roughly dragged her nearer leg wide apart from the other and, squirming onto his side and wriggling closer, attempted to find exemption from his nightthoughts.

Just a damn nightmare.

Chapter 16
1

Tuesday, January 24, 1911

Lazy damned bitch. It was her job to take care of the horse when he got in. So where the hell was she? Probably so full from eating all his food that she had to lay down and sleep it off.

Didn't she bother to think that he was cold and tired now? He'd been outside the whole damn day, riding a wide circle, opening gaps in the ice on the water holes and breaking stupid damn cows out of snowdrifts.

This was a shitty time of year for a line rider. The storms had been sweeping through every couple days since… he tried to think back… since sometime about the middle of December as near as he could recall.

The cold wasn't particularly bad this year, and there wasn't wind to speak of. But the snow. Damn snow just fell and fell and fell some more. And whenever some little bit of a breeze did spring up the light, powdery snow blew with it and accumulated in the lee of the slightest obstruction or depression on the ground.

It was a helluva task he had, and now the damn woman wasn't doing her part, damn her.

He crawled down from his saddle and stripped the gear off the horse, gave it a cursory swipe on the back with the dry side of his saddle blanket to get at least some of the sweat off the thing, and turned it loose in the corral to join the others.

He swung the outflow spout of the spring box to fill the water trough, then wearily clumped along the hard-beaten path to the hay pile to get some feed for the horses. He tossed that over the fence and figured he'd done enough for one day.

Dammit, with the woman lazing around indoors and all the snow out here he didn't even have Sarah to greet him.

He went in, stamping his feet on the empty burlap sack that had been laid in the doorway as a rug, knocking accumulated snow onto the rough cloth and kicking his boots off at the doorway before he continued on into the place in his stocking feet.

Like he'd damn expected the woman had been laying on the bed. She got herself up when he came in and went over, not too steady on her feet, to the stove.

Sarah's greeting was more to his liking. And a helluva lot more enthusiastic. The little girl screeched a welcome and came running to him, holding her arms in the air in a full, and accurate, expectation that he would lift her up and swing her about.

Joe set the child on his shoulder and glared at her mother. He probably should go over there and bust her one in the mouth. Would have except for the kids looking on. Well, kid then. Daniel was asleep in his box. Joe checked on him. The little guy looked all right. Clean and everything. At least the bitch hadn't got so lazy she was ignoring the kids.

"Coffee ready?"

She nodded and motioned with her chin in the direction of the table. While his back was turned, when he was making sure about Daniel he supposed, she had filled his cup and set it there for him.

Joe grunted... an acknowledgment, not a satisfaction... and sat to the table, Sarah sprawled across his left knee and leaning happily back against his torso. She was warm there and very small.

"What's for supper?"

"I will make hoecakes. You like those, yes?"

"Will make? Will make? You mean you don't have anything ready? I'm outside in this cra— stuff all day long and now when I get in I got to wait for my supper?"

"I am sorry. Very sorry. I will hurry now. The hoecakes, they will be all right? Some bacon, too?"

He cleared his throat and frowned. But what the hell could a man do? "Hoecakes, sure. And the bacon."

2

He woke to the sound of a high wind soughing past the cabin, building under the eaves and rattling the stovepipe. He could tell from the feel inside the protection of the cabin and the smell in the air that the wind carried more snow on it. No simple snowfall this time but a real handsome blizzard. It could blow for days sometimes. Or dissipate in a couple of hours. You never knew.

He had no idea what time it was. Middle of the night or thereabouts. It was still black dark out, that was all he could tell for certain sure. Not that it mattered. Not right now it didn't.

One thing he was sure of. He wouldn't be riding out anyplace today. Not again until the wind died and the snow quit falling, he wouldn't.

Good thing the woman got off her lazy ass and went out last evening to rig the guide ropes so you could feel your way from the cabin to wherever else a body might need to go, to the water tank and the corral and the haystack and the outhouse. And until this storm lifted those right there were the full and complete extent of their world. Nothing else was reachable; nothing else really mattered.

She was lucky she'd got that done when she did.

Joe rolled onto his back and lay there for a few minutes, wondering if he could put off moving until daylight and time to get up.

The steady, insistent pressure in his bladder—it hadn't been so bad until he started consciously thinking about it—soon drove him out from under the blankets.

He wasn't going outside, though. Not in a blow like this one. He used the lard tin that substituted for a thunder mug since they didn't have a proper vessel for the task, then while he was up anyway shoved some more firewood into the stove. The dry aspen burned hot and clean but too quick. Generally the woman got up a time or two through the night to stoke the stove, but it looked like she hadn't done it this time. Damn her.

Shivering from the chill that seeped through the walls like a stealthy invader, Joe closed the firebox door and hurried back underneath the blankets.

He was thoroughly awake by then and knew he wouldn't be able to get back to sleep right away. Not unless he was able to relax himself some. Which he expected he might just manage if he put his mind to it real hard.

He reached over and shoved a cold hand under the woman's nightdress, laying his palm on the rounded softness of her lower belly.

He snatched it back in sudden surprise. Then reached out again, slower and more deliberate this time, to feel of her flesh.

"Yes. Here. Let me..." She started to move onto her back to accommodate him, but he stopped her.

"Wait a minute, will you?"

"What is it, Joseph?"

"Is it just that I'm so damn cold or... no, that isn't it. You feel like you're afire. You know that? You feel like you're near to burning up. You don't have a fever, do you?"

It was a fairly stupid question. Damn right she had a fever. He'd never known anybody to have a fever so high. Not that he was any expert. But, Jeez...

"It is nothing. I will be all right. I know it."

"That why you were dogging it the other day, dammit?"

"I am sorry. Truly."

"Shit," he grumbled. Now see what trouble she was.

And what the hell was he supposed to do about a damn fever anyway? They didn't have any medicine. Aspirin might help, but he didn't know where to find any of that closer than fifty, sixty miles.

Whiskey, vinegar, and lemon juice was all right, too, but there wasn't any lemon juice for an even greater distance than the aspirin. He supposed he could make up some whiskey and vinegar toddies for her. Heat some water to put into the stuff and pour it down her throat whether she wanted it or not. But he suspected that would be a poor substitute for doctoring and real medicine.

Not that an Indian was worth actual doctoring.

But still...

He shivered beneath the blankets, and for the first time that either of them would be able to think of failed to respond when the woman, still intent on meeting his demands, felt of his crotch and tried to knead him to readiness.

Damn it anyway, he silently complained.

3

"I ask this as a favor, Joseph, not as a demand. I have asked nothing of you until now. I will ask nothing of you ever again. Only this."

"All right."

"Take the small ones to my people. Take them to John Blackwing at the reservation. You know how to go there?"

He shook his head, and she told him the watercourses to follow to reach her particular band.

"The uncle of my dead husband will take them. He will love them as his own. As you cannot love them." He thought he could see some tears forming at the corners of her eyes. "John Blackwing was right. He told me you would not love them. No, that is not true. He said you could not love. Not them, not anyone."

Joe frowned. He didn't want to listen to any of this shit. "Forget about this Blackwing, will you? You'll take care of the damn kids yourself."

"You do not believe this, Joseph. I do not believe this. When the wind stops blowing you must take the children. Find John Blackwing. The children are his kinsmen. He will provide for them."

"And Daniel? Is he one of John Blackwing's kinsmen, too?"

"You still ask me that, Joseph? Can you truly still wonder? I tell you true, Joseph. Daniel is the child of your flesh. No other. But John Blackwing will not turn a child aside. He will take Daniel in and care for him as one of his own even though he is not."

"And you think I'd turn a kid away. My own kid?"

She rolled her head, her eyes dark-rimmed and hollow with pain and fever. She looked at him for what seemed a long time. "Yes. You *would* turn a damn Indian child away, Joseph. I once thought..." She was silent then for a while. Finally she shrugged.

"You thought what?"

But she did not answer him. Not then. Not later.

He sat with a chair pulled next to the bed, sat with her dry, hot hand nestled in his. Sat powerless to do anything to help her.

He would have helped her if he could have. Damn it, he would have.

So why now... this one lousy time... ? There were no answers. He did not really expect any, nor was he disappointed in that expectation.

4

He saddled the grulla and put packsaddles on the other two. He loaded his trunk and bedroll onto the first packhorse and rolled the woman into the tarp they had used to cover the tack, then loaded her onto the second packhorse. It was a lousy thing for Sarah to have to watch, but there was nothing he could do about that. He didn't know if she was old enough to understand what was going on anyhow and didn't even know how much she could comprehend when he talked to her. The one thing he knew for sure was that she wasn't laughing and playing now. She was solemn and silent and so was Daniel.

Snow continued to fall, but the wind had stopped. The snow fell straight down now, covering the places that the wind had swept clean and hiding the contours of the ground so it would be difficult, perhaps impossible, to spot the drifts ahead.

If he had to he could switch the horses around, ride one until it tired of breaking through the snow and then put the lightest load, the pack with his trunk and gear, onto that horse so it could rest while another took up the heavy work of breaking trail.

They would manage.

Unless the wind came up again.

And if that happened... fuck it. He didn't all that much care anyway.

When the horses were set and the packs loaded, he went back inside for the kids. He bundled Sarah into practically everything she owned and wrapped a blanket around her in addition. Daniel he wrapped tight and cozy and stuffed inside his coat.

Balancing Sarah on the pommel with one hand and cradling Daniel with the other he had a helluva time worming his way onto the saddle, but eventually he managed it. It was a damn good thing the grulla was not spooky or they'd have all been in for it.

He raised up in the stirrups so he could tuck the bottom of his coat under him, trapping it between his crotch and the slick, hard leather of the saddle seat. That way he could be sure Daniel couldn't fall out the bottom of his coat while he was paying attention to something else. Then he settled Sarah against his stomach, wedging her there between the horn and himself so that she was secure. She was buried so thick in clothes and blankets that he could scarcely get a peep of her eyes and the bridge of her nose. Daniel was completely submerged inside Joe's coat.

"I reckon we're ready as we'll get, kid. Your mama teach you anything about praying? If she did, pray the wind don't come up again. Not until we get to the reservation, okay?"

He was positive the little girl could not comprehend all that.

Not that it mattered.

He was mostly talking so the damn kids would have the sound of his voice.

"Come on, horse. Let's get this over with." He reined the grulla eastward into the white snow curtain.

It was odd, he reflected after they'd gone a mile or so.

The snow-covered plain they rode across was dotted here and there with lumps. White hummocks where clumps of sage were buried or rocky outcroppings. He knew what was beneath the snow there. Hell, he rode this country over and over and had for the past couple years now. He knew exactly what lay underneath that snow.

But try as he could to tell himself that, he had the eerie impression that this field of white was much like another silent snowfield he could remember from the past. Fields of white. Fields of silence. Fields of death.

He shivered. And told himself it was only because he was cold.

5

It wasn't... what he expected. He expected a skin lodge or anyway a canvas lodge, which was what most of the bastard Indians had learned to resort to in recent years. You saw them everywhere, dirty white canvas cones substituting for the irreplaceable buffalo hides that rotted away—like their old way of life—years and years ago.

That was what he had expected. Something very like what he had known, well, years and years ago.

But this. This was a house. Shanty really. About ten by sixteen with a sheet-iron stove at one end. It was made of rough lumber, not logs. The inside was papered over with yellowing, brittle sheets of newspaper. That wasn't for decorative purposes, he knew, but to keep wind and cold out. Some old newspaper along with some flour-and-water paste would go a long way toward weatherproofing a bare-board wall.

That and the common, ordinary furnishings made it difficult for him to remember that this was a wild Indian's place. Or anyway a reservation Indian's place. It had been a helluva long time since there was such a thing as a wild Indian, he supposed.

He looked around and by the time he got done gawking realized that Sarah and Daniel were no longer in sight. One of the women must have carried them off someplace. To another house, he was sure of that. This place was only the single room. Just about the time he missed Sarah and Daniel he realized that the others were slipping out, too, and pretty soon he and John Blackwing were the only ones in the house.

Joe frowned. And peered closely for a moment at the dark, stocky man who stood in front of him. Blackwing had traces of silver in his hair at the temples and around toward the back of his neck but otherwise could probably have passed for thirty or thereabouts. He seemed…

"Do I know you?"

"Do you?" Blackwing countered.

Joe frowned again. Hesitated. Shook his head. "No. I don't expect that I do."

"We will take care of Mary and the children now."

It took Joe a minute to remember that that had been the woman's name. She had told him that. Of course she had. It just hadn't seemed important at the time. "Yeah, well…"

"You can stay, too, if you wish. You are welcome here."

Joe's frown became a scowl.

"Do not be so quick to refuse, Joe Potter. You could find healing here if you seek it. If you would allow yourself to accept it."

"I ain't sick, dammit. It was only the woman was sick. The kids and me, we're all right."

"It is not a sickness of the body that you need healed of, Joe Potter."

"I don't know what you mean."

"No? Do you not?"

"I said so, didn't I?"

"Your heart is very hard, Joe Potter. I tried to explain this to Mary, but she insisted she could find the good in you. I told her it was buried too deep for her to find. And if she did find it she would only destroy you."

"You're out of your damn mind, Blackwing."

"I? No, I think not. And in truth not you either. You have no choice. You must keep your true feelings locked out of reach. If ever you allowed yourself to feel the things you fear they would overwhelm you. You have no choice but to be hard of heart, Joe Potter. If ever you learn to cry again it will be too much for any man to carry. We understand this. But... you will not want to hear this, Joe Potter, but it is something I must say. It is something Mary would want me to tell you."

Joe gave the red Indian SOB a harshly skeptical look and backed off half a step, ready to wheel about and head for the door if he had to.

"We forgive you, Joe Potter. Our people forgive you, and if you would allow it we would help you to forgive yourself."

"I got nothing to forgive, dammit, and neither do you." He spat the words hotly, but there was a thudding in his chest and a rushing sound in his ears.

"It was an accident, Joe Potter. You did not mean to do the thing you did."

"You're one crazy bastard, you know that? You don't know what you're talking about."

"I know better than you do for I can look at that which you keep hidden from yourself, that which you do not dare to see without someone there to help take the guilt from you. There is such a one. He would help you. And we would help you to find him. The way is there, Joe Potter. If only you would take it."

"You're out of your fucking mind."

"It was an accident, Joe Potter. The boy the soldiers called Joey was running toward you. The guns were going off. Shells. Explosions. People were dying on every side. You were afraid. You heard someone run at you and you turned and you fired your gun before you saw who it was. Joey loved you, Joe Potter. Loved you as a brother loves an elder brother. Loved you as a child loves a favored uncle. And you, Joe Potter. You loved him."

"Loved some stinking Indian? I told you you're out of your fucking mind. I never loved any Indian. Not then and not now."

"You loved Joey, yes. And if you would allow yourself to heal you would love Sarah and Daniel just as they, too, love you."

"You're fucking crazy, I tell you."

"You remember that day, Joe Potter. It was an accident. The people saw. We know. You did not mean to shoot your gun at all. Not at any of the people. Especially not at the boy you knew as Joey."

"I shot my gun plenty, damn you. I killed a dozen of you bastards that day. Maybe more. I've killed my share of stinking Indians and then some."

"Not on that day, Joe Potter. We saw. We remember. You stood in tears when the people died in the snow. Your gun was cold that day and your heart overflowing. The other soldiers shot and stabbed and clubbed our people but you did not. The tears ran off your face that day, Joe Potter. You wept for us. And then the boy ran for you. For help. For protection. Perhaps to make you get down so you would not be shot by your own soldiers, who knows? He ran at you and you heard and you shot your gun before you saw who it was. You remember that, Joe Potter. You cannot tell me you do not."

"You lying son of a bitch," he spat back at Blackwing. "I never did any of that. I shot you

310

red bastards down until my rifle got too hot to let the empty shells out anymore and then I stabbed some more stinking damn Indians. I shot and I stabbed and I clubbed until I was wore out from the killing. Until I was too tired to kill no more."

Blackwing sighed. "Perhaps it is best if you remember it that way, Joe Potter. You are like a tall tree. Tall and strong but unable to bend. You would break apart if the pressures of the wind became too much for you to bear. Better the wall of ice you put around your heart, perhaps, than the bitterness of truth. It is not my place to judge. Only to tell you that you are forgiven, Joe Potter. Not one of the people holds that day against you. We forgive you. Will you forgive yourself?"

The sonuvabitch Indian stepped forward, hands extended, his expression serene and gentle.

Joe recoiled. Then lashed out. He hit Blackwing in the face.

He was sobbing. Damned if he knew why. He hit Blackwing with everything he had, then spun and bolted for the door.

He ran out into the snow.

The packhorse that had been carrying the woman was gone, taken off somewhere with the body. It didn't matter.

Joe scrambled onto the grulla and wheeled it away from the hitch rail. The packhorse with his things loaded onto it was still tied at the rail. He didn't turn back to get it. He could not. He did not dare linger. He wanted... away from there. Had to get away from there. Had to escape the horrors the stinking miserable damned Indians had in store for him if he tarried.

Lying bastard son of a bitch Blackwing. Lying damned Indian.

He booted the grulla into a walk and quickly into a lope and then into a bellydown run.

He had to get away.

He rode hard into the white curtain of falling snow. Rode blindly, letting the grulla have its head. Pointed the horse roughly north. Toward... no, that did not matter. It was chance, only chance that took him in that direction.

Toward the ghosts that awaited him there.

Damn them. Damn the living and damn the dead. Damn every stinking Indian there ever was.

He didn't need their forgiveness. Didn't need any absolution. Hadn't done anything to require it.

He rode across white, empty snowfields, rode away from human habitation savage or civilized. He rode erect and stiffly rigid in the saddle. Unbending and unmindful of the cold or of the fact that he had left bedroll, blankets, and coat behind.

None of that mattered.

It was all lies. All that bastard Blackwing said. Lies and calumny.

And as he rode blindly toward the far-off snowfield, a thin cold trickle of moisture rolled down his cheeks and into his beard where it soon froze in place and became a mask of ice that hid his face from view.

ABOUT THE AUTHOR

FRANK RODERUS wrote his first story, a western, at age five, and says he quite literally has never wanted to do anything else. He has been writing fiction full-time since 1980, and was a newspaper reporter before that. As a journalist, he won the Colorado Press Association's highest honor, the Sweepstakes Award, for the Best News Story of 1980. His novel *Leaving Kansas* (Doubleday, 1983) won the Western Writers of America's Spur Award for Best Western Novel. A life member of the American Quarter Horse Association, he is married and currently resides in Florida. Roderus and his wife, Magdalena, expect to divide their time between Florida and Palawan Island in the Sulu Sea.

If you have enjoyed reading this large print book and you would like more information on how to order a Wheeler Large Print Book, please write to:

 Wheeler Publishing, Inc.
P.O. Box 531
Accord, MA 02018-0531